MARTY VAUGHN

LORINE FORD

MARTY VAUGHN

LORINE FORD

Published by 1st World Publishing
1100 North 4th St. Suite 131, Fairfield, Iowa 52556
TEL: 641-209-5000 • FAX: 641-209-3001
•WEB: www.1stworldpublishing.com

First Edition

LCCN: 2004099920
SoftCover ISBN: 1-59540-907-6
HardCover ISBN: 1-59540-942-4
eBook ISBN: 1-59540-943-2

Dedication

To my son Michael Ford who is ill with cancer and his faithful wife Diana, my daughter Gerri Schilling who did my typing and encouraged me and her husband Francis, my nieces Wanda Mercer, Melba Smith and Shirley Meixner who gave me much encouragement to finish this book.

Dedication by Mayor Paul D. Pate

Welcome to the winning entry from the 2004 Cedar Rapids/Iowa City Book Publishing Scholarship Competition, sponsored by 1st World Library Literary Society. I salute all of the talented authors who submitted fiction, nonfiction and poetry for this contest that celebrates literacy and the value of reading of our Corridor.

I believe Mayor Lehman will agree that this contest also is illustrative of the strong economic and cultural connections that link our Corridor. As long as dedicated area residents keep asking, "What if?" we will keep moving our communities forward.

I hope you enjoy this novel that offers a picturesque perspective of 19th Century Iowa and the strong agricultural roots that contributed to our current economic strength and quality of life. Congratulations to Lorine Ford for winning this competition and sharing her talents with her readers!

The City of Cedar Rapids is proud of our rich literacy traditions, rooted in the leadership of our area school systems and our Cedar Rapids Public Library and our Metro Library Network.

The Cedar Rapids Public Library delivers more than 80

programs each month through two locations. The Combined research and pleasure reading resources of the Cedar Rapids, Hiawatha and Marion Public Libraries is an excellent case study in local government collaboration.

Today's users of these facilities will be tomorrow's leaders in Cedar Rapids and throughout our Corridor. When combined with additional outreach efforts like those of 1st World Library, our preparedness for tomorrow is only strengthened through appreciation of the resources available today.

Enjoy Marty Vaughn, and continue celebrating the joys of reading!

Paul D. Pate
Mayor
City of Cedar Rapids
www.cedar-rapids.org

Chapter One

Summer breezes rippled gently across the rolling prairies from the Wapsipinicon to the Mississippi. Smaller streams wound through the valleys where cattle grazed and switched their tails to discourage biting, pestering flies. Green foam formed on pools of stagnant water and fish swam lazily along the muddy banks. You could throw in a baited hook and catch a bullhead any time of day.

Cows and heifers, springing with calf, stood belly deep, seeking the coolness of the water against their feverish udders, swollen with milk. Horses, too, grazed on lush green pastures, enjoying a well-deserved rest from the spring field-work. The riding and buggy mares, along with the calves and half-grown geese, were allowed to roam and nibble grass in the orchards.

Cedar trees grew along the river bluffs. Oak, ash, maple, cottonwood, and piss elm offered shade on the hillsides and barnyards. Many other species grew wild in the wood lots and provided fuel, nuts, crabapples, chokecherries, and plums. Hedge fences divided the farms and fields and provided refuge for birds and small animals. This was 1882 and part of Scott County, Iowa, where I, Marty Vaughn, was born.

My birth was the consummation of a union between a maid of German descent and a young English gentleman. Perhaps *consummation*–the perfection of a union–is not the right word to use, for the marriage was fraught with dissidence. This is what Mama told me of their life in England.

I was conceived in the womb of Johannah Schwentzer, who was at that time employed as a maid in Vaughn Castle. Mama was seeking security when she married Frederick Wesley Vaughn. Frederick was the only child of Lord Frederick Vaughn and Lady Margaret Wesley Vaughn. They owned Vaughn Castle and the vast moors and pasturelands around it.

Mama was the eldest child of Dorothy and William Schwentzer. Grandpa Schwentzer died in 1879; one year later, Granny and her two younger children, Lena and Willy, sailed to America. Mama remained in England.

Papa was endowed with his father's name and an income from his maternal grandfather's estate. When he fell in love with Mama, his parents were displeased and forbade him to marry below his social level. They discharged Mama from their staff of employees, but Mama and Papa were already secretly married. When Lord and Lady Vaughn found out, they refused to let Papa bring Mama to the castle. Papa thought an heir might soften their hearts, but my birth did not accomplish that purpose.

To compound this situation was Mama's attitude toward me. An *object* is something tangible and visible, a material thing. Another meaning of this word, pronounced differently, is to object and disappove. Mama condensed it into one meaning and applied it to me, a thing of which she disapproved.

Mama and Papa left Europe before I was born. They had intended to establish a home in America, but Papa got homesick and discouraged quickly. When I was five months old, we returned to England.

Our home was a one-room flat on the third floor of the Turnbull House in London. The stairs leading to our flat were steep, and they folded against the underside of a trap door to which they were hinged.

Papa could not adjust to this way of life, and although I am sure he loved us, he was sad and out of heart most of the time. He started drinking and as time passed, he was drunk more often than not. This went on for five years. On the night of May 12, 1887, he came in late and either he forgot, or neglected, to close the trap door. He got out of bed that night, and in the darkness, he stepped into the opening and fell to the floor below. His neck was broken and he died almost instantly.

This happened two months before my fifth birthday, so my memories of him are dim and probably distorted; however, I seem to recall the events from the time of his death forth most clearly.

I awoke the morning of May 13, the same time as usual, but instead of Mama bustling about getting breakfast, she was sitting in a chair by the window, staring through the glass at the buildings that lined the streets of London's East Side. Papa's body had been taken away. Mrs. Tremble, the proprietor's wife, was preparing tea. It was a long day for me, because all Mama did was cry and repeatedly blow her nose, mumbling, "Fritz, mein Fritz."

Lord and Lady Vaughn claimed my father's body, and it was taken to Vaughn Castle. The next day a carriage called for us. On a high seat up in the cab were two men wearing high black hats and capes, their head and shoulders erect. They looked straight ahead. We rode in the carriage for quite a distance–how far I do not know–then we rounded a bend in the road and there before us was the castle, shrouded in mist like a picture from a fairy tale. We stopped under the portico. There, a footman helped us alight and he led the way inside.

We entered and were announced in a large room where

he drapes were pulled and candles flickered with a softness like the calm mellow of twilight. Lady Vaughn was sitting in a straight chair. The first thing that caught my eye was the cameo that was pinned at the neck of her black velvet cape. It was an odd gem, a black wreath of grain on a pure white background. Her eyes were red and bulgy, as though the cameo was pinned too tight and about to choke her. Her dress was draped to one side and her jaws were firm. Her hair was covered with a veil. When we entered the room, she stared at me for a long moment–then abruptly got up and left the room.

Lord Vaughn was standing beside her with his hand on the back of her chair. He was a tall man and a little paunchy. He had hair like Papa's, which was sand colored with a cowlick.

"We will be in the library, Hadley," he told the servant, and followed Lady Vaughn from the room.

Candleholders held thick, squat candles at either end of a long bronze box near the windows. Mama went over to the box and began to cry again. I did not see anything to cry about, so I stood on my tiptoes and tried to see into the box. Mama lifted me up and I saw Papa lying there. He looked strange with the candlelight reflecting the bronze to his face. I was afraid and began to cry too.

It seemed like we were there a long time, but it was less than an hour. Soon we were in the carriage again, which took us out by the stables and along a meadow, where other horses trotted along the fence, whinnying and keeping pace with our carriage.

The next day the same vehicle took us to a chapel for Papa's funeral. The days that followed passed slowly. Mama did not talk much or pay attention to me. She seemed to be in another world.

Papa had left a trunk constructed of wood. It was bulky and cumbersome. Whoever built it meant for it to last a lifetime or more. The top, bottom, and corners were reinforced with metal strips. It had sturdy iron hinges that closed it and latches that locked it securely.

Three months after Papa's death, Mama packed all my clothes and a lock of Papa's hair in the old trunk and shipped it to Aunt Lena in America. I accompanied it.

Aunt Lena had married a farmer, and they lived near Blue Grass, Iowa. I cried and begged to stay with Mama, but one day she put me on board a ship. I stood on the deck with my unwilling fist clasped tightly in the hand of a stalwart, bearded man, whose soft voice belied his appearance. He tried to soothe me, but I fought to free my hand and sobbed in a loud voice, "Mama! Mama! No! I don't want to go" As the ship moved away, I thought I saw her stretch her arms out to me.

The bearded man took me to a cabin that opened into a galley. I sat on the bunk and closed my ears and mind to everything and everyone. The lamp that hung overhead made a circle of light for a few feet that gradually diminished to grotesque shadows in the corners. My trunk held all my possessions, except for a stuffed doll that Mrs. Tremble had given me for my birthday. I held that tightly in my arms.

The first three days I did not eat or talk, but sat almost motionless staring at those terrifying shadows that moved as if they were alive. The man with the beard brought me food, returning later only to carry it away untouched.

On the fourth day out, a stowaway was put to work helping the cook. He was a young boy with unkempt hair the color of straw. His face was smooth and soft-the only sign of a beard was light reddish fuzz in front of his ears and around his chin. He was thin and his wrinkled clothes did not fit him well. But his blue eyes danced with merriment. Even when the cook grasped him by the ear and marched him over to a tub of cooking pots that had to be washed, his spirits were not dampened.

He worked hard the first day, and when the cook finally let him rest, he sat down next to me and asked, "What's your name?" I did not answer. "Do you know what my name is?" he asked, trying to get me to talk. I remained silent.

"My name is Tim Shannon. Look over there, see the rabbit?" He put his thumb and two middle fingers together, and raised his fist and little finger.

"See on your trunk? There's a rabbit on your trunk."

The shadow of his hand looked like an animal. I was frightened and began to cry. He was instantly concerned at my tears and pleaded, "Don't cry. Please don't cry. It won't hurt you."

He placed one hand over the other and manipulated his fingers into a shadow image of a horse's head. "See, now it's a horse."

Just then, the cook bellowed at Tim. "Come outer there ye lout and git about yer work." Tim made a face, stuck his thumbs in his ears, and waved his fingers back and forth in the direction of the cook's voice. Then he went out.

I raised my hand and found the shadow on the wall beyond the trunk. I moved my fingers and the shadow did too. I relaxed after that and went to sleep. Tim came again the next day.

"Well," he said, "are ya gonna tell me your doll's name?"

I shook my head.

"I know your doll's name," he teased. "Yep, your doll's name is Muggins." I shook my head, still unsmiling.

"I know," he stated, "*your* name is Muggins." He put his little finger in the corner of his mouth and made a wry face.

"No, it's Marty," I giggled, suddenly no longer shy.

"Oh," he exclaimed, laughing. "What's your doll's name, Marty?"

"Muggins," I replied.

That seemed to delight him. He laughed again, and I laughed to hear his high squeaky then low throaty laugh.

Tim was allowed to spend a couple of hours with me every day. He showed me what made shadows by changing the position of the light, and under the watchful eye of the man with the beard, he walked with me on deck when the weather and the sea permitted.

Eventually, the voyage ended and the bearded man placed me in the custody of a lady. Tim had to say good-bye on the ship before the cook locked him up.

"Good-bye, Marty," he said. "Now don't be afraid. The world's a big place with many friends in it."

The lady put me on a train and checked to see that I had my tag around my neck. Suddenly, I remembered I had left Muggins in the cabin. I screamed and cried out, but the lady firmly stood her ground. We could not go back for her because I would miss the train.

"Maybe Tim will take care of her," I consoled myself.

It was a slow journey from New York to Chicago. The train made frequent stops. I curled up in a corner seat as big silent tears streamed down my face. A short, pudgy conductor felt sorry for me and he dangled his ring of keys at me, as though I were an infant. I had a layover in Chicago, and then I was put on another train. I arrived at Durant, Iowa, twenty-six days after I left London.

It was a warm, sunny, fall day, September 29, 1889, when Aunt Lena clasped me to her soft bosom. She resembled Mama in many ways, except she was not quite as tall as Mama. Her hair was brown and she had it wound in a knot fastened to the back of her head with bone hairpins. Her eyes were violet-blue, and the light of faith and calm tenderness shining in them dispelled my fear.

"Du ist Marty, ja?" she asked, taking me in her arms. "My, my, du ist a big girl. I'm du Tante Lena." She tucked my hand in hers and led me from the train. "Uncle Hans get du trunk," she told me.

Uncle Hans was of medium height with slightly stooped

shoulders. His homely face, brown from the summer wind and sun, broke into a welcoming smile.

"My, my, du has grow. Du no look like der kinda we haf five jahrs [years] ago," he said, squatting so he was nearer my height. "Du like der trip?" I nodded, but I was more interested in the rig than I was in the journey I had just completed.

"Are we going to ride in this?" I asked, pointing to the rig.

"Ja," said Hans.

"Are they your horses?" I asked.

"Ja," he said again.

"What are the horses' names?"

"My, my, so many questions," he laughed. "Dis ein ist Nollie und ist one ist Prince. Komm, I put du up," he said, lifting and swinging me up to the back seat.

"Why is that one Prince?" I asked.

"Well, he halt hiz head high, so we call him Prince," he answered.

"Doesn't Nollie hold her head up?"

"Ja, but nicht so handsome," he answered.

I pondered over that. Meanwhile, Tante and Hans visited with other people who had come down to the station to meet the train. They proudly told their friends, "Dis our nishte [niece], from London she komm. She will live mit uns."

Finally, after I had been thoroughly inspected and discussed, and as it was getting late, we started for the farm.

Along the way, the roadsides were yellow with goldenrod and the trees were wearing the bright hues of autumn. In a pasture two squirrels were busily making trips from a hickory tree to an old hollow maple. As the horses' hooves clapped on the plank floor of the bridge that spanned the creek, the squirrels sat up and listened, unaware of a pigeon hawk soaring lazily against the blue sky overhead, looking for some hapless prey for its supper.

When we reached the farm, Hans unhitched the horses and began choring. Tante took me inside. The kitchen was warm and stuffy. Tante poked at the coals still glowing in the kitchen range and put some wood on them.

"Komm," she said, "Tante show du your room."

We went up the wide stairway and into a large room. What first caught my eye was the bed. The frame was wooden and the mattress a large tick filled with straw. A billowy feather bed lay on top. It seemed monstrous to me. Tante poked it with her fist.

"See kinda, ist a big soft bett, du schlaf [sleep] gute hier."

Mrs. Kelly, the midwife who had attended Mama at my birth, had said I was born with a caul. She said the veil bestowed the power of a clairvoyant and an insight of the spiritual world. I was blessed with a rare gift. This proved to be true. With Mama I had been an "object," but with Tante and Hans the feeling of being "people" transformed me into a healthy inquisitive youngster. I was allowed to sit between them on the buggy seat and would announce proudly, "I am people."

The first week of school, however, I became an "object" again and crawled back, briefly, into a shell of silence.

"Komm, kinda," Aunt Lena coaxed, "dere ist many jung in der schule. Du must learn like other people."

It took a great deal of coaxing, but finally I sat on the raised platform with the other first graders. The teacher gave us beanbags to toss back and forth. The McGuffey reader was full of pictures and letters that transformed into words and sounds. Thus began my life in Iowa.

Tante and Hans Kleinart owned their farm. The large house was a two-story frame building with four stately colonnades supporting the roof over the front porch. The wide front door led into the parlor and used only when they had special company. The kitchen was comfortable and homey, with a small butry. In the winter the top of the stove was a cherry red and the kitchen was warm with the smell of "kaffee kuchen"–you could smell it as soon as you stepped on the back porch. The teakettle was singing and the fragrance of coffee predominated when you opened the door.

My room upstairs was next to Tante and Han's room. At night I could listen to the sound of their hushed voices as I lay on top of a mountain of straw and feathers, yearning silently for Muggins. There were times when Tante tiptoed over and closed the door between us when she thought I had fallen asleep. I lay there tense, listening hard for any sound from their room. One night, after she had closed the door, I slid quietly from the bed and opened the door so softly I did not think she heard me, but the bed creaked as she sat up.

"Marty," her voice was sharp and commanding, "wot du dun? Get to bett." She came out of her room to swat me firmly on my bottom and tuck me back in bed–then determinedly closed the door.

In the morning I picked at the fried mush Tante put before me and ignored the crispy fried bacon. Inwardly, I was bracing myself for a scolding because of last night. I was remembering another night in London. I had gotten out of bed because I had a bellyache. I sat in the rocker and soon fell asleep. Mama missed me out of bed–suddenly I was across her knee while she spanked me with her open hand on my bare bottom, smacking me until the stinging felt hot. I howled, first with terror at being awakened so abruptly, then with rage at the injustice of it.

I watched Tante out of the corner of my eye. She was pleasant and acted as though nothing had happened. Hans came in from chores and rumpled my hair.

"Nau, nau, wore ist jo smile?" he asked. He scrubbed his face with his hands, dribbling water from his elbow and splashing it out of the basin.

"Acht, du swine," scolded Tante in a mild voice, handing

him a towel. He reached over and twinged her nose affectionately, and sat down next to me. He slid several pieces of bacon to his plate with a fork.

"Today we make apfelwein. Du helfe Hans?"

"Oh goody! May I Tante?"

"Ja, go mit, kinda," she smiled, turning to clear the dishes from breakfast.

With my hand clutching one of his fingers, I tried to match his long steps. He harnessed a shiny black horse with a clipped mane and a patch of white over his nose, then hitched him to the wagon. We went to the orchard, picked up the windfalls, and hauled them to the cider mill in the backyard. Hans put the apples through a grinder and they fell into a wooden tub. When it was full, he turned a wheel that had a round pressboard attached to it. The board fit snugly in the tub and he turned the wheel until it was tight and then wedged a paddle in the wheel. With the added leverage, all the juice was extracted. He carried it to the cellar and poured it into a wooden barrel. It took about a year for it to turn to vinegar.

Mister Clausmann, a neighbor who lived on a farm about a half mile down the road, was a robust man with a big smile and a hearty laugh. Sometimes he and Hans drank from the cider barrel. They would laugh and talk in German, slapping their knees at jokes I did not understand.

On Saturday, I went with Hans to load the cane that he and Tante had stripped the day before. I held the reins and pretended I was driving, but the old horses were so used to working with Hans that they knew every command he gave them. He had a couple of skittish mares, but I never got to hold the reins when he hitched them. It was a hot day and Hans frequently drank from the earthen jug that was tied on the front endgate. I watched as he twisted out the corncob that had been used a long time to stopper the jug. He turned it over his hand, supported it with his arm, and spat out his cud of chewing tobacco. He rinsed his mouth, spat that out too, and took a long drink.

"I wanna drink too," I told him.

"Ja ist too heavy fur du. Come, Hans halpen."

I took a drink and made a face. It tasted like corncob.

Hans laughed, "Nitch so gute?" he asked.

"No, I don't like it."

Tante had made a lunch for us to take on the trip to Moscow, where the sorghum mill was located. It was fun sitting under a big shade tree to watch the mule that was lashed to the pole sweep go around and around, grinding and mashing the stalks. He never seemed to tire and walked at the same gait hour after hour. We did not stay long. Hans wanted to get home before dark, so we would return later to get the jugs of green molasses.

The trip seemed longer and the sun hotter going home. I wanted to take my bonnet off, but Hans would not let me. He stopped and fixed the sideboard over the top of the wagon.

"Nau, komm unter out ov der sun," he told me.

It was rough and jolting after sitting on the high spring seat, but I sat and watched the fluffy clouds overhead. Some were bunched together like big feather beds and others were shaped like animals. One looked like "Old Red," a rooster in Tante's flock. Old Red was a big show-off. He would strut around the chicken yard, fan out a wing, and sashay around a hen–then flapped both wings and crowed about it.

"He ist verruckt [crazy]," Tante would say.

Old Red tried to be boss around the farm until "Mr. Wicket" came up from the creek. Mister Wicket was a big gray gander. He put Old Red in his place. I had a lot of respect for that old bird, too. He chased me every time I went in the barnyard. He would stick out his long neck and *th-th-th* at me all the way to the gate. He caught me once and I had the black spots from the thrashing for a long time.

Tante rescued me when she heard me scream.

When the team turned into our lane, I got up sleepily and stood behind the seat.

"Du sleep gute, kinda?" asked Hans. I shook my head. I felt cross and tired.

Tante had supper ready. "Wot ist los [wrong], Marty, du hungry?" she asked. I shook my head and began to cry, for suddenly I had a longing inside me for something or someone. I didn't know for what or whom. Sitting in the rocker, Tante took me on her lap and wiped the sweat from my face with her fresh clean apron. I was asleep before Hans came in. When I awoke, the house was quiet and dark.

October came and with it, cornhusking. For a long time Hans had been tying ears together, then slinging them over the clothesline and checking the moisture in them. One day he said to Tante, "Ve start hasken Monday."

Every day after school, I skipped out to the field where they were husking and climbed on the wagon. They let me ride until we got to the creek. Then I had to get off because there were rocks, mud, and water. My extra weight might just be enough to keep the horses from getting the load through the creek. If that happened, Hans would have to bring out the mares and put a four-horse hitch on them. He did not like having to bring the mares out, for they reared and seesawed, so he had quite a time to get them to pull together with the old team. Then, too, he always had to mend the harness after they'd been stuck. Sometimes there was too much corn on the wagon and it would mire down anyway.

Tante and I got the cows and gathered eggs, slopped the hogs, and filled the horse mangers with hay. It was dark before we were done. Tante lit the lantern and I carried it so we could see. After supper, Hans hung the lantern high in the crib and scooped the corn off the wagon, so it would be ready the next day when the first rays of sun streaked across the dawn with a rosy haze and topped the horizon like a huge orange ball.

By Thanksgiving, the corn was all cribbed. Hans worked in the woods getting the wood ready for fuel, for it was not long before winter was with us. The snow fell deep and fluffy over the prairie. Tante and Hans lowered the bobsled that hung overhead in the granary, and put the wood rack on it.

"Komm, kinda, du wont to go mit Hans to haul wood?" he asked.

"Are you going, too, Tante?" I asked.

"No, du go mit Hans, Tante has bread to bake," she said. "Hans, du see she hangs on fast."

"Ja, sweetheart, du bake der bread, ve bringen der wood," he answered, pressing a kiss on her nose. "Go in, der schnauze ist cold."

The bobsled glided smoothly to the timber as I held tightly to the wood rack, the sharp wind biting my cheeks and making my nose cold. My hands were tucked inside warm woolen mittens that Tante had knitted for me. Hans loaded the wood with the large butts to the front and the small ends hanging far out the back. The snow was deeper in the timber than it was around the buildings–it came over the top of my one-buckle overshoes. I made paths from tree to tree, examining tiny tracks of chickadees and snowbirds and trying to follow a bright flash of scarlet as a cardinal flitted from bush to bush. A covey of quail were roosting under a gooseberry bush, and they looked so much a part of the dead leaves that I would not have seen them had they not moved.

"Komm, Marty, du feet bekammen wet, sit hinder and hangen fast," said Hans putting me on top and showing me how to sit tight. We zipped across the field to the house. Tante met me at the door and swept me off from head to toe with her broom.

"Du snowman," she laughed. "Komm, we make jo feet dry." She put me in front of the oven, which was pouring heat from the open door. She had just taken crusty brown loaves out, which were cooling on the table, the crust shiny with butter.

"May I have the crust, Tante?" I asked. When the bread was hot, the crust was my favorite piece, with gobs of butter melting into it. Add a big glass of milk, and it was the essence of bake day.

"Ja, und when du feet ist warm, du helfe Hans mit der wood bringen."

Hans was chopping when I went out, shuffling my feet in the snow to make a path to the door. He picked up a big load and I struggled with one-half the size of his, first trying to carry it, and then rolling it in the path. He carried four loads while I was rolling mine, giving me a word of encouragement each time he passed me. When I finally got it to the porch, it looked more like a big snowball then it did a chunk, but he brushed it off and put it in the wood box too. Then Tante came out with her broom again.

"Auch, du ist snowman," she said. "Du helfe gute, nau we haben kuchen."

At night, sitting beside the cozy fire, Hans told us stories about his childhood home. I sat wide-eyed, leaning my head against Tante's knee while she knitted. I do not know if his stories were true or not, because of the twinkle in his eyes, but his ruddy face was stern as he talked, and he seemed to be reliving the episodes. He must have seen Indian raiding parties as well as the friendly tribes that lived near his home. He talked about the herds of bison that roamed the Nebraska plains, within sight of his father's sod house. The cattle on the ranch ranged for many miles. It was unusual, but occasionally a buffalo bull would take a heifer, if the time was right and the female had strayed from the rest of the herd.

One spring, a heifer belonging to his father gave birth to a buffalo calf. It was pure white, probably due to an ancestor on the heifer's family tree. Anyway, Chief Wannetata made a bargain to give his father twenty horses for the white calf. It was a good bargain for his father, so they made the trade and turned the horses into the corral. The evening was quiet, except for an occasional hoot from an owl and the wail of a coyote calling for a mate and an answering wail miles away that told the bitch the male was on his way. But the next morning the horses were gone, silently, as though they had sprouted wings and flown away. The rustlers had effectively dusted out all their tracks and his father never saw them again.

Christmas was near and a vague mystery prevailed about the house. Tante made me go to bed, sometimes by seven o'clock. The kitchen smelled spicy and good, and I strung popcorn on thread to drape over the Christmas tree.

"Santy bringen fine present, if du ist gute. If du is bad he bringen stick," Tante threatened.

I waited expectantly and tried to remember if I had always been good. There was the time last summer. Hans had told me not to play in the manger where the cows were stanchioned or I might get my head fast between the boards. But I had to see for myself, so I put my head through one of the spaces. It slipped in easy, but when I tried to get out, my ears were in the way. No matter which way I twisted, I could not get loose. I began to cry. It was just a whimper at first as I struggled, then it got louder and louder.

"Hans, Hans," I shrieked. "GET ME OUT! TANTE! HANS! GET ME OUT!" I struggled and pulled and cried. Hans came back with a hammer, a quizzical expression of amusement and stern authority on his face. He knocked the board off as gently as he could.

"See's du? Next time du mind nau."

And, of course, I was always forgetting to close the garden gate. Several times Mr. Wicket and his hens went in and gorged their necks with Tante's flowers and vegetables. I was always playing with Connie Clausmann after school instead of coming straight home like Tante told me to. The Clausmann's were our nearest neighbors. Connie was eight, almost the same age as me.

"How does Santy know if I'm good or not? I asked Tante.

"He know if du ist gute," she replied.

"But, gee, how does he know? He must be like God," I thought. "Tante says God knows everything we do, and we can't hide from Him. Maybe Santy is like God, only he lives in the North Pole instead of Heaven."

It was one of those mysteries that Tante talked about, like "cast your bread upon the waters." I had not figured that out either. I could not see what throwing bread on the water had to do with putting my nickel in the collection plate on Sunday, especially when I wanted to keep my nickel. She explained if we give in the name of Jesus, we cast our bread upon the waters. It helps build the church, pay the preacher, buy the organ and hymn books, and helps poor people.

"So," she said, "we get back much more dann we give."

We chored early on Christmas Eve because the school program was being held that night. I went with Mrs. Clausmann and Connie, because the children had to be there by 6:30. Tante and Hans would bring Mr. Clausmann with them.

The schoolhouse seemed strange and unfamiliar at night. Three boys who I saw every day were dressed in black robes and high hats. Instantly, a picture of two men in high black hats driving a carriage flashed across my mind, and suddenly I was alone among strangers. I began to cry hysterically. The familiar surroundings had changed and I so wanted everything to stay rooted. There was nothing Miss Alice, the teacher, or Mrs. Clausmann could do to calm me.

I had stopped crying by the time Tante and Hans arrived, but my breath came in heavy sighs. I was an "object" again. I did not recite my pieces–I just went to sleep.

I awoke in my own bed. It was Christmas morning. Tante came in and pulled the covers back.

"Komm up, komm up, Marty, Santy–e komm! Komm, we go see wot he bringen." I was walking across the icy floor in my bare feet before I was fully awake.

The tree, resplendent with beads, berries, cardboard stars, and popcorn, stood in the front room. It had a golden star on the very top. I stared in fascination, then my eyes fastened on a doll. A stuffed doll with an embroidered smile.

"Muggins! Muggins!" I shouted joyfully. I clasped her to me and hugged her tightly. The soft cotton body was cuddly, and her yarn hair was golden and soft against my face. Although it was not my true Muggins, I accepted her.

The week of Christmas was cheerful, lovely, and good. A light snow had fallen, and it made everything sparkle in the bright sunlight. Everybody wished everybody they met a "Merry Christmas."

Mama sent me a package, and in a letter to Tante, she said she hoped I would like the dress goods. She had not made the material up into a dress because I had probably grown. The material was a drab green, better suited to an older person, but Tante said, "Dis be a nice dress. Dis no show der dirt."

The holidays did not interrupt the routine of farm chores that had to be done. Meals and lunches were always on time. On New Year's Eve, everyone who was able gathered at a large hall in Blue Grass. They danced and sang the old year out, and welcomed the New Year with much shouting, kissing, and backslapping.

Chapter Two

The winter of 1888 had been one of the worst Iowa had ever experienced. A howling blizzard had roared across the prairie and caught many farmers unprepared. Snow piled into drifts so high the livestock could not get through to the shelters. They struggled in the deep snow until they were exhausted and froze to death. Farmers could not get to them with hay and grain, and some animals starved. This winter was different–they were ready for any kind of weather. The moisture from the snow combined with the cool spring had grown an excellent oats crop and the heavy blanket of snow had protected the winter wheat. Bedding was plentiful. Even though farmers had lost some livestock in the blizzard, they were compensated with a bumper crop of grain and plenty of straw.

When the barn was kept closed, the heat from the animals kept it comfortable. Hans started a fire in an old steam boiler that he had salvaged and put it in the stock tank to keep it free from ice. White smoke puffed from the small pipe and swirled around the tank in the brisk wind.

The young geese had been sold. Mr Wicket and his hens stayed in the barn where they kept their feet warm in the hay. Hans filled a slop pail from the tank and carried water to them. He looked like he had a fire going inside himself as his breath fogged around his face from the exertion in the cold wind. When he opened the barn door, Mr. Wicket scolded with loud honks. After Hans poured the water in the wooden tub, that ungrateful goose jumped in and took a bath, before he would let the hens in.

Tante took care of the chickens. On a cold snowy day, the hen house seemed cozy and friendly, with the hens singing the way they do when they are contented. They scratched in the straw, busy with the chicken business of laying eggs and growing fat for the stew pot. The hens did not lay many eggs in the winter, but Tante had put some away in dry salt during the summer when the flock was laying.

Spring came late this year–the March wind blustered until mid-April. The cold wet weather, however, did not prevent the baby animals from arriving on schedule. Tabby and Ginger, our two calico cats, had litters in the hayloft. Tabby was in a warm nest in a tunnel under the hay. Ginger was up on the hay where it was piled to the roof.

Pigs seemed to arrive mostly at night. Hans got up frequently and went out to the hog house. Sometimes he did not return to the house until morning. Then he would have a squealing, squirming pig to put by the range and keep warm until the sow finished having her litter.

The calves were born in a box stall in the barn. The cow got to stay for one day with her baby before she was turned out to pasture, but she spent a full week standing by the barn bawling for her calf. It was not fun for Tante when she had to break a calf for bucket feeding. It was fun for me to watch, though, as she straddled him and pushed his back end into a corner. She stuck two fingers in his mouth and pushed his head in the bucket until his nose was down in the warm milk. He sucked her fingers and wagged his tail and butted the bucket, so there was as much milk on Tante as there was in his belly.

Mrs. Wicket laid an egg every other day in the barrel by the hen house. Mr Wicket stood guard to see that no one bothered her. Tante watched for them to leave the barnyard, and then she brought the egg in so it would not chill. She wrapped them in an old pair of Hans's woolen underwear and turned them every day until it was time for Mrs. Wicket to set. Tante said that was the way a goose hen would take care of her eggs, if they were left in the nest. She would scooch around until she had every egg turned, and cover them carefully with straw.

School was out in May. I passed to the second reader. Tante and Hans arose at four in the morning and went to bed at nine in the evening. Saturday, we went to town and on Sunday we went to church. When there was heavy work to do, there was always a neighbor to lend Hans a hand. Mostly, it was Henry Claussmann. Tante belonged to the Prairie Girls sewing club, and Hans was a member of the Mason Lodge.

After walking behind the plow all day, Hans relaxed after supper. He sat on the porch and looked out across the prairie, where he could see the freshly turned sod, an expression of well-earned accomplishment on his face. Often he would fall asleep and Tante would tickle his nose with a blade of grass.

"Komm to bett, Hans," she would urge, running her finger through his wiry brown hair. He pulled her down on his lap and held out his free arm to me. I avoided his arm and sat on his foot for a bouncy ride. Then, with his arms around both of us, we went indoors.

July was hot and humid. Tante had not been feeling well. She had a bad spell right after haying in June. Now she was pale and rested a lot. Hans was worried when he told me, "if Tante get sick, du komm and bringen Hans."

"I'll take care of Tante," I told him.

"Das ein gute girl." To Tante he said, "Liebchen, du nitch dings das too heavy for du.

"Ja, I be careful," she said.

That afternoon Hans stayed close to the house. He fixed the evening meal. I put some marigolds in a tiny vase and set it on Tante's tray. I skipped alongside of him when he carried it to her, and I was rewarded with a smile and a hug.

In the night, I woke up to voices in Tante's room. I got out of bed and opened the door. Dr. Miller was working over Tante and I could see blood. I was terrified.

Hans said, "Go back to bett."

I whispered, "Hans, is Tante hurt ? Is she going to die?"

"Nau, nau, kinda, Tante be all right. Don't cry, du stay in bett and Dr. Miller will make Tante better," he soothed.

Alice Clausmann came over every day to bring food and sit with Tante. I mooned around like a lost puppy.

One day I heard Tante say to Hans, "God ist nicht ready to give uns baby jet."

Three years passed since I had come to live with Tante and Hans. I was nine and in the third reader. It was early in June. Tante and I sat on the porch. Tante had the churn between her knees and was plunging the dasher up and down in the thick cream. It was a warm day, and she had thrown a bucket of cool water over the porch floor and swept it off. The pungent odor of marigolds mingled with the smell of bread baking in the kitchen. Off in the west, thunderheads were building into a summer storm. Tante was quiet and thoughtful. She did not seem to hear the rumble of the thunder.

"Marty," she said, "ich get brief [letter] from du Mama." She hesitated. "Du Mama komm here."

"Uh, uh, my Mama's far away," I said.

"Nau du haben another Papa," she answered.

"I don't want another Papa," I stated.

"But nau du kann be mit du Mama and stay by her," she

said, trying to sound enthusiastic.

"No," I said as a matter of fact, "I'll stay with you and Hans."

Before she could answer, the wind began to lash the big tree that shaded the porch. The branches swung low and the leaves brushed the ground. They raised and bowed again. I thought of Tante shaking her apron at the chickens when they got in her garden.

"Komm Marty," she said, picking up the churn, "we beta go in."

The storm raged and I forgot about Mama. I did not want to remember, because remembering gave me an odd feeling in my stomach, like being scared. Tante did not mention her again.

True to custom, when guests were to arrive, the house was cleaned from the attic to the cellar. The feather bed in the spare room was hung up to air and the straw in the tick was stirred and freshened. An old cradle that had been used by Hans when he was a baby was brought down from the attic.

I wanted to ask Tante why, but for some reason I just could not mention it. I just watched and rejected it. Tante still did not say anything more about Mama and my new Papa.

Mama and Heinrick Heldt arrived a week later. I watched from the window in the kitchen behind the curtain. They were coming up the lane in a buggy. It had rained again, so the unshod horses plodded in the soggy road, slipping and plunging against one another and the tongue of the vehicle. Mama was holding a bundle wrapped in a blanket. I thought to myself, maybe she's bringing me a present, maybe it's a doll.

The rig stopped near the front gate. I giggled when the man, dressed in a dark suit and black hat, threw back his head while his chin whiskers, trimmed neatly to a point, stuck straight out.

Tante came to the door and turned to me, "Komm, Marty," she said. "Diese is du Mama."

"No," I said, hanging fast to the curtain. She did not insist and went out to welcome them.

Mama was fat and did not seem to be as tall as I remembered. Tante hugged her, looked in the blanket, and smiled as they walked together up the path to the kitchen. I pulled the curtain around me and hid my face. Tante disentangled me gently.

"Komm, Marty, und see du Mama," she insisted firmly.

Mama held out her arms, "Mein kinda! Mein kinda! How big du grow." She tried to pull me over to her, but I shoved her away.

My new Papa squatted beside me with the bundle. "So du ist Marty. See Marty, we bringen du ein bruder." He showed me a sleeping baby. The doll I was sure was in the blanket turned out to be a baby. A real live baby! I turned away and fled to my room, where threw myself on the bed and cried.

Papa came in and sat on the bed beside me. He patted my shoulder and stroked my hair gently until my sobs ceased. Then he lifted me to a sitting position and raised my chin with his finger. I looked into a pair of brown eyes that had funny little laugh wrinkles around them. His face was kind, and his goatee did not seem funny anymore. It made him look the way a Papa should.

"Nau, nau, why du cry, ist du afraid?" He picked up the end of the sheet and dabbed at the tears on my cheeks. "Du no like baby Peter? His Mama und his Papa no can keep him, so we bringen him to haus mit uns."

I was silent except for a smothered sob. I went to a chair to hug the softness of Muggins, hiding my face in her yarn hair.

"Das ein pretty doll. See! I kann smile like jo doll." He crinkled his face in a ridiculous smirk. I moved my head so that I could peek at him with one eye.

"See, I can cross mein legs, too." He sat there with his chin whiskers jutting out and a foolish grin on his face, one leg curled around the other. He looked absurd and I was reminded of Tim. I smiled in spite of myself.

"Komm, nau we see Mama," he insisted, quietly. Mama was talking when we entered the kitchen.

"Heinrich is gute man," she was saying. "He was staying by Turnbull haus when Fritz was toten [killed]. I sprechen [spoke] mit him und he make me forgess Fritz and his femilie. Der name Vaughn ist dead. Heinrick asked me to marry mit him, I think dis is gute ding. He have geld [gold] from his vater [father]. We go to Ipswitch for zwei [two] jahr, und den we go to Holstein. Den Heinrich get brief [letter] about Peter, so we komm to America."

She stopped talking when she saw us in the doorway. Papa had his arm around my shoulder and guided me to her arms. She kissed me on the lips. I did not like it and rubbed them hard with the back of my hand. I did not like her either, for she had just said the name Vaughn is dead.

In the days that followed, Mama tried to make me love her. I turned from her, instead giving Tante my good-night kiss. I would take my slate to her for praise or encouragement. Mama resented my rejection, and soon she was giving a barbed reply whenever Tante asked her a question. A tension grew between the two women. I think it was a great relief to Tante when Papa bought a farm near Yankee Hollow.

I fought desperately to stay with Hans and Tante, but Mama insisted I live with her and Papa.

So, my trunk was again packed and I accompanied it. For days, I was an object again, deep in depression. Gradually, I did adjust to a new life with Mama and Papa.

Yankee Hollow was a one-room school built in a hollow where Mud Creek wound toward the Mississippi. Roy and Elsie Glenney lived a mile south of the hollow. Their four children were Martha, whom everyone called Mate, eleven,

Sam, seventeen, Tom, sixteen, and Gibson, fourteen.

Past Yankee Hollow and farther south was Henry Mason's place. Caroline and Henry had four children also–three girls–Teresa, nineteen, Kate, fifteen, Ann, thirteen–and a boy named Joe, who was seventeen. Henry Mason was deaf and almost mute. He could make a few guttural sounds that no one understood except his family. He used sign language to communicate with others.

Martha and George Sheldon lived across the field to the west. The teacher, Harvey Tompkins, boarded with them. Within a ten-mile radius were four other farms. Minne and Al Gates and their eight-year-old twin boys, Stella and Clay Hemper and their seven children, Joe and Jenny Goss with five kids, and Pearl and Jim Cleggar, who were older people whose children had grown. The school enrollment was twenty-three.

Everyone was friendly in the new school and helped me adjust to the new routine. I missed Tante's companionship and the things we had done together–like exploring the hillside where we found the first Dutchman's-breeches and shootings stars in the spring. We had discovered the plants first. Every day that followed we watched for the buds to appear and finally bloom. When the blossoms burst forth, I was allowed to doff my shoes and stockings and walk in the cool grass–then dip my toes in the icy water of the spring-fed creek.

I had watched the cats near milk pails, and hauled them out by their tails when they crawled over the side and lapped at the foam while Tante and Hans were milking. I climbed in the horse manger to gather eggs some crafty hen thought she had hidden. I had helped Tante set the brood hens and shared the thrill of the eggs pipping on the twenty-first day.

Life was different now. Peter was growing and doing cute things that I termed mischief. He liked to climb, but he was so clumsy he fell more times than not. He was fat–no wonder the way Mama shoveled food into him. He had good lungs, too. He knew if he used them, Mama would come running to him and kiss his hurt place, even when it was on his bottom, crooning, "Nau, nau, Mama make es besser." But when I stubbed my toe, she yelled, "Du dumb kopf [head], watch what ju du ungeschickt [clumsy]." She would frown and bumps came out on each side of her face.

The bumps reminded me of Mearl, the boxer hound that belonged to Ernie Prettel. Ernie owned the general store in Blue Grass, and I had been there with Tante. Mearl was a big fierce-looking canine who growled whenever anyone touched him. When he opened his mouth to yawn, it looked like a small cavern with a passageway to dark mysterious depths. I always clung to Tante's skirt and kept my eye on him, for I had seen Ernie give him a large bone to chew on. He had growled, wrested, and chewed. I was sure he would do the same thing to me if I ever got in his way.

Mama assigned chores for me to do. I had to get the cows from the pasture and milk two of them. I gathered the eggs and fed the chickens, filled the wood box and the reservoir on the side of the cook stove. I did the supper dishes, and once each week I scoured the bottom of the pots and the silverware with wood ashes.

I was rebellious. I soon learned that the wood box filled up faster if I did not rank the wood. The dishes were done sooner if I hid some of the dirty pans in the cupboard. It was more fun to get the cows. If I timed it just right, Mate Glenney would be after her family's cows at the same time. The Glenneys' pasture was next to ours, so I would crawl through the hedge to play with Mate. The cows always started for home when they saw me coming. By the time I got home, they were standing at the gate bawling to get in and milked.

Papa shook his head. "Kinda, kinda, why du make tricks on Mama? Du know she catch du sooner oder later? Den she licks du und du get no supper."

"Mama don't like me. She only likes Pete," I pouted.

"Well, kinda, try nitch to tease du mama-dan she no be so cross," he said.

Sometimes Mama scolded Papa and treated him badly too. Whenever she sent me to bed without my supper, he always managed to smuggle something up to me.

Mate Glenney was my best friend. She was an eager conspirator to all my mischief, and thought up quite a few tricks of her own. Her eyes were the color of blue lupine and her innocent gaze was deceptive. She wore her blonde hair in braids that hung over her shoulders. My hair was dark and my eyes were blue-green. We were both at an awkward age. My arms were too long and I did not know what to do with them. My legs were skinny and my knees knobby beneath my petticoats.

In the fall, Mate and I started in the fifth reader. Mister Tompkins was a tall man with graying hair and piercing blue eyes. He wore thick, gold-rimmed specks well down on his nose and looked over the top of them. He said he could not see a thing without them. We agreed, for when his back was to us, he could not see a thing we were doing without those mirroring spectacles. We did not catch on until Joe Mason hid them behind some books in the reference library. Mister Tompkins had to keep turning around to see what was going on behind his back.

He kept everyone after school every night trying to find the guilty one. Finally, Joe confessed and the rest of us were allowed to go. Mate and I stayed around outside to see what would happen to Joe. Mister Tompkins came out and proceeded to cut a good stout hickory stick from the tree by the rail fence. When he reentered the schoolroom, the howls that emitted from within convinced us that Joe was feeling the full brunt of the stick.

"Did it hurt much?" I asked Joe, when he came out.

"Naw," he said. "I just hollered loud to make him think he was hurting me. I shoulda broke his old specs, then he couldn't see nothing." He jumped over the fence and cut across the field toward home.

"I'll bet it did so hurt," said Mate.

"Yeah, I'll bet it did," I agreed, starting toward home.

"Look! Horse beetles Marty," said Mate, picking up a stick and poking a manure ball they were rolling.

"Here, this one's yours and this one's mine. Let's have a race and see which one gets to this stick first." She laid the stick across the dusty wagon track several feet ahead.

"But you've got three beetles pushing yours, I've only got two," I protested.

"Yes, but mine has a little farther to go," she answered.

"Maybe two inches is all," I said.

The beetles pushed the balls with their back legs, tumbling and rolling along with them. We watched their efforts for some time, and they rolled them about six inches.

"I've got to get home Mate, or Mama will get after me," I said starting down the road. "Are you comin'?"

"Yeah," she said, pulling her stick along in the thick dust. "But mine beat," she added.

"They did not. They didn't get to the stick," I said.

"Yes, but mine was ahead of yours," she contended.

"I'll tell you what, I'll race you to your lane. Whoever gets there first is the winner," I challenged.

"Oh no, you can run faster than I can," she answered.

"All right, then it's even," I said.

Walking side by side, we did not talk very much. Suddenly, she darted ahead and got to the lane first.

"Ha, ha! I beat. I'm the winner," she crowed.

"That's not fair. You said you wasn't gonna play," I reminded her.

"You didn't Kings X or anything, so I won." She ran up

the lane with her hands over her ears, chanting, "I'm the winner, I'm the winner."

Oh well, I thought, shrugging my shoulders. Then I started to run, for I was already an hour late getting home. Mama was waiting for me with Papa's razor strap near at hand.

"Next time du komm to haus when school ist aus," she hissed, between whacks across my shoulders. I was determined I would not cry, and went about my chores dry-eyed with a little more resentment.

Mister Tompkins tried to set a good example and would have us believe he had no bad habits. He kept his cigars hidden under some papers in his desk drawer, and his spirits locked up with the chalk. One day, when he was out of the room, Joe swiped three of his cigars. Everyone laughed and giggled. I thought for sure he would get caught, but when Mr. Tompkins came in the room, everyone immediately stuck their nose in a book, pretending to study. Mister Tompkins looked around suspiciously, giving Joe extra close scrutiny, and decided everything was in order.

At recess, Joe strolled nonchalantly out with the three cigars hidden in his shirt.

"Who wants to smoke a cigar?" he asked the group that surrounded him.

The boys all yelled, "I do."

But he said, 'No, I'm gonna teach the girls to smoke. Marty and Mate's gonna help me smoke 'em."

"Not me," said Mate.

"Come on, Mate,' I coaxed, thrilled that Joe had picked us. "Come on, I dare you."

"We-ell, all right," she said hesitantly.

Mate could be dared into doing anything I wanted her to do. We climbed over the rail fence and walked deep between the rows in the cornfield. We sat down, far out of sight of the schoolhouse, and Joe lit the cigars. I puffed on mine and had it about half smoked when my stomach began to feel queasy. I grinned a sickly half-hearted grin and looked at Mate. She was positively green. I glanced at Joe. He did not look well either. Mate rubbed her stomach and groaned.

"Ooh, I'm sick." She got up and staggered over several rows before she began to retch.

Joe pretended he was feeling fine, but his sickly grin told us it was all he could do to hold his lunch. "I guess we better get Mate back," he said, trying to give me the impression this was old stuff to him. By the time we got to the fence, everything seemed to be moving in circles. I grabbed for a rail as the fence went by and hung on.

Mate's brother Gib carried her to her seat. Joe and I staggered to ours.

Mister Tompkins looked at us over his specs. "What's the matter here?" he asked. "Did you eat something?"

Joe just shook his head and groaned inaudibly. I put my head on my folded arms–that way things stopped spinning.

"Gibson, hitch up my rig. We had better take them home," Mr. Tompkins said, puzzled.

Joe had ridden to school on horseback. He assured Mr. Tompkins he was able to ride home. Gib took Mate and me in Mr. Tompkins' rig.

Papa was coming from the barn when we drove in. "What ist los [wrong] mit ju, Marty?" he asked.

"I'm sick." I answered.

"So," he said, "what make ju sick?"

I shook my head. "I don't know." I was beginning to feel better, but I had to bluff it through.

Papa got the whiskey bottle and poured about a half cup in a glass. "Nau, drink," he instructed.

The whiskey nearly strangled me. I had managed to keep

from vomiting until now, but this was too much. I heaved until I was so weak I could hardly wobble to my bed.

Mama was concerned too. "Du stay in bett, du feel besser in das morgen."

The next morning I was weak, but felt better and went back to school. Mate and Joe were there also. Mister Tompkins had a suspicious nature. He thought we had recovered too soon; he had discovered his cigars were missing as well. He put two and two together, and got three guilty people. When school took up after lunch, he had a steely glint in his eyes as he walked down the aisle and stopped in front of Joe.

"Joe, how do you feel today?" he asked.

"I feel better," answered Joe.

"And how are you feeling, Marty?"

"I feel pretty good," I answered.

"Martha, how do you feel?"

"I feel better," she said.

"Well now, I'm glad the three of you made such a quick recovery. Now," he ordered, rubbing his hands together with anticipation, "I want the three of you to help me with an experiment. Come to the recitation bench."

I wondered why he wanted us to come before the class, but I followed Mate and Joe and sat down.

"Now then!" he said, in his most experimental voice. "I'm going to give each of you a cigar to smoke." He took them from a box in the drawer and handed us each one. "Now, light up and start smoking," he snapped.

There was a twitter among the others. Mister Tompkins looked over his specs and demanded, "Silence in the classroom! Miss Vaughn, Miss Glenney, and Mr. Mason will entertain us with a repeat performance of yesterday's episode. I will call on your parents this evening and inform them as to the nature of your illness yesterday, and further inform them you will be detained after school for the next three weeks for thirty minutes while you write 'I will not steal,' one hundred times on the blackboard."

I guess the punishment fit the crime, but I thought it was an injustice when Mama walloped me just to let me know she thought Mr. Tompkins discipline was fair.

Mate and I was fourteen the fall Sam Glenney had to marry Lillian Thompson. Sam and Lillie had finished school in the spring. We knew they were sweethearts, because we had seen them kissing behind the schoolhouse. Mate informed me of the approaching marriage on the way home from school one day.

"I had to get up in the night, and I heard Mom and Dad talking," she said. "Lillian is going to have a baby."

"How do they know?" I asked.

"I heard Dad tell Mom that Lillian is in a family way and she is blaming it on Sam, and God only knows who it belongs to. Sam told Dad he was guilty once and that was the only time he had anything to do with her. Mom said more than likely it would have to happen more than once for her to get caught, and she didn't see why she was blaming it on Sam."

I thought about what Mate had told me, as I walked alone after Mate had turned at her lane. When I got home, I said to Mama, "Lillian Thompson is gonna have a baby and Sam Glenney is gonna marry her."

Mama looked shocked. "How du know about dat? For shame du not talk about est, she bad woman."

"Why is she bad?"

"Sie nau hast a man jet. If du let man vergenralliger [rape] du und du mek scandal to uns und get schwanger [pregnant], I toten [kill] du and bury du hinter [behind] der stall [stable]."

Mama had never told me about babies and how they

came into the world. Now she was threatening to kill me if I got pregnant and disgraced her. I did not even know what *vergenralliger* meant.

It was a bad year for the Glenneys. For several days Mate had not been in school. Mister Tompkins asked her brothers if she was sick. They told him she had a sore throat. The next day the two Glenney brothers were absent also.

I decided to stop and see Mate on the way home from school, so I hurried faster than usual after we were dismissed. I left my lunch pail at the end of the lane, went up to the house, and rapped. A white paper attached to the door read, "Quarantine." Hmm . . . , I thought. I wonder what that means. Oh well, that piece of paper doesn't concern me. I rapped again. No one seemed to be around, so I opened the door and went in. Mrs. Glenney was not in the kitchen, and I could see through the double doors leading into the sitting room that she was not there either. I went up to Mate's room. Her door was shut and I turned the knob quietly. I did not want to wake her if she was sleeping.

She was lying in bed, facing the window. When I came in, she made an effort to turn her head to see who had entered.

"Hello, Mate," I said cheerfully, "how's your sore throat?" She tried to reply, but I could not understand her. I moved nearer to the bed. She struggled to get a deep breath and coughed. Her face was gray with pallor, except for an unnatural flush in her cheeks. Her eyes looked wild with feverish brightness.

"Do you think you will be well soon enough to be in the Halloween program? If you're not in it, I'm not going to be in it either," I said. She tried to say something. "Don't try to talk if your throat hurts," I said.

Mrs. Glenney must have heard my voice. She came into the room and when she saw me, she threw up her hands. "Marty, oh my goodness, Marty! What are you doing here?"

"I just stopped on my way home from school to see how

long before Mate can come back," I answered, but she had me by the shoulders and was pushing me out of the room.

"Didn't you see the quarantine sign on the door? That means you are not to come into this house," she said.

"I saw a sign, but I didn't know what it meant," I replied.

"Is means that Mate has diphtheria. Even her father and brothers aren't allowed to go in there. Diphtheria is a very bad sickness. It spreads from person to person when they come into contact with it. Mate is very sick, Marty." She began to sob, but with an effort she said, "You go on home, Marty, and tell your mother that Mate has diphtheria and you were in her room. You understand Marty? It's very important you tell her the minute you get home, because now you are exposed."

"All right, Mrs. Glenney, I'll tell her," I said, puzzled at the fuss she made, and a little scared too. Mate looked awfully sick, and Mrs. Glenney acted like she wasn't going to get well.

When I got home, I went in the kitchen door. Mama hollered from the front room, "Ist dot du, Marty?" Her voice sounded like she had bumps again.

"Yes," I said.

"Where was du? Du late from schule," she said irritably.

"Mate is sick and I stopped to see her," I answered, debating whether or not I should tell her about Mate having-about her sickness. I couldn't remember what Mrs. Glenney said it was.

"What ist der sacht [matter] mit her?" she asked, coming to the kitchen.

"I don't know. She has got an awful sore throat," and deciding I had better tell her, I added, "they've got a sign on their door so nobody will go in."

"Diphtheria!" Mama shouted. "Mate haben diphtheria?"

"Yes, that's what Mrs. Glenney said she is sick with,"

I answered.

"Du nau go in, did ju?"

"Yes, but Mrs. Glenney made me go right out again."

"Himmel! Why du go in? HEINRICK! HEINRICK!" she screamed out the back door toward the barn, at the same time pushing me out on the porch.

Papa came running. "Nau, nau, what ist los [wrong]?"

"Mate Glenney haben diphtheria, Marty was by her haus."

"So, so?" said Papa.

Mama filled the wash tub from the range reservoir and poured Lysol in it. She stripped off my clothes. Papa took them out and burned them. He cut a big hunk off his chewing tobacco and made me chew it while Mama scrubbed me. I put on fresh clothes. Then Papa got his whiskey bottle and poured a half glass; he stood right there to see that I drank it. After all that, I was sure no respectable germ would have me, and I did not think the disease would have been as bad as the preventative measures they put me through.

Mate died at dawn the next morning. Sam brought us the news of his sister's death. It was hard to believe Mate was gone and I would never see her again. With the shock of her death, I was seized with panic at the thought I might get the dreadful disease and die too. Already I thought my throat was beginning to feel sore. If I could have gone to Tante, she would have reassured me even though she would be worried about me.

Papa and Mr. Mason dug a grave for Mate in the little cemetery on a knoll not far away. There was no public funeral for her, because nobody wanted to go near the Glenney place. Papa helped build the coffin. Mister Glenney and the boys had to take it inside and lay the body in it.

I walked over to the cemetery a week later. As I stood by Mate's grave, the wind moaned and sighed through a tall pine nearby. It seemed to echo the lonely feeling of the dying summer and to re-echo an aching emptiness in my heart.

Time has a way of healing all hurts, but I never walked past the Glenney farm without a feeling of sadness and depression.

Chapter Three

Spring burst forth as the melting snow turned the land soggy and the roads axle deep in mud. The willows by the creek blushed green and burst their swollen buds into tiny leaves. The hillsides were covered with shooting stars and other wild flowers.

The last day of school was celebrated with a program and a box social. All the women in the district made a box for the auction. I was about to turn fourteen in July and in the fifth reader, so I spent a lot of time on mine to get it to look just right with satin ribbons and artificial daisies. I packed the lunch with great care and a secret wish in my heart that Joe Mason would buy my box. The men were not supposed to know whose box they had bought until they opened it and found the name inside. It would be a tragedy if Mr. Tompkins or a married man would happen to get a box that had been fixed up for a certain boy.

That night the boxes were wrapped in newspaper and deposited on a table in the cloakroom. Mister Tompkins brought in the artistic creations and handed them to the auctioneer one by one. My box was the sixth one he held up. "Now, what am I offered for this one?" He balanced it in one hand. "Mm-mm, there's a lot of goodies in this one, fellows. I'll bet there's a piece of Carrie Mason's chocolate cake in here. Who'll give me a quarter?" He turned so everyone could see it.

Joe looked at me and asked a question with his eyes. I barely nodded and dropped my head coyly. He smiled and started to bid. The auctioneer began to chant, "I got a quarter, a quarta, who'll give a half?" Gib Glenney raised his finger and the chant was "I got a half," he pointed a finger at Joe. "A dolla?" Then to Gib, "I got a dolla, now a quarta, a quarta," to Joe, "now a half," to Gib, "two, now two." Gib shook his head. "Come on, Glenney, there's a pretty girl comes with this box, see the daisies?" He started pulling on the petals. "She loves me, she loves me not, she loves me-do I hear two dollas?" He pointed at Joe, "Going, going, gone! Sold to Joe Mason for a dollar and a half."

I would have been disappointed if Joe had not gotten my box, but I was embarrassed, too, at the way the auctioneer had pulled the daisies, making everyone laugh. This was the first time I sat next to Joe, like a girl with her fella. The twins, Jimmie and Jonnie Gates, ran around in a circle, chanting, "Joes's got a girl, Joe's got a girr-l." Joe's brown eyes smiled at me. I did not dare look at him because my face got hot, so I looked at my lap.

"You're bashful," he teased. I blushed. "I like bashful girls," he laughed. "Say! How about an after-dinner cigar?" he whispered mischievously in my ear.

"Ugh, don't mention cigars to me. I can't even stand the smell of them."

"They make whiskers grow," he laughed, stroking his face proudly, where there was a faint trace of red fuzz beginning to show.

"Wouldn't I be pretty with whiskers?" I asked sarcastically.

"You could let them grow and braid 'em," he teased."You

could be a bearded lady."

I put my hands on my hips and turned to him with a smart, "Well."

With an impish grin, he added, "I'd like you even if you did grow a beard."

"That's pretty nice of you," I said dryly.

"You mad?"

"No."

"Since I'm out of school now, Pa will give me a two-year-old gelding if I stay and help him on the farm."

"Are you gonna stay?"

"Yeah, I guess so. A year or two anyway."

"Is the gelding broke to ride?"

"Not yet, I put a saddle on him the other day and led him around the yard. He bucks a little. Tell you what, I'll bring him over to your place and you can ride him."

"Thanks! I'm not a bronco buster," I said flatly.

"That's all right," he grinned, "my horse isn't a bronco."

The women had gathered in small groups, putting on their wraps, and the men were out at the hitching posts waiting to go home. Joe whispered, 'I wish I had my own rig, then I could ask your Pa if I could take you home."

"I'd like to see your horse sometime," I said boldly.

"I'll be over," he answered.

With school out, Mama found a lot of work for me to do, but every chance I got, I went off by myself and made friends with Molly, a red heifer we had raised from a calf. I was trying to break Molly to ride. Whenever I went after the cows, I petted and groomed her, coaxing her to let me ride on her back. The day I thought she was ready for my first ride, I climbed aboard. She stood quietly until I was on her back, then she kicked up her heels. With her tail flying in the air, up the hill and down dale we went. I tried desperately to hang on while Molly tried to get me off her back. I lost the battle and flew off head over heels.

Slowly, I picked myself up and gingerly felt my neck and back to be sure my bones were all together. I turned when I heard a loud chuckle. There was Joe, sitting on the gate, waiting for me to bring the cows in.

"You sure can ride, Marty," he laughed. "All I could see was heels and red petticoats a-flyin'."

The chagrin I felt turned to anger at Molly and–topping that–at Joe having to see my tomfoolery. I stomped my foot at him. "Joe Mason! What are you doing spying on me?" He was laughing at me and I was furious.

"I don't think it was funny, I might have broken my neck."

He got down and dusted me off, still laughing. "The next time you try to ride her, you had better *tell* her what you have in mind."

My anger turned to embarrassment. I ran to the house and did not come out until he went home.

The next time I saw him, he still had that teasing grin. "Have you got that heifer broke yet?" I knew he was imagining me fly off Molly all over again.

It seems I was always at a disadvantage when Joe was around. He was sitting with me atop the board fence that enclosed the hog pen the day Mama and Papa were ringing the hogs before turning them out to pasture. Papa was catching the hogs and holding them, while Mama inserted the ring in their nose. The boar was the last of the herd to be rung. He weighed more than three hundred pounds. Papa backed him into a corner of the fence and straddled him. He grasped the boar's ears and pulled his head up. The hog did not like that much, and he swung his head trying to avoid the ring. Mama followed his movements with the pliers, trying to thrust the ring in his nose. Her long dress, apron, and petticoats were no help.

The boar was stubborn and refused to cooperate. He made a lunge and knocked Mama off her feet, taking off with Papa on his back, who hung on for dear life. His feet and his stiff, trimly tailored goatee stuck straight out. Hanging tightly to the boar's ears, he rode piggyback around and around the lot, kicking up a small cloud of dust as he and the hog went.

Mama was trying to kick herself loose from her confining skirts. She got to her knees, but they pinned her skirt so that she could not get slack enough to get on her feet.

Papa was astride the boar. Mama shook her head to clear it and get her bearings, and spotted Papa and the hog. She picked up her pliers and started after them, shouting, "Halt, Heinrick! Halt! Setzen [get him] in der ecke [corner]!"

"I see now where you learned to ride, Marty," said Joe, laughing so hard I thought he was going to fall off the fence. It made me laugh to see him laughing.

On her third swing around, Mama spied us. She swept me of the fence and boxed my ears so hard that they rung. I guess Joe thought he might get it, too, because he leapt off the fence and made tracks for home.

The boar found a hole in the fence and Papa rolled off just in time, as he ran to the pasture. Papa picked himself up and was none the worse for his undignified ride.

The summer was hot and dry, but in spite of the parched soil, there were days of pulling weeds and hoeing along with regular chores. Mama's favorite saying was "waste not, want not." With this in mind, we cut corn from roasting ears and spread it on cloth to dry. There were apples to peel and spread in pans, butter to churn, and schmierkase [cottage cheese] to make.

August 23 dawned with the temperature already in the seventies. Mama and Papa started to town before the sun got too high, leaving Pete and I at home to keep water in the hog troughs and chicken pans. The broiling sun compelled the hogs to seek shade. They lay along the board fence, taking advantage of what shade it offered. A few hens were taking dust baths to combat the lice that tormented them. Pete and I were lying on a horse blanket under a shade tree in the yard. As the day wore on, we were getting pretty bored. Old Tom, our gray cat, was swinging his paw at a piece of hemp that Pete was dangling in front of him.

I had some matches in my apron pocket. I lit one and held it up, watching the sputtering yellow flame until it burned down to my fingertips.

"I want one, Marty," said Pete.

"No, you'll burn yourself," I answered.

"I won't either. I'll tell Mama you were lighting matches," he threatened.

"Look," I cajoled, putting a lit match to the end of the hemp entangled in Tom's claws. "I'll bet he lets go when he feels the heat from this."

It burned to Tom's paw. He felt more than the heat, because it burned up around the fur on his leg. He arched his back and made off, spitting and yowling, straight for the straw pile, dragging the burning hemp with him.

Panic seized me and I dashed after him, but there was no catching that burning, terrified cat. As he leaped up into the straw, I stopped short, aghast! Flames flickered up in several places. The blood in my veins ceased to course, and I collapsed. I was unconscious only a short time, but when I came to, Pete was screaming and the straw pile was a mass of flames. Getting to my feet and grabbing a slop pail, I ran back and forth between the tank and the straw pile, tossing water on the flames, but it was like throwing a drop at a time on that inferno. White smoke belched from the flames and turned black as it puffed skyward.

The straw was piled against the barn and the flames were licking the side of the building. I still carried water, even though I knew my efforts were useless. After a time, help began to arrive. First to get there were Henry and Joe Mason. Almost immediately after came George Sheldon and the Glenney boys. Soon the yard was full of neighbors. They formed a bucket brigade, but it was to no avail.

"How'd it get started?" asked Mrs. Glenney.

"Probably combustion from green hay, could have been burning for a long time and just got air to it," said Clay Hemper.

"Naw, it didn't start in the barn," said George. "The stack was on fire first."

"The sun reflecting on a piece of glass could have started it," said Joe.

"Could of," they agreed.

Mama and Papa drove in with the horses at a gallop. They had seen the smoke when they were several miles away. By the time they reached home, the barn was a pile of burning embers. Papa looked old and tired as he sat staring at the ashes that had once been a barn, his shoulders sagging. I vowed to myself that I would never *never* do such a foolish thing again.

One by one the neighbors left, and I had to face Mama and Papa.

"Nau!" said Mama, "Wot make der feuer [fire]?"

"Mar-Mar-Marty did it. S-s-she burned T-Tom'n-n-n he run in the h-h-hay," said Pete, stuttering with excitement.

"So," said Mama, the bumps beginning to show, "dit ju make der katze on feuer?" she asked.

"We were just playing," I said trembling, backing toward the door.

"Du huzzy! Nau we have no-no scheune [barn] for der-der herdes [horses] und- und kuhs [cows]," she said furiously. She raised her hand to cuff me.

"No, Hannah!" Papa caught her hand and stepped between us. "Ist was accident."

"She ist teufel [devil]," hissed Mama. "Next jahr she go out to work."

I kept out of Mama's way as much as possible the next several months. When school was out in the spring, my trunk was again packed and I left the farm to work for a family who owned a large hotel in Fairport, a small village on the Mississippi.

Abby and Jim Hooverman owned the hotel. They had three children. Bill was the eldest, he was eighteen; Kate was next, she was my age, sixteen; and John was fourteen. Abby was an invalid, confined to a wheelchair. She was a tiny, good-natured person with large dark eyes and hair that was soft and white. Abby was forty-eight, but her hair made her look older. Jim was fifty-three. He had dark hair that was only beginning to turn gray at the temples, and his eyes were blue-gray. He was tall and youthful looking. His love for Abby showed in his eyes when he looked at her and in the tender way he took her in his arms and carried her from the wheelchair to the bed. Bill was tall, redheaded, and freckled, with eyes like his father's. Kate and John were both dark eyed, and their hair was the same color as Jim's.

There was a legend about the hotel that Bill told me at his first opportunity. He said a sailor had been murdered in a room on the third floor. Once a year, on the anniversary of the murder, lights could be seen and strange things went on in that room. They had closed the third floor and no one ever went up there. The legend intrigued me, so on my afternoon off, I climbed the narrow stairs. The room was right at the top and the door was closed. I pushed lightly against it with the palm of my hand, and turned the knob with my other hand. Slowly, it opened. It was an ordinary room with a bare wood floor and an old iron bedstead with springs. There was a washstand, a bowl and pitcher, and an old chest against the wall. The windows were bare. As I stood there looking into the room, an excited, tingly feeling came over me. I closed the door and ran down the stairs. In the days that followed, I tried to forget about the room on the third floor, but over the next year or so, it held a strange fascination for me.

Bill was a medical student at the state university. He teased me from the time he arose in the morning until I went to bed at night.

"Marty," he said, "I'm going to be a doctor. When I get through medical school, I'm going to cut you up in inch pieces and sew you together again, and if you are still as pretty as you are now, I'm going to marry you."

"Well, if you're as dumb as you are now, you won't know where the pieces belong," I retorted.

"And you wouldn't be afraid," he jeered.

"Of course not," I answered.

"You see, I'd save your blood and put it in a jug so I could pour it back in your veins. It might take quite awhile on your face and I'd give you a little turned up nose," he teased.

"I like my nose the way it is, Bill Hooverman," I said.

"See, I knew it, you're afraid," he laughed.

"I'm not afraid of anything." I stated.

"I'll bet you are afraid to sleep in the haunted room," he said.

"I am not! That's just a silly old story."

"All right! Sleep up there if you're not afraid."

"I will sometime."

"How about tonight?" he persisted.

"All right, tonight," I said, as little tingly thrills chased up and down my spine.

Kate was horrified when she found out what I was going to do. "Don't you do it Marty. Something terrible will happen to you. Don't you know there are ghosts up there?"

"Ah-h, pooh! Did you ever see them?" I asked, sounding much braver than I felt.

"No, but Marty, there was a man murdered up there," she told me.

"You don't have to go through with it, Marty," said Bill.

I suspected Bill was beginning to feel a little worried, but I knew if I backed out, he would always tease me about being afraid.

"You get me some blankets to put on the springs," I said.

"I'll sleep on the floor at the bottom of the stairs, so if anything happens, I'll be nearby to help you," he said.

After the supper dishes were done and the kitchen was tidied up, we went into Kate's room until bedtime. We were careful so that Abby and Jim did not know what we were up to. At nine o'clock, with an odd feeling in the pit of my stomach, I picked up the kerosene lamp and climbed the stairs. I pushed open the door, hesitated a moment, and looked back. Bill was as good as his word, and arranged a blanket and pillow at the bottom of the stairs.

I went in, set the lamp on the chest, and put on my nightgown. I left the door open and blew out the lamp.

I could see a dim glow of the lights in the street through the window. I lay there a long time trying to distinguish objects in the room. Suddenly, the window was dark and a flickering light was coming from a candle in an old brass holder of intricate design. It was atop a large highboy, along with a fully rigged model of a sailing vessel. I looked toward the window and heavy drapes covered it. My bed had changed; it was now an old four-poster wooden bed, and I was covered with a heavy spread that matched the drapes. There was an oval braided rug on the floor. I glanced at the door. It was closed.

I laid there, not moving a muscle. Suddenly, a paralysis

started to creep up my legs, like a cold, damp hand. I could not move–it seemed as though I had turned to stone. Slowly, the hand crept toward my throat. As it reached my chest, I made a desperate effort and let out a piercing scream. Blackness engulfed me as I lost consciousness.

Slowly, I opened my eyes. Jim was rubbing my arms and Bill was bathing my face with cold water. "What happened, Marty–why did you shut the door?" Bill asked.

I began to recall what happened, and my eyes must have mirrored the horror of my experience. I tried to sit up, but Jim pushed me gently back. "Lie still, Marty, I'm going to call Dr. Quinn."

Evidently, they thought I had some sort of nightmare, for Bill repeated, "Why did you shut the door?"

"I didn't shut the door."

"It was closed when you screamed."

"It was terrible, Bill, the whole room was changed."

"What do you mean, 'the room was changed'?" asked Jim, coming back into the room.

"Everything was changed. There were drapes–and a rug on the floor–and a candle and-and-and–oh, everything was changed!" I sobbed.

"Now, now," soothed Jim, "just stay quiet until the doctor gets here."

"I told you something terrible would happen if you went in that room," said Kate, rubbing my arms.

"Kate, go see if this has awakened your mother," said Jim. "John, you go to bed."

Doctor Quinn was at the door. Jim went to beckon him to my room. The doctor took my hand, and his deft fingers instantly found my pulse.

"What's the trouble, Jim?" he asked.

Jim seemed hesitant to reply. "The kids were foolin'

around, I guess. Seems something must have scared Marty pretty bad."

The doctor put his stethoscope inside my gown and listened. He straightened up, removed the listening apparatus, letting it hang around his neck. "What scared you, Marty?"

"It was my fault," interrupted Bill, gallantly. "I dared her to sleep in that room up on the third floor, the one that's haunted."

The doctor looked at me with an expression I could not fathom. "Oh, what happened up there?" he asked Bill.

Bill shrugged, "I don't know. She screamed and I guess I got scared–well, you know all those stories about that fellow who was killed up there. I ran and got Dad and we carried her down here."

"Did you see anything in the room?" he asked.

"No, Marty was laying there unconscious," said Jim.

"How long was she in there?"

"Maybe an hour, or an hour and a half," said Bill.

"Marty, what did you see that scared you?"

"I was just lying there, trying not to think about the story Bill told me, and things just gradually began to change. First, it was the window, when I blew out the lamp. I could see the window, but the rest of the room was dark. Then, I could not see the window, but there was a light in the room, from a candle on a highboy. There was a ship with white sails, a little one about three feet long, which looked just like a real ship. I tried to get up. I was going to relight the lamp, but I could not get up. There was a weight on me, and then I saw it was a heavy bedspread. It was dark red, and so were the drapes that covered the windows. The bed had changed, too. It was a wooden bed with posts and there was a braided rug on the floor. Then the weight got heavier on my feet, and–and–then I knew it wasn't the bedspread that was heavy–it was-was hands!"

"Why did you think it was hands? Had you been thinking about this before you went to sleep?"

"I didn't go to sleep! I was awake! I knew it was hands because they were cold, and all the time I was trying to get up, but I could not move. When the hands got to my throat, I knew they were going to strangle me."

"Hm-m." Dr. Quinn leaned over and examined the skin on my neck. "Hm-m, what do you make of this, Jim?"

"My God, Doc! That looks like finger marks around her neck," exclaimed Jim, exchanging a look of dismay with the doctor's look of inquiry.

"I'm going to make an investigation of this, Jim. Marty, tell me again exactly what you saw in that room."

I repeated the whole story again, while the doctor wrote everything I had told him in a book. "I'm going to leave a sedative for her. She'll be all right–she should go to sleep shortly. I'll be back tomorrow." The doctor closed his bag and tucked his little book in his pocket.

Jim followed him out. They were still talking out in the hall when I drifted off to sleep.

The next day Jim made me stay in bed and I was glad to, because I was weak and shaky. The doctor came about eleven o'clock. He pulled up a chair by my bed. "How do you feel this morning?" he asked.

"Just weak," I replied.

"Marty, who described that room to you? How did you know how that room was furnished twenty-three years ago?"

"Nobody described it to me, that's the way the room looked last night."

Jim came in and stood at the foot of my bed, "Good morning, Doc."

"How're ya, Jim? Jim, do you know how that room was furnished when the murder was committed?"

"No, ya know, I bought this place from Jess Cooley, fifteen years ago. Those stories about the murder didn't worry me none, but people were a little leery about renting either of the rooms up there, so I just closed up the third floor. There's nothing but junk up there. No, I don't recall anybody telling me how that room was furnished."

"Hm-m, tell me again, Marty, exactly what did you see in that room, every piece of furniture."

I repeated every detail I could remember.

"Jim, this is an amazing thing-she has just described that room exactly the way it was when Pete Nordike was strangled to death. I went to the newspaper office and looked up the file on this. The only thing she didn't describe was a portrait of George Washington that hung over the highboy."

This was my first experience with the unknown, extrasensory perception, or ghosts–whatever it was.

Chapter Four

I attended school in Fairport with Kate and John Hooverman, and in the spring of 1898, I finished my education with the completion of the sixth reader. The hotel was home to me, and I had developed affection for the Hooverman family. Abby and Jim were like mother and father to me, even to the point of scolding when I did not learn to spell all of the words in the spell down. Bill was like a big brother. When he arrived home on weekends, he tugged my braids loose and let them fall to my shoulders.

"You're prettier with your hair down," he said. Kate and I shared secrets we would not think of divulging to Abby. John was a typical kid brother, playing tricks that sometimes turned out to be more serious than he anticipated. Like the time he tied string across the stairs and I tripped over it. I tumbled down the steps, hurting my back. I spent the next two weeks lying strapped to a board!

Henry Mason had died the winter of 1897, and Mrs. Mason had moved her family to town. Joe was a handsome man now. His hair was black, and he sported a black mustache and side burns. His brown eyes still twinkled with mischief, and the tallness of him dwarfed me by comparison.

His horse and buggy were the envy of the young men in the community. His buggy was shiny black with red wheels, and his horse, Fannie, was jet black, slick and curried until her coat gleamed. The harness was fancy with gold rivets and hung with red celluloid rings.

I saw Joe one day when I went to the store for Abby. He asked me for a date and I accepted. When I told Abby, she said I must have a new dress, it being my first date. I did not have any money, since Mama came every month and collected my wages from Jim, so Abby gave me five dollars and told me to pick out the material. She would have her dressmaker sew it for me. My first party dress was the most beautiful gown in the world!

Our date was Saturday night. On Saturday morning, I got up early and fixed breakfast for Abby and Jim; they always had breakfast together in their room. I carried it on a large tray and Jim followed with the coffeepot. Kate was eating when I came back to the kitchen and I sat down with her.

"What's he like, Marty?" she asked.

"Who?"

"Your Joe. The boy you're going out with."

"Oh, he's nice. I went to school with him."

"Will he try to kiss you?" she teased.

"Oh Kate, of course not. Besides I wouldn't let him."

"Why don't you want him to kiss you?" she giggled.

My face was beginning to burn. Secretly, I was hoping Joe would kiss me. Kate was reading my thoughts.

"We have to get the work done," I said, trying to change the subject. "How about you giving your mother her bath?"

"Yeah, I guess so," she replied rather gloomily.

I did not think about Kate's swiftly changing mood, I was walking on air. Dinner was always early on Saturday night, because Jim liked to go to the corner saloon, or stand on the street corner and visit with his friends. By six o'clock the dishes were done, and I went to my room to get dressed. Kate came in to help me button, a wistful expression on her face.

"Gee, Marty, I wish I could go to a party with a boy."

"I'll bet you'll get a date one of these days, Kate."

"Somebody has to stay with Mother, and Daddy just takes it for granted I will. Boys never get a chance to see me," she sighed.

"I'm sorry, Kate, I wish you could go too."

She smiled a little crooked smile and gave me a push toward Abby's room. "Come on, let's show Mom your dress."

"Marty!" Abby exclaimed. "How nice you look. Doesn't she look pretty, Kate? Marty, remember, it's good girls who get husbands, so don't let that young man go too far with you." She patted my hand and smiled. I leaned over and kissed her cheek.

"Thank you for the beautiful dress."

I went back to my room and stood before the mirror. The reflection I saw was of a dark-haired girl with sparkling eyes and a flash of excitement in her cheeks. The dark red velveteen dress, with the white collar and cuffs, made me look at least two years older. I did a little pirouette before the mirror and went back to Abby's room. Kate was sobbing in her mother's arms. This made me feel bad. I put my arms around her. "Kate, please don't cry. Do you want me to stay home?"

She shook her head and pulled away from my arms, and left for her room. Abby's eyes filled with tears. "Marty, if only I could get out of this chair."

"Bill is going to make you well someday, Abby," I said. He was always saying, "When I get to be a doctor, Mom, I'm going to make you well."

"Yes, God willing, maybe he will, Marty," she answered. "Come, smile now, we mustn't spoil your first party," she added.

Joe arrived a short time later. He was wearing a blue serge suit and black shoes with tan spats.

"My, my, he looks like a dude," said Abby, peeking out from behind the curtain. I went to the door.

"Hello, Marty," he smiled. He nodded to Abby, who had wheeled herself to the door. "I'll bring her home as soon as the party's over," he said, taking my arm.

"Joe, this is Abby," I said, tugging him around to face her.

"Hello," he said. "I'll bring her home right after the party," he repeated, confused under the scrutiny of her gaze.

The evening air was heavy with the fragrance of spring. A cooling breeze wafted against my cheeks, as Joe helped me step in the buggy. He got in beside me, took the reins, and trotted the horse out of town. His rig looked smart; he had braided red and white ribbons in the horse's tail and mane.

The party was at a farmhouse five miles from town, and as we drove in, we could hear fiddle music. Every window in the house was lit. Joe gaily threw the reins to the attendant and asked, cheerfully, "Hi'ya Seth, are you elected liveryman or did you volunteer?"

"I been hired, Joe," he answered. "G'wan in and have a good time."

I learned later, if the attendant was hired, he was paid out of donations from a hat that was passed around among the gentlemen–the musicians were also paid out of the donations; when the liveryman volunteered, you tipped him for taking care of your horse.

Inside, a lot of people were dancing in a large room that must have been the dining room before they moved the furniture. In another room, ladies and children were visiting. Joe escorted me into this room and introduced me to the hostess, Mrs. Kocher. She took my arm and introduced me to the other ladies. They did not make any bones about looking me over from head to toe. I suppose they reserved judgment until they saw how I conducted myself. While I was being properly presented to everyone, Joe disappeared, but I barely had time to miss him before he was back.

After our first dance, I was able to follow Joe's waltz with perfect rhythm. With his face close to mine, I could smell the faint odor of spirits. I danced with a dazed feeling–this was a dream world. I went from Joe's arms to those of his friends, through the circle two-step and quadrilles, which were a confusion of bumping, laughing mistakes, until I learned to understand the lingo of the caller, and followed the guiding hands of do-se-do and promenade.

All too soon, the music changed from a lively turkey trot to "Home, Sweet Home," and we were waltzing in a special embrace, Joe's arm firmly around my waist. My heart was pulsating in my breast at a rapid rate that he must have been aware of, because he looked down at me and smiled, then held me a little closer.

In the buggy headed for home, Joe wrapped the reins around the buggy whip and pulled me close to him. I wriggled free and stretched my arms above my head.

"Oh, that was fun."

"Yes it was. Marty, will you be my girl?" he asked, pulling me close again.

"Kate and I dance sometimes when Abby isn't resting . . we turn on the gramophone," I said, embarrassed and pushing him away again.

"Marty?"

"Yes?"

"You didn't give me the right answer. Are you afraid of me?"

"No."

"Then why are you pushing me away?" He pulled me into his arms again. I relaxed against him and we drove in silence, enjoying the early morning stillness. A faint streak of dawn was appearing in the eastern sky as we entered Fairport. A bird twittered somewhere in a nearby tree, as we walked up the path to the door.

"I hope you won't get scolded for getting in so late.

"I don't think they will say anything."

"Will you go riding with me tonight?"

I nodded. "Tonight."

He tightened his arm around me and drew me against him, touching my lips lightly with his. "Goodnight."

"Goodnight, Joe."

I floated into my room in a cloud of ecstasy, undressed, and got in bed. I relived again every detail of the evening, and touched my mouth with my fingers, where he had pressed his kiss, as I drifted off to blissful slumber.

"Marty, Marty, wake up!" It was Kate, and it seemed I had just gone to sleep. I pulled the sheet over my head.

"Marty, Marty! Did you have fun? It's time to get up." I raised up on my elbows. I knew Kate was not so much concerned about getting me up as she was to hear about my date.

"Was it fun–did you have a good time?" she asked, settling beside me on the bed.

"Uh-huh," I said drowsily.

"It was morning when you came in," she whispered in awe, like she thought we did something we should not have.

"Yeah, the dance lasted until two o'clock."

"It was four when you came in. Tell me about it, Marty," she urged, fascinated.

"There isn't anything to tell. We went to a dance."

"I know that. Did he put his arm around you? Did he try

to kiss you?"

"You can't dance with a boy unless he puts his arm around you."

"Oh, you know what I mean," she said disgustedly. "Did he put his arm around you on the way home?"

"Well, sort of."

"Did he kiss you, too?"

"Yeah, once."

"You aren't supposed to let a boy kiss you unless you're promised," she said, her eyes sparkling.

"I am promised in a way. He asked me to be his girl."

"Already! You've only been out with him once–besides, he has to ask you to marry him before you're promised."

"C'mon Kate, we have to get breakfast," I said, getting up and pulling my dress over my head. I buttoned it on the way to the kitchen. She was making my date seem like something to be ashamed of.

Bill was sitting at the table drinking a cup of coffee. "Well, someone is trying to beat my time, eh?" he teased. My face began to feel hot and he laughed at my confusion.

"Well, if I have to share you with another fellow, I hope he's a nice guy, Marty."

I put four slices of bread in the wire toaster, slipped the clamps over the handles, and laid it on the hot stove. I was in for a lot of teasing about my beau, I could tell. I decided to ignore him. I spooned oatmeal into two dishes and flipped the toaster over. I set up the tray while it browned, and then buttered the toast and carried the tray to the bedroom.

"Good morning, Marty–my, you look pretty and rosy cheeked this morning. Did you have a good time last night?" asked Abby.

"It was getting daylight when you came in," said Jim.

"I had a wonderful time and the party wasn't over until two o'clock," I said, answering both of them.

"That's all right. I know you will take care of yourself," said Abby.

"May I go out again tonight?"

"With Mason?" asked Jim.

"We're just going riding," I answered, nodding.

"Well, if you get in early," he consented.

"I will."

Joe took me to his home that evening. Carrie Mason greeted me warmly. "Hello, Marty, it's nice to see you again. You've grown since you left the farm–filled out, too. How's your mother and father?"

I blushed when she mentioned my being filled out while Joe was present, but it was true. I was no longer the gangling, skinny girl with the bony legs and arms too long. My bust was rounded and firm, and my waist was slim.

"It's nice to see you, too, Mrs. Mason. Hello, Ann," I greeted his sister, who was sitting at the table doing some mending. "I haven't seen Mama and Papa for almost a month, but I guess they're all right."

Mrs. Mason was the same thin, gaunt woman, with thinning gray hair and green eyes. Her hands were strong and work roughened. There was an awkward silence while I tried to think of something to say while Mrs. Mason discreetly looked me over.

"How's Kelly and Teresa?" I asked, finally.

"Come in and sit," said Mrs. Mason, leading the way to the sitting room.

"Ann, put that up now, we have company. Kelly and Teresa are both married, you know. Teresa lives in Texas. She married a rancher, Christopher Ladehaus. Kelly lives on a farm close to Durant. She married Ted Miller and they have a son, Thaddeus. He's almost a year old, they call him Tad."

"Oh," I said, ill at ease.

"You still work at the hotel where your ma sent you?"

"Yes, for the Hoovermans."

"Do they get many people there?"

"Oh yes, it's the stopping place between Davenport and Muscatine."

"You must meet quite a few people," said Ann.

"Jim doesn't let Kate or me go into the rooms until the guests have checked out. Then we clean it and get it ready for the next customer."

"They don't board anybody, do they?" asked Ann.

"No, they used to, but not since Abby's been paralyzed."

"What was it that happened to Mrs. Hooverman?" asked Ann.

"She was hurt in a runaway, wasn't she?" asked Mrs. Mason.

"Yes, it happened when Kate was six years old. Abby was driving to the country to visit friends. There was a train coming when she crossed the tracks and the engineer blew the whistle. It scared the horses and they bolted. When the buggy upset, Kate flew out–she didn't get hurt much. But Abby was dragged with the buggy and it hit a tree," I said, remembering the details Abby had told me.

"People just take too many chances. Women shouldn't drive horses that shy easy, not until they're broke good. Henry used to hitch a colt with an old horse, so if the colt got skittish, the old horse helped hold him down," said Mrs. Mason.

"You have to know how to handle a spirited team," said Joe. "Keep a tight rein on them, and the check rein fastened, so they can't get their head down. Never speak loud or make a sudden noise."

"Hm-ph," said his mother. "Just give me a good reliable team. Let the young fellows break the wild ones."

"I guess that's best," I said.

"I'll boil up some coffee," she said, going to the kitchen.

"You're through with school, aren't you?" asked Ann.

"Yes, I finished last spring," I replied.

"I wish I was, I've got another year to go," she said.

"The last year isn't so bad, you do a lot of review work," I told her.

"It gets monotonous, anyway, I don't like school. I wish Ma would let me quit and get a job."

"I didn't want to go to school either, but Abby and Jim insisted I finish grade school. Abby said school days are the best part of life. Once you quit, you're no longer a child and you had better have a strong back with which to face the world."

"School or no school, ya gotta have a strong back, anyway," she answered. "There's nothing for girls to do anyhow, except scrub floors and wash and iron, and you don't learn that in school."

"There are other jobs for women, Ann," said Joe, breaking into the conversation.

"Like what?" she asked.

"Like a store clerk in a ladies' fashion shop, or if you can sew a straight seam, you could be a seamstress," he answered.

"In this town?" she scoffed. "Every woman in town makes her own clothes and buys whatever she needs from Miss Tucker's Fashion Salon. Miss Tucker sure don't need any help," she added. "I can sew as straight a seam as you can plow a furrow, Joe Mason."

"Well, finish school, then you can teach," he said.

"Who wants to be an old maid school teacher?" she answered.

"Come on, there's cake and coffee," called Mrs. Mason.

"Sit here, Marty," she said, indicating a chair next to Joe.

"Ma's special," said Joe, seating himself and passing me a plate of chocolate cake with a hard sugary frosting.

"Looks good," I said.

"If they keep on registering boys in the Army, the women will have to take over the men's work," said Mrs. Mason, picking up the conversation where we had left off.

"Yeah, I suppose I'll join up one of these days," said Joe.

"Course, you got your job at the slaughterhouse, said Mrs. Mason. "Ben Fritz couldn't run the slaughterhouse alone, not the way he hits the bottle and goes off to God knows where. The last time he went on a toot, he was gone for a week. If it hadn't been for you, he wouldn't have had anything to sell in the butcher shop."

"The last time, he was sure on a binge. It took him a week to sober up," said Joe. "I work for Ben Fritz, Marty, he has a slaughterhouse out by the frog pond, and a butcher shop in town."

"Oh, is that the butcher shop next to Klaseman's General Store?" I asked, surprised because I had not seen Joe in there.

"Yeah, when I'm not in the slaughterhouse, I cut meat in the back room."

I had seen old Ben Fritz. He was a red-faced man with freckles and a barrel chest. His arms were big and muscular, and his hair was almost as red as his face. He always wore greasy overalls and blood-soaked rubber boots. He bought hogs and cattle, and kept the animals on dry feed in bare pens. Jim had been complaining all summer about the awful stench from the slaughterhouse when the wind was blowing from the southwest.

"I think Ben needs Joe," said Mrs. Mason, interrupting my thoughts. "It isn't every young fellow that knows how to skin a critter."

"Well, Marty," said Joe, "I suppose I had better take you home." His chair made a rasping noise on the soft pine floor as he slid it back from the table. He took a pipe from his pocket and filled it from a sack of "corn-cake" tobacco.

Mrs. Mason and Ann said, "Good-bye, Marty, come again," as we went out the door.

The horse was tied to the hitching post and his checkrein was loose. Joe spoke softly to her and started humming as he fastened the rein. I could not make out the tune. The aroma from his pipe had a masculine appeal that set me tingling from head to toe.

"When did you start smoking a pipe?" I asked.

His eyes twinkled, "Since I gave up cigars."

"Oh," I laughed.

"Seems a long time ago, doesn't it?" he asked.

"What seems a long time ago?"

"Since that day we smoked Tompkins's cigars."

"Oh, yeah."

"Remember the day your Pa's barn burned? How did that fire start, anyhow?" He was looking at me with an unfathomable expression. I did not know if he really knew or if he was curious.

"It got started accidentally," I answered.

"I heard something about a cat settin' it on fire," he said, with a teasing grin.

"Joe Mason! How did you find out about that?" I asked, vexed.

"Your pa told me. Boy! Your eyes are shootin' sparks, just like the day the heifer bucked you off," he laughed.

He got in beside me and headed the horse east out of town, instead of taking me home. We stopped in a wooded area, he got out, and loosened the checkrein again, so the horse would be content to munch grass. I was still smarting a little, because Papa had told Joe about the cat. Joe got back in beside me, and with his finger under my chin, he turned my face toward him. "You mad," he asked.

"Well, it was an accident," I pouted. I had tried hard to forget that episode. I am tenderhearted where animals are concerned, and the last thing I would have wanted to do was deliberately burn a cat to death.

"Sure it was, honey," he soothed, pulling me into his arms. "I wouldn't give a hang for a woman without spunk." He kissed me hard. "You are my woman, aren't you?" He breathed against my ear and kissed me again, long and passionately, bruising my lips against his. "Are you, Marty?"

I nodded and struggled free. His arms and lips were awakening a consuming desire that was enveloping me. The way he said *woman* was like, well, like he was not thinking of me as a virgin, but rather as a female he could mate. The laughing, teasing Joe was the boy I went to school with, but the brown eyes of this lean, firm-jawed man made my blood race, and told me I would have a fight or yield to his passion.

"Please don't, Joe," I begged, "take me home."

"Why, are you afraid of me?" he whispered, pulling me back into his arms and repeating the same question he had asked last night.

"No, but I have to get home. Jim told me to get in early," I answered. Abby had warned me again to be a good girl, just this afternoon when I was pinning her hair up. "Marty," she said, "don't let him get the best of you. If a man can get the cream for nothing, why should he keep the cow?" Well, it was crudely put, but it drove home her point, and then I remembered Mama's threat to kill me and bury me behind the barn if I got in a family way.

"All right, Marty," he said. "But you know I wouldn't hurt you, don't ya?"

"I know you wouldn't," I said, but in my heart I was not sure I could control him and myself too. This was only our second date. I would have a fight on my hands to remain a virgin.

The weeks passed swiftly, and we were together as much as Jim and Abby would allow. One night we were sitting in the buggy, near the edge of Joe's favorite wooded area. The horse was nibbling grass. Joe sat there, quietly, listening to me prattle about the day's routine at the hotel. Finally, I realized he was waiting for me to get through talking, and I fell silent.

"Marty, will you marry me?" he asked, abruptly.

Those were the words I had been praying to hear. He had asked them at last. His proposal was so unexpected at that moment, I suddenly was shy and tongue-tied. I had practiced a hundred times or more in front of the mirror saying, "Yes, Joe, I'll marry you" or "Yes, darling, I'll be your wife." Now I could not get a simple little "yes" to leave my lips.

"Joe, Joe," I breathed fervently.

He gathered me to him, and held me in his arms. "Marty, are you going to give me an answer?" he asked at last.

"Yes, Joe," I whispered.

"Yes, what?" he asked, his eyes twinkling and holding me at arm's length, so I had to look at him.

"Yes, I will," I answered simply.

"I love you, honey. You love me, don't you?" he asked.

"Yes, Joe," I answered.

"Yes, what?" he asked again.

"Yes, I love you," I answered.

"When dear?" he asked.

"When what?" I asked, stealing his line.

"When shall we get married?" he urged.

"I don't know, I suppose I'll have to ask Mama," I said.

"We'll ask your folks together," he said. "We'll drive

over Sunday."

The next morning, when I carried Abby and Jim's breakfast tray in, Jim commented, "You look radiant this morning, like the cat who just swallowed a canary. What have you been up to?"

"Now, Jim, quit your teasing." chided Abby.

"Joe and I are going to get married," I told them.

"Well, now, when did you decide all this?" asked Jim.

"Last night," I replied.

"You're very young, Marty. Have talked to your mom and dad?" asked Abby.

"No, but Mama will be glad to get rid of me," I told her.

"You better talk to them, Marty, then you won't be sorry later," said Jim. I know they were right. We should say something to Mama and Papa. After all, I was underage and they could make us wait until I was eighteen, and that was two years. Abby and Jim knew I was sixteen; they also knew I did not have much affection for Mama. Tante and Hans seemed more like parents to me.

Joe agreed when I told him what Abby and Jim said. We decided to go the next week on Sunday.

It was a long week. I worried every day about what we would say to Mama. I could see her brows getting wrinkled and the bumps coming out.

It was about a six-mile drive and the black mare could not have looked any nicer as she pranced along the dusty road. We did not talk much. I cuddled up with my head against Joe's shoulder. It was nearly noon when we arrived at the farm. Joe drove up to the hitching post by the front gate. Papa came out on the porch, and when he saw us he came down the path and took my hand to help me down. He greeted me with a pat on the shoulder.

"Go in, Mama ist cook," he said.

Papa went to help Joe water the horse and take him to the barn. I went in. Mama was puttering around in the kitchen. When she saw me, she said, "Ist Marty! Komm in, komm in, we get some eat."

"We came to talk, Mama," I said.

"So we talk, und we eat. Wot we talk about?" she asked.

"When Joe comes in, we'll talk then," I told her.

"So ist about ju and Joe," a statement rather than a question, but the question was in her eyes. I knew what she was thinking. Joe and Papa came in, and I helped Mama put the dishes on the table. The four of us sat down to eat and nothing was said for a while.

Papa sensed the tension. "What ist los [going on]?" he asked. "Everybody so quiet."

Mama looked expectantly at me. I looked at Joe. He had a twinkle in his eye and he winked at me.

"Henry, Marty and I would like to get married," said Joe, smiling at me.

"So," said Papa, "so du hear det, Hannah? Marty and Joe want to get married."

Mama did not look surprised. "Du kinda, sechrehn [sixteen], too janj [young]." She looked at Joe, "Ju tink ju want to marry mit Marty?" She know nichts [nothing] aboudt geld."

"We'll learn together," said Joe.

Mama looked thoughtful and turned to me, "Ju want to marry mit Joe?"

"Yes, Mama," I said, "I've learned much from Abby and Jim."

"Ju get married, ju get babies and a lot of work. Make garden and can food, help mit chores. Ju always be busy, sew, mend, wash, and clean haus."

Mama was telling us all the things we should have talked

about long ago, things Tante had taught me and I learned firsthand from the Hoovermans. Papa sat quietly while Mama went on and on about raising chickens and milking cows. When she paused, Papa said, "Ist no so bad kinds. Ju love Joe and ju work together. Mama work hard, but I work, too, sometimes from sun up 'til sun down, ist not right, Hannah?"

Mama nodded, "When du get married?" she asked.

I looked at Joe, the first real look since Mama had started about all the work marriage meant. He took a handkerchief from his pocket and pretended to wipe the sweat from his brow. "Whew, that was some day's work," he laughed. We all joined in the laughter. That seemed to ease the tension. We finished eating and I helped Mama clear the table. Together we washed the dishes.

"Marty, komm, I give ju some things ju need when ju get haus." She led me into the bedroom and took some quilts out of a box she pulled from under the bed.

"Ditz tings I du when snow komms. I keep busy. Ju pick ein, I give to ju when ju get haus. Much tings ju need when ju start housekeeping. I give ju some tings."

"That is nice, Mama. I know we will need things. Mama, where is Pete?" I asked.

"Ju miss him? He go back to his Papa in Fenton. His Papa komm and ask him he want to go home mit him and Peter, he go. I miss him too. He be mit uns for twelve years. Peter no make friends much, he quiet. He no like to du chores, he no like to go to schule, he not happy here. Heinrich say let du boy go mit his faider [father]."

I wondered if Mama had treated him right. It sounded to me like she treated him like she did me.

"Lena and Hans speak about selling ihr [their] farm, maybe they move, too," Mama continued. That was news I did not like to hear. I did not want to think about Tante moving away. Mama is telling me some news, and I'm thinking, "Mama's treating me like a person."

The afternoon was pleasant, but it was getting time for Joe and me to start back to Fairport. Papa stuck his head in the door, "Marty, Joe say he want to start back."

"Well, we glad du komm," said Mama. Mama and I went out where Papa and Joe were hitching the horse to the buggy. I said good-bye to Mama, and Papa took my hand as I climbed into the buggy. Papa shook hands with Joe.

"Komm back soon," he said.

We drove for a while, not saying much, until Joe wrapped the reins around the buckboard and pulled me into his arms.

"Hello, Mrs. Mason," he said, "I love you. I have loved you since we went to school together. I think I was born to love you, Marty."

Joe's kisses were long and passionate, and now his mouth was devouring my lips with kisses that left me weak with a desire I had not felt before. I pulled away when his seeking hands starting fumbling to get inside my blouse.

"No, sweetheart, I love you," I said pulling my blouse down. "We mustn't do this."

He took the reins and urged the horse to a fast trot. The sun was setting when we reached Fairport. He kissed me good-bye as soon as we got back to the hotel. He was so quiet, I wondered if I had made him angry. I realized we had not talked about when we would be married or made plans of any kind. He did not say when he would see me again. Abby and Jim were anxious to find out how our visit turned out, but I went straight to my room. I felt more like crying.

Kate came into the room. "Mom and Dad want to know if you're feeling all right, Marty."

"Yes, I'm all right. Tell them I'll be down in a minute." I poured some water in the washbowl, picked up a washcloth, and washed my face. That made me feel refreshed. I drew a deep breath and went downstairs. I forced a smile, "Did you want me, Abby?"

Abby smiled, but there were questions in her eyes. Jim was reading the paper. He looked up and went back to his paper.

"How was your trip?" she asked.

"It was good. Mama and I talked, and she told me she would give me some things for my house when we get married. She let me pick out a quilt."

"Sounds like your day was good," she said.

Bill came in. "What are we having to eat tonight?" he asked.

"Kate is cooking tonight, ask her," said Abby. "Marty and Joe went to Marty's folks today and Marty just got home.""

"You mean Joe Mason took my girl out again?" he teased.

"I'm not your girl, Bill Hooverman," I protested. He laughed and went toward the kitchen.

We ate big bowls of stew that Kate had made. After supper, I went back upstairs, and I wondered if Joe had the same let-down feeling I did.

The next day Abby could tell I had something on my mind. She kept trying to talk to me, but I guess my answers were not very good. Finally, she asked, "Marty, is something bothering you?"

"No," I replied.

She insisted I did not seem like myself.

"Marty, did you and Joe have a quarrel?"

"No," I said.

This was something between Joe and me, and we had to work it out ourselves. We were just finishing up in the kitchen, when there was a knock on the door.

"Marty, Joe's here."

My heart leaped. I walked into the parlor. "Hello, Joe."

"Hello, Marty. Are you through with your work?" he asked.

"Yes, I think so."

"Do you want to go for a walk?" he asked.

I looked at Jim. "Go ahead. You better wear a coat, it gets chilly at night."

We walked down to the river, sat on a bench, and watched a ship as it slowly made its way up the river.

"Marty–Joe," we both started at the same time. We laughed.

"You first, Joe, what were you going to say?"

"No, you go first, what were you going to say?"

"I was going to ask if you were angry with me yesterday."

"No, why should I be angry with you?"

"I thought you got angry with me when I pushed you away."

"No, I didn't get angry."

"Why were you so quiet and wouldn't talk to me?"

"You don't know me very well. Kissing you brought on feelings I could barely control. I love you. I want us to get married, soon–right away–tomorrow!"

"I love you, too, and I felt that way too. If we get married right away, where would we live? We will need our own home," I said.

"I've been thinking about it all night," Joe said. "Farmers have tenant houses for hired help. I know a farmer over by Wilton Junction. He hires part-time help in the spring. I might be able to make a deal with him."

"But you have a job," I said. "What about the slaughter-house?"

"Ben don't have that much work, not enough to live on. Charles Kettleman might let us have the house and work for him when I'm not working for Ben," said Joe. "What do you think, Marty?" There was a long pause as I thought about it.

"Well?" asked Joe.

"Joe, Wilton Junction is a long way from here," I said.

"Not that far by horseback," he said. "Ben has been talking about a meat house in Wilton, he might open a butcher shop there. I think the only reason he don't is because he has the ice house handy here, and he would have to buy ice up there or haul it from here."

"I don't know, Joe," I said.

"I don't know if it would work out like that, but I'm going to see what happens. If I can work something out, then we can get married. We can live with Ma for awhile," he said, as an afterthought.

I did not like the thought of living with his Ma, but I did not say anything. "Joe, we're talking about getting married and we don't have any furniture," I said.

"We don't need much," said Joe. "We can get things as we go along. We've got each other." Joe's arm tightened about me and I felt those urges returning as he tipped my head back and put his lips to mine. Abruptly, he released me, stood up, and pulled me to my feet.

"We better get back," said Joe. We walked slowly back to the hotel, arm in arm. I did not see Joe for the next few days. My thoughts were filled with a home of my own to cook and clean. I imagined it must be heaven living with Joe. Joe came back on Saturday morning.

"There's a party this evening and I'll pick you up," he said.

Supper was about four o'clock on weekends and I was free to do as I pleased, after the kitchen was put in order. By the time Joe arrived, I was ready to go. This time we did not drive very far. The party was in a building at the edge of town. Unlike the first dance, there were no women sitting together, minding children, exchanging recipes and ideas. And a regular dance band–with drums, trumpets, and piano–provided the music. To get in, you had to pay a door charge. Everyone had a partner, and most of them were dancing quite differently than the first party we attended. Some of the couples switched partners to dance, but Joe and I danced together every time, or just sat along the wall and watched. Once Joe talked to a couple of men he knew. He introduced us–their names were Alex and Frank–and we exchanged pleasantries.

When the band played "Home Sweet Home," we danced the last dance and left. Joe drove to our favorite spot and we talked again about getting a house.

"I think Charles will let us have the tenant house. He told me he would think it over and I should come back in a week or so," said Joe, taking me in his arms. "I don't know what he wants to think about . . . I know farming. Pa was a good farmer and he taught me how to handle a team and plow and harrow and disk–and that's about all I have to know," he added.

Joe stepped out of the buggy and pulled me down into his arms. We took a short walk in the cool grass and felt the cool breezes against our faces. We finally decided it was probably getting very late, so we got back in the buggy and he drove to the hotel. We had a passionate kiss that left me weak, and we parted.

We spent Sunday at Joe's. Ma Mason was inquisitive about Mama and what she had been doing. Mama and Mrs. Mason had not been very neighborly when the Masons had been on the farm. They competed at the Wilton Junction fair with bread and cakes, and Mama thought the judges were making the wrong decisions when she did not win. Ann asked about Kate Hooverman–how old she was and if she still went to school. The day passed swiftly, and soon we were back in the buggy headed for our favorite spot to be alone.

Joe spread a horse blanket on the grass and said, "Come

on, sit here."

"Oh no, you have to catch me first," and I started running through the trees and around an old log. I had forgotten how fast he could run, and before I knew what had happened, he had me in his arms, carried me over to the blanket, and sat me down.

"Now, young lady, I can make you pay, you know.'

"You wouldn't , would you?"

"Oh, wouldn't I?" He grabbed me by the shoulders and pushed me down, his entire body covering me.

"Please, Joe, let me up," I begged. Instead, his lips covered mine and I was clasped in an embrace that I could not free myself from.

"We're not waiting–we're getting married right away. We can stay with Ma until we get a place of our own," said Joe. Sitting up, he pulled me to a sitting position.

"We can't go on like this, Marty."

"I know, I feel the same way"

"My birthday is coming up next week, we could get married then. What do you think?" he asked.

"What day is your birthday?" I asked.

"The twelfth." he said.

"That's only three days away . . . that doesn't give us enough time, sweetheart."

"Well, what day do you think we should do it?" he asked.

"Why don't we do it on the eighteenth, that gives us another week," I replied.

"That sounds good. It'll give me enough time to talk to Ben and tell Ma we'll be staying with her and Ann for awhile."

"Yes, and that gives me time to tell Abby and Jim–and I should let Mama and Papa know. I wish Tante and Hans were here, but they moved."

The ride back to the hotel was quiet. We were each busy with our own thoughts. Joe kissed me good night at the door and turned to leave, but one kiss was not enough. I ran after him and pulled his head down for another kiss, and he held me close.

"Soon, Marty, we'll be together, always."

Monday was always a quiet day at the hotel–not many people around, just routine work–washing linen and cleaning rooms. There were only two rooms occupied over Sunday.

I told Abby over lunchtime. "Joe and I are getting married the eighteenth,"

She looked startled. "Oh, Marty, you are so young to get married. You and Joe should wait at least another year–besides I hate to lose you–you are part of my family."

"I'll miss you, too, but we will be here in Fairport for a time–besides I'll be seventeen in July."

"You think about it. Marriage is a big responsibility" she said.

I picked up her tray of dishes and went to the kitchen. I did not even think about what Abby was telling me. I was too excited about our wedding day.

The days seemed to drag by. Joe and I were together whenever we got the chance, and the weekend was spent at Joe's place.

Ma Mason told me, "Joe said you would be staying with us for awhile after you get married. When you get a house, I have some things I'll give you–of course, you can have the furniture in Joe's room–and I have a rocking chair, some dishes, and just some other things that Ann and I don't really need."

On Sunday, we drove to Wilton Junction, to see about the tenant house Charles Kettleman had. Joe tied the horse to the hitching post by the front gate and went up the path to the house. Charles must have seen us coming, because he opened the door before Joe had a chance to knock and came out on the front steps. They talked for a minute, and Joe motioned for me to come, too.

Charles was a muscular man of average height and ruddy complexion, with a ready smile and full beard. Joe said, "Charlie, this is Marty. We're getting married the eighteenth."

"Well, well . . ." he smiled. "Hello, Marty, I'm pleased to meet you. So, you two are getting married...come on in." He opened the door and we walked into a large kitchen. Charlie's wife was bustling around putting something in the oven to bake. The big wood range was throwing out a lot of heat and it was making the kitchen quite warm. Pauline was a heavyset woman. Her hair was done in two braids, wrapped around her head, and fastened with bone hairpins. She had a pleasant face with laugh wrinkles and a double chin.

Charlie said, "Polly, this is Marty and Joe Mason."

She picked up her apron and wiped sweat from her face and hands. "Good morning, Marty and Joe. I'm not very dressed up for company, but come into the parlor, it's cooler."

We walked through the dining room with a long table, a dozen chairs, and a large buffet type of cupboard, and into the parlor. The parlor had a woolen rug on the floor and four wooden platform chairs that stood stationary on the floor but that rocked when you sat in them, and several other chairs, a smaller table, and a settee that would seat several people. It was home that spoke of wealth.

When we were seated, Charles said, "Well, Joe, you came to see about the tenant house, is that right?"

"Yes," said Joe. "Have you thought about renting it?"

"Well," he said, stroking his beard and looking

thoughtful, "the family that is living there wants to stay until the first of March, next year. They have been good workers, but they want to get farming for themselves, so I'm going to give them a start on my farm over by Stockton. I know that's a long time to wait, but I will need the help this spring and through the fall, so I need the house for them. Next year, I will need another good hired hand to take his place, and maybe you would be interested in coming to work for me."

Mrs. Kettleman asked, "Where do you live now? Can you stay there until we have a house for you?"

"Oh, we're not married," I said. "We're getting married a week from this Wednesday."

She looked somewhat confused. "Oh, I'm sorry. The way Charlie introduced you, I thought you were married."

"No," I said, "my name is Marty Vaughn."

"I'm sorry I interrupted,' she said.

"That's all right," Joe said, "but that's almost a year. We thought we would stay with my mother for awhile, but that will be an awful long time."

"You work for Ben Fritz, don't you?"

"Yes, I work at the slaughterhouse."

"Well, think about the offer I made you. It's the best I can do for you until the house is empty."

"Marty and I will talk about it," said Joe, getting up. "We'll let you know."

Mrs. Kettleman and I got up. "Well, we didn't get to visit, Marty, but think about Charlie's offer and maybe we'll be neighbors next year."

"Thanks, Mrs. Kettleman," I said, "we will."

"We'll let you out this door," said Mrs. Kettleman. "No use going back in that hot kitchen." They both walked us around to the buggy.

"Do you remember last year helping out with the

threshing?" asked Charlie. "You ran the steam engine and kept the belts oiled. I remember you were a friendly kid and worked hard. You were kind of tricky, though. When we got done for the year, you went around collecting all the straw hats. You waved your hat in the air and threw them in the separator. Some of the fellas got mad, but they didn't do anything but chase you. You had everyone laughing before we went in to eat."

"Yeah, I remember that," said Joe, laughing. "I outran the two fellas who were mad at me." Joe helped me in the buggy and said, "We'll see you again. Bye now," and we were on our way back.

"It looks like we'll have to find a house in Fairport, Marty," said Joe, clucking at Fanny and slapping the reins on her back, so she moved to a trot.

It was early afternoon when we got back. We ate a bite at his Mother's and took a walk along the river. We did not talk much, just walked hand in hand. As time passed, we watched the sun sink in the west, with yellow, pink, and rosy colors around a big red ball, as it slowly sank in the river. We walked further down the river than we realized. It was getting late by the time we returned.

"I better go back to the hotel, Joe." We said good night with our usual good-night kiss.

Even though the days were busy, they still seemed to drag until it was evening and I could see Joe again.

Chapter Five

Our wedding day was a beautiful, sunny day. Abby and Jim had been trying to get us to wait another year, but when they found out we were serious, they gave in and gave us their blessing. Today, they were taking us in style in their surrey, which Jim had cleaned and decorated for us. Abby and Jim were in the front seat and Joe and I were in back. Joe was clean shaven; he had slicked his hair back and was wearing a dark blue worsted suit. Abby and Jim had bought me a beautiful dress in a shade of blue that matched my eyes. It had a bustle in the back and a skirt that fell in pleats to my ankles.

The mares Jim was driving seemed to be prancing down the road. It was a happy foursome who rode in the surrey that morning, but my stomach was beginning to feel like it had butterflies inside. I cannot describe my feeling of happiness, wonder, and fear. It was a mixture of feelings I had never felt before.

We were married before a justice of the peace. Abby and Jim were our witnesses. We had our picture taken by a local photographer, Joe sitting handsomely in an armchair, and I standing behind his chair, with my hand on his shoulder.

We did not stay long in Wilton Junction. It was twelve miles from Wilton Junction to Fairport. We were not far out of town, when Jim produced a bottle of wine and passed it to Joe. He laughed and took a drink from the bottle, and handed it to me. I shook my head, laughing, but Joe said, "Oh, go ahead, it won't hurt you." I took a swallow; it was sour and I did not like it. Abby took a drink and asked, "Do you like it, Marty?"

I said, "No," and she laughed. They urged me take some more, but I could not get much of it down.. Abby and Jim were passing it around frequently, and I found they were laughing too loud and too long and having too much fun, so I pretended to have fun too.

We arrived home about 7:00 P.M. to find the house surrounded by people with pans and buckets. They were pounding on them with spoons, and some of the boys were setting off gunpowder, laughing and shouting. Joe said they were shiveree-ing us. He left me standing there and went to the house. When he returned, Joe had cigars and candy in a box. He handed them out to the crowd. Everyone shook hands with us. One man said, "Good cigar, Joe, you can keep your wife."

I said, "What did he mean, 'you can keep your wife'?"

"If I had not given them a treat, they would have taken you and kept you all night somewhere, and I would not have been able to find you. They would have brought you back in the morning. It's an old custom. They take the bride so they can't be together on their wedding night. If you give them a treat, they won't do anything. We'll be expected to have a wedding dance, later."

Everything was so confusing, but so much fun. By the time everyone had left, we were very exhausted. We said good night to Abby and Jim, and Abby said she would miss me. Ma Mason put her arms around me and kissed my cheek. "Welcome to our family, Marty," she said.

Joe's room was neat and clean. The bed had a homemade

spread on it. A nightstand by the bed had a kerosene lamp on it that burned very brightly. There was a large oak wardrobe with double doors–a beautiful piece of furniture. There was also a table with a bowl and pitcher on it; a door to the bottom concealed the enameled chamber pot. There was an oval braided rug by the bed that matched the blue wall. A large framed portrait of his father hung on the wall along with several other family pictures. My old wooden trunk was over by the window. Joe had moved it yesterday, and it had all my clothes and possessions in it.

We sat on the bed, each waiting for the other to make a move to undress. When I just sat there, he started unbuttoning my dress and pulled it down over my shoulders. I stood up and stepped out of it, and finished taking off my underclothes. Joe removed his clothes, blew out the light, and we collapsed on the bed in each other's arms.

I awoke early the next morning. Joe was still asleep. I studied his face, such a firm, strong chin. His eyes were closed, but I knew they were warm brown with a mischievous twinkle. His lips, full and firm, always sent thrills through me when we kissed. He opened his eyes as though he felt me looking at him.

"Good morning Mrs. Mason." he said, kissing me.

We lay there talking for a while. Joe had the week off from the slaughterhouse. We decided to have our wedding dance on Saturday night before he went back to work on Monday.

After breakfast we went to Davenport and put a notice in the daily paper, and we let Alex know so he could put up a notice in his pool hall, that building on the edge of town. This was the Alex I had met at the dance there. We rented the hall for Saturday night. Joe knew the boys who played the instruments at other parties and he asked them to play for our party.

It was a busy week. Ma Mason and Ann were planting a garden, and they spent a lot of their time outdoors. I helped in the house and tried to be useful, although Ma said I did not need to help. It felt better when I was busy doing things. Joe was gone some of the time. He looked after his team of horses, and was always doing odd jobs for a few dollars. He spent one day helping a farmer make hay. He got a couple of loads of hay for helping. He stored it in the barn for the winter.

Saturday night arrived. Joe and I dressed in our wedding clothes, and went to the dance hall. People were arriving, carrying packages all wrapped in colorful paper and storing them at one end of the hall on a long table. By the time the dance started, the table was overflowing. Mama and Papa arrived soon after the music started. Papa was carrying a washtub full of wrapped presents. The first song they played was the wedding march and it went into a waltz. Everyone clapped and called for us to dance. We danced alone on the floor for two rounds and then people began to join us. Soon the floor was crowded with people dancing. That was the last dance with Joe until they played "Home Sweet Home." I think every man and woman there insisted on dancing with the bride and groom.

At about 10:30, they had an intermission. Joe and I were escorted to the gift table. I noticed Joe was talking and laughing a lot, walking a little unsteady; he helped me with the wrappings, however. We were so amazed at the things people were giving us: dishes, pots and pans, cutlery, linens, towels, soaps–even a washboard, washtub, ironing board, and iron. We tried to thank everyone.

By 1:00 A.M. the dance was over, and I could tell Joe was more than a little drunk. I wondered how we were going to get all the gifts home. Ma told me not to worry, we could get them tomorrow.

Jim said, "The horse knows the way home, Marty," and indeed the horse did know the way home. Alex had brought Ma and Ann, and when we got home, he helped put the horse in the barn and unharness him.

Joe passed out on the bed with his clothes on. I removed

his shoes and socks, and crawled in beside him. I lay awake a long time, thinking what life was going to be like, and it was after 4:00 A.M. before I went to sleep. When I woke up, it was after 8:00 A.M. Joe was sitting on the edge of the bed with his head in his hands.

"Sweetheart, I'm sorry I got drunk last night," he said. "Are you mad?"

"No, I'm not mad," I answered.

"Several of my old friends were there, and we were drinking together," he explained.

"It's all right," I repeated. I got up, removed my wrinkled clothes, and poured some water in the washbowl. Thoughts were running around in my head and I just wanted to be left alone for now. I washed my face and the cool water made me feel better. I slipped into some fresh clothes and went out to the kitchen where Ma Mason was making breakfast.

"Good morning, Marty."

"Good morning,' I said. She looked at me and my expression must have told her I was upset or maybe an infraction in my voice.

"Marty, Joe doesn't drink very often. Last night was the first time I've really seen him drunk. I think it was getting married and seeing old friends, and it just happened," she explained.

"It's all right," I told her, dipping some water from the reservoir on the stove. "I'll take some water for him to wash up."

I went back to the bedroom. Joe was washing in the same water I had washed in and was getting dressed. I poured the water in the pitcher and turned to go out, but he caught me by the arms and pulled me to him.

"Honey, I'm sorry, I won't do that ever again, I promise."

"Joe, I guess I understand. It's all right, we'll forget it," I said, putting my arms around his neck. I pulled his lips to mine and we went to the kitchen together.

Ma was nervous as she poured coffee. She said, “How do you feel this morning, Joe?”

“Don’t ask,” said Joe.

“Do you want something for a headache?”

“No, I’m fine,” Joe replied.

“How are you going to get all those presents down at the hall?” she asked.

“We’ll take the spring wagon and go down when we get through eating,” he said, sounding a little irritated. Ma did not say anything else, but she kept glancing at us nervously. Ann came down from upstairs.

“Morning,” she said. “Yow-ee, were you drunk last night,” she teased, looking at Joe. No one answered her or paid any attention to her.

“*Excuse me!* I must have slept in the wrong house last night.” She said no more, but she kept glancing at Joe and me.

Ann and I cleared up the dishes from the table while Joe went to harness the team to the spring wagon.

The three of us went to the hall and packed everything we had unwrapped last night, into the wagon. It was almost full.

“Marty, we will have to find a house to rent.”

“Yes, we need our own place.”

“Shall we go looking tomorrow?”

“Don't you have to work tomorrow?”

‘Not if I tell Ben I want to look for a house.”

“Then let’s do it,” I said.

“The Jacksons are moving to California. You might be able to rent their house,” said Ann.

“Jacksons? Where do they live and how do you know them, Ann?” asked Joe.

"They are the people who have the boy that walks funny. His one leg is all twisted to one side and his foot turns to the side. They live on the corner where we turned up the hill. It's a brown house. I don't know them–I just know where they live."

"Well, there ought to be houses to rent somewhere. I've seen the boy you're talking about."

"What will your Ma and Ann do if you are not here to help them?" I asked.

"There's not much to do. They take care of the cow and chickens, and they have the garden and the house. The only thing I really do is see that the animals have feed and take care of the horses. And about the only time I'm really busy is hay making and threshing, and I give farmers a hand, then, when Ben ain't busy. Well, here we are. What are we going to do with all these things?" asked Joe.

"You can put them upstairs in the small room," said Ann.

"That's gonna to be a job."

It was a job, and it took the three of us over an hour to pack everything up the stairs. By the time we were through, it was after five o'clock and near suppertime. Ma Mason had made a kettle of stew and we enjoyed the meal together.

Joe went to work in the morning. I was left alone with Ma Mason and Ann. It felt strange to be there without Joe, and I really did not know what to do. Ma Mason was tending chickens and Ann went out to milk the cow. I picked up the breakfast dishes from the table and heated some water to wash them. Ann came in with a bucket half full of milk. She strained it, took it to the cellar where it was cool, brought up last evening's milk, and skimmed the cream from it. She took the skimmed milk out and gave it to the cats who lived in the barn. Joe came home about ten o'clock.

"Ben says there's a house about a half mile from here we might be able to get. I think we should go over and see what the deal is."

The house was one-and-a-half stories, white with brown trim around the windows and doors and dorms in the half story. It had a front stoop with a roof over it. The house was empty and there was no one around. We walked around the house to the back, where there was an enclosed porch with windows across the front. The floor was slightly sloped to the door, and windows alongside of the house indicated about four rooms downstairs. There was a big garden, yard, and stable.

"I wonder where the owner is? Maybe we should go over to that house over there," said Joe, indicating a small house some distance away. "They will probably know who owns the house. He must have been watching us. When he got closer to us, Joe said it was Frank Karns, the man with Alex at our party.

"Hey, Frank, how are you?"

"Good," said Frank. "How are you, Mrs. Mason?" He did not wait for me to answer. "You looking' to buy a house, Joe?"

"We aren't thinking of buying, yet, but we want to rent a house for awhile."

"Well, let's go in and you can look around," he said. He unlocked the front door and we stepped into an empty room, with clean painted walls and a double opening that led into another room, slightly larger with the same kind of wallpaper. A bedroom was off that room. The kitchen was medium sized and a door on the opposite side opened into it. The first thing I noticed was a cupboard built in the corner with a glass door. I thought, "What a nice place to keep dishes."

The kitchen walls were painted a light yellow and the floors throughout the house were painted a medium tan color. There were round holes in the ceiling of the kitchen and living room for stovepipes to reach the chimneys in the upstairs rooms.

After looking the house over, Joe turned to me and asked, "What do you think?"

"I like the house, don't you?"

"How much is the rent, Frank?" asked Joe.

"You aim to stay working for Ben?" he asked.

"Yeah, for another year, anyway."

"Twenty dollars a month, can you handle it?"

"Well, I don't make much money, but I expect I'd have to pay that anywhere. Shall we take this house, Marty?"

"Yes," I said.

"All right Frank, can we move in this week?"

"Sure, anytime you're ready," he answered.

"Joe, we don't have any furniture or a stove, yet," I protested.

"We'll get along," said Joe, taking some bills from his pocket and handing them to Frank.

"Honey, we don't have a stove or table," I repeated. I felt Joe was not thinking about furniture.

"Come on, Marty, let's go. We got a lot to do."

I got in beside him, "Joe, what are we gonna do?"

He did not answer; instead, he lit his pipe, started to hum, and slapped Fanny with the reins. We started back home, but then we turned the other way toward town and stopped at a store. A sign over the door said new and used furniture. When we entered, an old, bald, whiskered fellow came out of a small office.

"How're ya, Bert," said Joe, not waiting for him to answer. "We need a stove–do you have any used ones?"

"Well, let's see what I have," he said, leading us into another room. "I have a Home Comfort, nice stove I just got in."

It was a nice-looking stove, but it was dusty and seemed

like it had been there for some time.

"How much, Bert?" asked Joe.

"I can let you have that one for eighteen dollars."

Joe opened the oven, took the lids off, and turned to Bert, "I'd like to have this stove, Bert, but I can't afford it. I'll give you ten dollars for it."

"Nope, can't do it, Joe."

"Have you got a table and chairs?" asked Joe.

"I'll tell you what I'll do. I'll sell you the stove and a table and two chairs for twenty-five."

"I'll look at the table and chairs," said Joe.

Bert took us into another room, where he had several tables and a bunch of chairs. He showed us an oblong table painted a dark green.

A round oak table caught my eye and I said to Joe, "Honey, this is really a nice table."

Joe looked at the table and asked, "How about this one, Bert? This table, four chairs, and the stove, twenty dollars, best offer I can make," said Joe.

Bert shook his head. "I wouldn't make a cent, the table is worth fifteen," answered Bert. "I'll give you the green table and throw in the extra chairs and the stove for thirty dollars."

Then Joe shook his head. "I'll give you twenty-five, but we want the round table, take it or leave it."

"Well, all right, since you're just getting started, but just remember if you need anything else, where you got such a good bargain."

"Thanks, Bert, I'll pick them up later. I have to get someone to give me a hand with the stove."

"Walter can give you a hand with it," said Bert. Walter was Bert's son, a husky kid of seventeen.

We drove home and Joe threw the reins to one side.

"Unharness Fanny and put her in the barn, Marty, while I harness the other team."

"I don't know how to unharness a horse, Joe."

"Get Ann to help you, she knows how," he answered.

Ann was not at home when I went in. "Oh well," I thought. "Ann knows how, it can't be that hard." I went back and unhooked the single tree and let the shaft down. So far, so good. I loosened the rein from the bridle and led the horse to the tank to drink and put her in a stall. The rest seemed to be a cinch. I unfastened the belly straps, hames, and anything else I could find that had a buckle on it. I pulled it off and was surprised it was so heavy and cumbersome, but somehow I managed to get it on a hook and hung up. I looked at Fanny and she was shaking her head. I started out the door. She whinnied, then shook her head and whinnied again, but I went out and back to the house.

It was suppertime when Joe got back. Ann still was not home.

"Honey, did you get things moved over to the house?"

"Yeah, got the stove set up–had to buy some pipes, though–where's Ann and Ma?'

"I don't know. I haven't seen them since we got back."

"Who helped you get Fanny in the barn?"

"There wasn't anyone around to help, so I had to do it myself. I had a hard time getting the harness hung up."

"You didn't take the bridle off and put a halter on Fanny."

"Oh-h, I thought it was the same thing as long as I could get her tied. What's the difference?"

"Honey, a bridle has a bit that goes in the horse's mouth–that's to help control them. The bit would be uncomfortable for her to eat."

"Well, I learn something new everyday. I never had to do much except feed them. Papa always took care of the horses when I was at home."

Ma and Ann came in. "Where have you been?" asked Joe.

"To the meetin'. Marty, you'll have to join," Ann replied.

"What meeting?" I asked.

"It's the Ladies Aide Society. We do a lot of different things. We roll bandages, raise money for crutches and walking sticks, knit caps and mittens for orphans, and help with the money we raise to buy shoes, overshoes, and coats. We just do a lot of good things."

"Sounds good," I said.

Chapter Six

Moving everything into our first home house was hard, but when we were finally through and had everything in place, we walked hand in hand through each of the rooms. Strange feelings flooded my body, a lonely feeling of "this is my house, Joe's and mine"–no Abby, Jim, Kate, Bill, or John, no Ma and Ann, just Joe and I. It was a thrilling yet odd feeling that I just could not explain. Joe sat down in the rocking chair in the front room and pulled me onto his lap. We sat there quietly, each with our own thoughts.

Days came and went, and we soon settled into a routine–Joe leaving for work at the slaughterhouse and me working in the garden. Joe had plowed the garden with the sulky and harrow from Ma's. Ma had some seeds left that she did not use and I planted everything I could. I cooked and baked and kept house. It was a busy time. Soon it was June and the garden had grown, along with the weeds. It was all I could do to keep up with it all. Peas and beans were coming on and that meant canning–and I was not feeling well. I got up in the morning feeling sick and would lose my breakfast. I did not feel like doing anything. I did not say anything to Joe, but he noticed I was not acting as spry as usual.

"Marty, are you sick? You look pale," he asked.

"I don't feel very good. I guess I'm just trying to do too much."

"Where do you hurt?"

"I don't hurt anywhere. I just feel sick to my stomach. I'll be all right."

Joe did not say anything else, but when he got through eating, he said, "Marty, are you going to have a baby?" The thought of a baby had not occurred to me.

"I don't know. Do you think I am?"

"I'd bet on it. That's the way women feel when they get in a family way.

"I know, and come to think of it, I haven't had my monthly."

"We're going to have a baby. How do you feel about that?"

"I guess I'm happy if you are, Joe.'

"I'm happy if you are, Marty." He kissed me and left for work. I sat at the table thinking about having a baby to care for. I hoped the sick feeling would go away. As the days and weeks passed, I began to feel much better and by August was feeling like myself again. Canning and preserving was in full swing, as the garden vegetables and fruit were maturing. Ma and Ann helped me, and I helped them. Soon we had rows of tomatoes, corn, beans, and pickles in jars. Before we knew it, October was upon us and it was time for farmers to start corn picking. Joe helped a farmer with corn picking and made enough money to buy material for baby clothes and a sewing machine.

"I don't know how to work a sewing machine," I said.

"Ma will help you learn. It will be better than making things by hand," said Joe.

By Thanksgiving the corn was picked and cribbed. Joe

started getting firewood by helping a couple of men cut wood. Before I knew it, Joe announced we would have the men who did the sawing cut the wood into stove lengths. So that meant I would have to cook a meal for the three men. I was beginning to see what Mama meant, when we had asked her and Papa if we could get married, and she recited so many things that were expected of a wife. Wow, what was that I felt in my belly–tap, tap, tap–could it be I felt the baby move? I put my hand on the spot and patted it, but I felt nothing more right then. As I started supper, however, I felt it again. A sensation of surprise, elation, and fear engulfed me. I wanted to run to Joe and tell him and feel his arms around me, but Joe was not home yet. I went to the window–he was due home a half hour ago–well, he must have worked later today, I thought. It was nearly six o'clock when Joe got home, almost an hour late. He came in the door, threw his cap on a hook, took off his coat, and pulled me into his arms.

"You're late," I said.

"I know, I told Ben about the baby and he thought we should celebrate, so he got his whiskey bottle and it just got late." I could smell the liquor on his breath, but I did not say anything, I just felt warm and comfortable in his arms.

"I felt the baby move, honey, right here." I took his hand and put it on the spot where I felt the baby move. He leaned down and put his lips to the spot, then we sank to the floor in a passionate embrace.

Days were getting much shorter now; even so, the time seemed to drag for me. I missed Kate, John, and Bill. It would be nice if I could see Abby and tell her about the baby. I know she would be happy for me, and I know Kate would have many questions. Joe did not seem to want to take me to the Hoovermans' and I could not hitch the horse to the buggy myself. I wrote them a letter and told them everything since I left. We visited often with Joe's mother and Ann, and went to the farm to see Mama and Papa several times, but with the fall work and the longer hours Joe was putting in to make some extra money, we did not have much time for visiting.

Soon Christmas was only a few days away, and we decided to have our first Christmas tree. Joe went to the wooded area where we used to go when we were dating. He cut a limb from one of the evergreens that grew there and trimmed it up to look like a tree. Together we strung popcorn and made cardboard stars, and added colorful candles and a few other ornaments that Mama gave us.

Christmas was a chilly day with a snowflake now and then falling softly to the ground. We were on our way to Mama and Papa's.

"Isn't this a perfect Christmas Day, sweetheart?"

Joe smiled, "Perfect, but I hope it doesn't snow too much." I snuggled closer to him.

Mama had the kitchen smelling of delicious Christmas goodies. A big goose roasted with apple and raisin stuffing and mincemeat pie was in the warming oven. Pete was there–so were Tante and Hans. They had arrived yesterday. Papa had picked them up from the train in Blue Grass. The trip from Fenton had taken more than twenty-four hours. It was good to see Tante and Hans again, and when the goose was served, we even laughed that it might be a descendant of Mr. Wicket. We relived some of the good times we had when I was living with them. Pete was very reserved and quiet, and I thought he seemed ill at ease; he did not enter into the conversation unless we asked him a question. He also did not offer any information on his life since he left the farm, except to say he did not go to school anymore and was going to get a job with a blacksmith. He was a big man with dark hair and sideburns, and did not look anything like the Pete I called my half brother. I wondered why he had come back to visit; he did not look like he was enjoying himself and I really wondered if he was happy. I asked Tante, when we had a moment alone, and she told me he was a hard one to get to know, but he seemed interested in business and was learning all he could about wagons, transportation, and such. He seemed to spend a lot of time in the blacksmith shop. Hans and Tante were going to stay until New Year's, but Pete was going back to Fenton tomorrow.

Tante had not said a word about the baby. I saw her looking at me several times and finally she asked as a matter of fact, "When du haf baby?"

"Tante, I thought you were never gonna ask about the baby!"

"Du Mama tell me du haf baby when she send brief. I tink ju still baby, yet, now ju get to be mama so soon."

"I've grown up, Tante," I told her, giving her a big hug.

"Ja, du big girl, Joe gute man." It was half question and statement.

"Yes, Tante, Joe and I are happy about having a baby."

"Marty haf baby in March, nay Marty?" asked Mama, getting up to clear off some dishes and carry them to the workbench in the kitchen. I picked up some plates and followed her.

"Doctor Quinn thinks it will be around the middle of March."

"Ju haf to get woman to hilfe ju. I tink I can stay by du haus."

"Joe's mama is going to help out," but I added, "If you can stay awhile, that would be good. Then Ma Mason wouldn't have to stay the whole time."

I really did not know about Mama taking care of the baby and me. I did not think it was best for us. Mama's disposition was not reliable, but I did not want to make her angry by telling her I preferred Ma Mason. Tante's eyes pleaded with an expression that said, 'Don't make your Mama mad." I knew what she was thinking, and remembered all that happened after I went to live with Mama. Let bygones be bygones. Mama seemed to take it all right. Even though I knew she did not get along well with Ma Mason, she did not say anything. Mama had changed since I got married. She seemed more like a mother should. We finished the dishes and joined the men in the parlor. The rest of the afternoon was pleasant with Papa and Hans talking about roads and wagons.

Mama had outdone herself with trimming the tree; it was full of ornaments that she had brought from the old country. I had seen them several times, but to Joe they were new and beautiful, with the pretty colors of candles with holders, angels, and Santa's.

"The tree is very pretty," he told Mama. "I've never seen candleholders like that. All we can get are the ones with snaps that you snap on the limbs."

"So, dis ist snaps, too, dey hide," she laughed, and showed us how they snapped to the tree so you could not see where they fastened.

There were several wrapped packages under the tree. Mama picked them up, one at a time, and handed them out. When I unwrapped mine, it was a white flannel nightgown, and for Joe a pair of gloves. For Pete, Hans, and Papa, each a pair of gloves, and for Tante a white flannel nightgown. Everyone laughed and told Mama it was just what he or she needed. I thought how typical of Mama. Tante and Hans had brought some dress and shirt material, very pretty gingham for dresses and blue chambray for shirts. She gave me a package with white flannel material for the baby and the gingham was my favorite color of blue to match my eyes. I felt we could not bring presents, but Mama and Tante both told me they did not expect me to bring presents with the baby coming and all.

The time passed so swiftly, before we knew it, it was time to leave. Saying good-bye to Tante and Hans was tearful for me. It had been such a good day of remembering, and I wrapped my arms around Tante's neck and kissed her. Hans put his hands on my shoulders and gave me a little shake.

"Kinda, ju grow too fast." He pressed a kiss on the top of my head, turned to Joe, and shook hands. "Name baby Hans," he said.

Joe laughed, " It might be a girl."

Pete shook hands with both of us. Mama and Papa kissed me and said good-bye to Joe. Papa helped me into the buggy. Fanny trotted out to the road and we waved good-bye to everybody. We were silent for a time, each with our own thoughts.

Finally, Joe put his arms around me. "Are you tired, sweetheart?"

"Yes, I am tired, but it was such an enjoyable time. I am so glad I got to see Hans and Tante, and I was really surprised to see Pete. What did you think of Pete?"

"Seems like a smart fellow. He seems to know a lot about horses–he sure thought Fanny was great."

We were quiet again. It was cloudy, but the snow had stopped. There was just a skiff on the ground and it was getting dark. We should have left a little earlier. It was near four o'clock and we were only halfway home. Fanny knew the way, so we did not worry. The aroma from Joe's pipe and the tune he was humming put me to sleep.

"Wake up, Marty, make some coffee." Joe was already out of the buggy and unhitching Fanny. I got out slowly, and went to the house. I could not believe I had slept most of the way home.

The house felt cold. Joe had stoked the fire in the heater, but it was almost out and the cook stove was out, too. I kindled the fire in the cook stove and put the coffeepot on, without taking off my coat. Joe came in with a basket of corncobs and threw them on the coals in the heater. Soon it began to warm up. Supper for Joe was a couple of slices of bread buttered with gobs of apple butter. I did not feel hungry, but I drank some coffee with cream–it tasted so good.

We sat at the table, lingering over our coffee. I recalled more of the time I had lived with Tante Lena and Uncle Hans. Joe got a good laugh when I told him I had caught my head in the cow manger and when Mr. Wicket would chase me out of the barnyard. Joe recalled some of his encounters at school with teach Tompkins and we laughed again at the cigar episode. I guess we will never forget that day.

It was ten o'clock when we climbed into bed. I was soon asleep. I awoke with the smell of coffee cooking. Joe was already up and dressed. He came into the bedroom. "Are you awake, sweetheart? I have to go to work you know."

"I know, I'm sorry, I didn't hear you get up. I'll get you some breakfast." I dressed quickly and went to the kitchen. I sliced some side meat from a side of salt pork and sliced some potatoes. Then I let them cook while I set out some bread, butter, and apple butter. Once we had eaten, it was time for Joe to go to work and I was alone. I cleaned up the breakfast dishes, wondering what I should do the rest of the day.

I picked up the package with the pretty blue material and held it up to me. No, I thought, I should be making small garments and I had material to do that. I opened the package with the flannel material and I looked it over. Diapers, or little gowns? The diapers seemed the better choice. I laid the material out on the table and cut squares. I opened the sewing machine and threaded it. Then I pulled my old trunk out of the bedroom, opened it, and as I laid the lid back the queerest feeling came over me that I could not fathom. I felt both scared and excited at the same time. I did not know why I felt that way. Oh well, I shrugged it off, and began to hem the squares I had cut out, forgetting about the trunk. I hemmed a dozen squares and still it was not late enough in the day for me to get supper, so I folded the diapers and laid them on the trunk. Again, that feeling came over me, scared and excited. Why, I wondered, did that happen when I touched the trunk? It must be the lock of hair still in the trunk all wrapped in tissue. It must be a feeling about my real father that was affecting me. That's it, I thought, it brought back memories. I finished placing the leftover material in the trunk and pulled it back in the bedroom, soon forgetting all about it again as I set about doing some chores.

I went out, fed the hens, and gave them some water. I should have done that this morning, but I was not accustomed to going out to feed chickens or the animals. Joe, however, told me to take care of the chickens, because if they laid an egg I should bring it in or it would freeze. It was not likely they would lay an egg in the winter–it was not egg-laying time. Ma Mason told me this when she gave us two dozen young hens and a rooster; she said they were dominickers. I did not know a dominicker from a Rhode Island Red or leghorn. Mama's chickens were a mixture of several of them. I gave them corn and warm water, and looked in all the nests for eggs–there was none. Better get supper, I thought.

Joe came home early, and after supper we had a long evening.

"I made some baby clothes today," I told Joe. "Come in the bedroom, I'll show you what I've got done. I opened the lid of the trunk and instantly that scared, excited feeling gripped me.

"Joe, it's funny, but I get the oddest feeling when I open that trunk. It's never happened before, but when I opened it this morning, I felt so scared. It must be I'm remembering everything that happened when my father died and then coming over on the ship and all."

"Yeah, I don't know why it should affect you now–it hasn't done that before, has it?"

"No, I can't figure it out. What else would make me feel that way?"

"Imagination–you're pregnant, you know."

We both laughed. "Yeah, that's probably it," I said.

I did not open the trunk again for several weeks. The days

passed slowly, but I did not want to open that trunk again. I used excuses such as, "I have no ambition to sew."

When I was not busy with housework, I read a book, or mended some of Joe's socks. I had not gotten the washing done between Christmas and New Year's, so I spent one day getting caught up on the washing. I vowed to myself, someday I would have a washing machine like Mama has, one that you can sit down at and use one foot and one hand, instead of using a washboard and both hands and my back.

Another week passed, and I kept thinking about the baby clothes I still needed to sew. I made up my mind to get the flannel material out of the trunk and pay no attention to how I felt. Taking a deep breath, I slowly raised the lid. I felt nothing but expectation. I spent the day happily cutting out little gowns, getting them ready to sew.

When Joe came in from work, I was humming a tune as I put things on the table for supper. "What are you so happy about?" he asked, as he tipped my head back and looked into my eyes.

"I'll tell you after we eat, Come on, get washed up," I pulled his lips down to mine and pushed him toward the washbowl.

"What's the big secret?" he asked, drying his face.

"You'll see, eat." I slid a sausage cake onto his plate and passed him the bowl of potatoes as he sat down. He said no more, but kept glancing at me now and then. We finished eating and I started to clear the table.

"Come on Marty, tell me."

"I need the table to show you." Together, we cleaned off the table and I took his hand. "Come with me."

"I thought you needed the table."

"Come on," I said, pulling him into the bedroom.

"Not tonight Marty, I'm tired," he teased.

"No, not that," I said and slapped his arm.

He laughed, “Well, show me,”

“All right.” I picked up the little garments I had cut out and lifted the lid on the trunk. Joe said nothing, just stood there. “See, it doesn’t do that anymore.”

“Do what?” he asked.

“Give me that scared feeling when I open it. Remember the first time I opened it?”

“Are you still thinking about that?”

“Joe, you don’t realize that terrible scared feeling I had when I opened the trunk to take out the material for the baby’s clothes. You weren’t there.”

“And I told you it was your imagination.”

“But it did it both times I opened it.”

“Well, it doesn’t do it now, does it?”

“No, and I feel a lot better about it. Come on, I’ll show you what I got done.” I spread the little pieces of gowns I had cut on the table.

“Look’s like they're gonna be pretty big,” he commented.

“They have to be sewn Joe. Besides, it’s the pattern I got from Mama.”

“Going back to that trunk, how long have you had it?”

“All my life. It came with me from England.”

“Well, you see, why should you suddenly feel like you’re scared of it? Did you feel that way about it before?”

“No.”

“So forget about being scared of it. It's just a wooden trunk.”

“I know, I’m being crazy, I guess.”

I tried to put it out of my mind as I sewed the little gowns and bellybands, but every now and then I would think about that trunk. As the days passed I forgot it, and my thoughts were more with Joe and the baby, who was due in about six weeks.

Joe had come home, smelling heavily of whiskey several times as the weeks passed. I felt he was drinking too much, but I tried to think it was because of the baby and because he was frustrated with our relations. Then there was the night he did not come home at all. I was beside myself with fear. What could have happened to him?

There was a blizzard raging all day, a typical March day. The sun was shining through the swirling snow, then disappeared, and the howling wind blew it into big drifts around the house. I walked from window to window, trying to see out into the darkness. I opened the door and the wind blew a big gust of snow into the kitchen. I quickly closed it. Finally, I put on my coat and overshoes, and set out for Ma Mason's. Our baby was due in a week or so, and I was awkward with my big belly as I made my way through the deep snow and pounded hard on Ma Mason's door. The house was dark; she and Ann were in bed. I pounded again. At last I saw a flickering light from a match, as she lit the lamp on the table. She opened the door and saw me.

"Marty, Marty, what's the matter? Are you all right? Where's Joe? Has something happened to Joe?" There was alarm in her voice.

I was crying. "I don't know. Joe didn't come home tonight."

She pulled me into the kitchen and pushed me into a chair. "My goodness, you're shaking. You shouldn't be out in this weather in your condition. Here, get those overshoes off." She helped me pull them off and shook the grates in the stove until the glowing coals burst into flames. She opened the oven door so the heat would warm the room.

"You say Joe didn't come home. Did you have a fight?"

"No, but sometimes Ben gives Joe whiskey and he gets drunk."

"Don't worry, he'll be home. You stay here tonight. When

he comes home and finds you gone, he'll come to his senses."

When I saw how calm she was taking Joe's absence, I wondered if she had been through this before. I spent the night there and Joe did not show up. The next morning, Ma told Ann to take me home in the buggy. She told me, "Joe is probably with Ben and he'll be back today," she soothed.

The house was cold. Ann helped me fire up the stove. "Don't worry Marty," she said, "he'll be home."

Joe was gone for three days–three days of crying and worry–wondering what had happened, had he gone off and left me, and would I ever see him again. He came home the afternoon of the third day. He looked terrible and I thought he was ill.

"Joe, where have you been? I've been worried sick about you." I flung myself in his arms.

He pushed me away. "Ben had to go to Chicago. He wanted me to go with him." Guilt and anger was in his voice.

"Couldn't you have told me so I wouldn't worry?"

"I didn't have time. You gonna be one of those naggin' wives?" This was a side of Joe I had never seen. I was scared, worried, and a little angry myself.

"We need some things from the store," I said.

He did not answer. He put his coat back on and stalked angrily out the door. He was gone a long time. When he returned he had a sack of coffee and sugar. We ate supper in silence.

In bed, he turned to me. "Marty, I'm sorry. Please don't be mad at me." He put his arms across my belly and tried to draw me close.

"Why did you go with Ben?"

"I know I shouldn't have, sweetheart, but Ben and I had been drinking. When he said he had to go to Chicago, he asked me to go along. I told him I couldn't, but he said I must be henpecked and I was just drunk enough that I told him, 'All right, if you want me to go, I'll go.' Him saying I was henpecked is what did it. Marty, I'm sorry, forgive me?"

"What were you doing in Chicago and why were you angry?"

"I was so drunk by the time we got there, I didn't know anything. When I sobered up, I was in a small room down by the waterfront. It must be a place where Ben always goes. Honey, I'm so sorry for acting the way I did. I'll never get that drunk again."

I was heartbroken. As long as I knew Joe, I had never heard him plead for forgiveness, nor did I ever have a reason to think he was a man with a weak character who would do something so foolish on the spur of the moment. I just did not want to hear any more. If Joe had been unfaithful, I did not want to hear him say it.

"Go to sleep, Joe," I said, pressing a kiss on his cheek. "It's just that I was so worried about you. Just forget it, sweetheart."

But I could not forget about it as I lay there in the darkness, tears running down my face. I thought, "How could he do this to me, making me a laughingstock with Ben? It would probably be all over Fairport, and telling me he's sorry is supposed to fix everything?" I could not go to sleep. Every time I closed my eyes, I pictured Joe in the arms of another girl. I could not get comfortable. I turned one way and then another. I had a queer feeling in my back.

"What's the matter, honey, can't you go to sleep?"

I did not answer and laid as still as I could. When I was sure he was asleep again, I crept cautiously out of bed and made my way through the darkness to the kitchen. Closing the door, I groped my way to the cupboard and found the matches. I lit the lamp and sat down at the table, just as that queer feeling came in my back again. This time it felt like a muscle spasm. Oh! A contraction–I'm gonna have my baby!

Should I wake Joe? No, I would sit there and suffer. When he finds me, he will be twice as sorry. I waited, tensely, for the next contraction. Doctor Quinn had said when the contractions were five minutes apart, to let him know. Well, they were a good ten minutes apart now. I sat there until the gray light of dawn began to outline the houses on our street, and the pink rays of the rising sun began to appear in the eastern sky. Suddenly, the door flung open, and there was Joe in his baggy underwear, a look of fear on his face. Seeing me, his expression relaxed.

"Are you sick?" I nodded. "Why didn't you wake me . . . shall I get the doctor . . . how long have you been up?"

"Since about midnight," I answered his last question first.

"Are you having pains?"

"Yes, about every seven or eight minutes."

"You stay right there, honey, I'll get Ma." Grabbing his coat, he was out the door before I could stop him. I got up and went to the door; he was already coming back.

Sheepishly, he said, "I guess I better put my pants on." This time he had his clothes on, and his coat and cap, he stooped to kiss me.

"It won't take me long, honey. I'll be right back with Ma and then I'll go get the doctor."

"You'll have to get Mama, too."

We had planned on Mama coming around the fifteenth, and it was only the ninth. A short time later, Ma came in.

"The baby is ready to come, huh, Marty? Joe went to tell Dr. Quinn. How do you feel?"

"I feel all right until I get that pain in my back."

She sat with me at the table. I could see she was curious about something. Finally she asked, "When did Joe get home?"

"Yesterday afternoon."

She hesitated. "Was he all right, was he sober?"

"Yes, he was all right."

"Did he say where he had been?"

"No!" I said sharply.

My clipped answer must have told her I did not want to talk about it, and she asked no more about it. Let her ask Joe where he had been and what he had been doing. I wanted to pass it out of my mind.

Ma got up, put kindling in the stove, pumped some water into a pot she found in the cupboard, lit the kindling, and put some wood on it. Soon it was crackling and burning, heating the water.

It was almost an hour before Dr. Quinn came in, stomping the snow off his boots and leaving them by the kitchen door.

"Well, Marty, what's happening with you? How often are you having contractions?"

"About eight to ten minutes apart," I told him.

"I need to examine you." After making the examination, he said, "It doesn't look like this is going to happen for at least a couple of hours. I'll be back then. In the meantime, if your contractions get to be two or three minutes apart, let me know."

Mama and Joe arrived about eleven o'clock, and the two grandmothers-to-be visited about what had happened in the old neighborhood since the Masons had left Yankee Hollow.

Joe came in from stabling the horses and Mama said, "We better put der bett out by der stove, nay Joe, it be warm for baby."

"Humph, you can't put her bed out here, what will people think, who come in?" said Ma.

"I no care what people tink. I take care of her. Der bett comes out here," retorted Mama.

"She's right, Mrs. Mason, you can't hatch a chicken out of a cold egg," said Dr. Quinn, who had just came in.

"Yes, and believe me, it's cold. If you don't think so, try going out without your pants on," said Joe.

Doctor Quinn looked at Joe with a raised brow. Joe explained, "With the excitement of getting up and finding Marty in pain, I started out to get Ma in my underwear. It was a little breezy, I can tell you."

Doctor Quinn laughed. "Wait until you have a half dozen. By that time you'll be taking it quite calmly."

I could see Ma did not like being outvoted the way she stomped out to the kitchen. Joe and Mama quickly tore down the bed and moved it into the front room.

I did not much care what they did, as my pains were closer together now. I barely made it to the bed when Dr. Quinn handed Mama a gauze-covered strainer with chloroform on it. She held it over my nose. I drifted into darkness. Slowly, I floated back to hear faraway voices say it was a girl. I awoke to full reality to see the two grandmothers' actually beaming at one another, as they examined the baby for traces of family resemblance.

"We name her Isabelle, nay, Marty?" asked Mama.

"Isabelle," shouted Ma. "That's not a name for a baby. Clara is a good sensible name, don't you think so Marty?"

I looked beseechingly at Joe. He was looking from one to the other in exasperation. "Marty and I have already picked a name. We are naming her Maybelle Josephine."

The two grandmothers grumbled but did not object. I dosed off and slept. When I awoke, Ma was gone and Mama was sitting in a chair by the window. My baby was lying on a pillow beside me.

"Where's Ma Mason, Mama?"

"Eir cum back and fix some supper. Joe cum eir haus."

So Mama was taking care of me and Ma was taking care

of the house. The two seemed to be getting along all right. Ma went home.

The next day started off all right until about eleven o'clock, then I heard them disagreeing about something. I heard the door slam and silence. I wondered what on earth happened now.

I called to Mama, "Where did Ma Mason go? She didn't even come in to see me this morning."

"Oh well, she be back. When Joe comes, he take me haus."

"I thought you were going to stay until I get on my feet?"

"Let that uder one stay. I no can do tings der way she likes."

"You're not doing it for her."

"Nay, I go to haus."

When Joe came, he did not say anything, and he took her home. Ma came back and got supper for us. Joe finally had a chance to really see his daughter, look into her brown eyes, and touch the yellow fuzz on her head.

"I think Ma really got mad when your mother insisted on moving the bed out here."

"Mama isn't an easy person to live with–that reminds me, how did you come up with a name for the baby so quick?"

"I don't know," he said. "It just popped into my head and it came out my mouth. If you don't like it we can change it."

"No, I think Maybelle is a pretty name. It fits her–don't you think it does?"

"If you say so, honey," he said kissing me repeatedly. My hurt and angry feelings were gone. I felt loved again. I had a baby to love and take care of.

The next morning Joe gave me some coffee, and laid out a couple of diapers so I could reach them. "Ma will come over after while. I better get to work." He kissed me and left.

I lay there all morning, wondering when Ma Mason was going to show up. Finally, I heard someone come in. "Is that you, Ma?"

"Ist me, Marty." Papa stuck his head around the door. "I come to see the little one."

"Come in, Papa. Did Mama come too?" I asked, thinking Mama had changed her mind and was going to stay with me.

"No, don't worry, kinda. Mama get over it when eir fuss awhile. I bring ju und der little one old Molly, she haf calf pretty soon. Ju drink lots of gute milk so ju haf lots of milk for der baby."

"Oh, Papa, you mean you brought me Molly? I can have her?"

"Sure, but ju no try to ride her, nay?'

"No," I laughed. "I won't ride her."

"Gute, I go now."

"No, you haven't seen the baby. Here you hold her," I said, pulling the blanket aside so he could see her face."

"No, no, she too small. I break eir."

"No, she doesn't break." We both laughed at the way he held her. "Thank you for Molly."

"Sure, sure, ju get feed for eir?"

"Well, we will have to keep her at Joe's mother's because Joe has feed in the barn at his mother's."

"Ja, we talk, Joe and me, he knows I bring der cow."

After Papa left, I waited for Ma to come, but she did not show up. I used the last diaper and I went to the drawer to get some. It was empty. There was no sheets for the bed, either. I went to the back porch. There I found all the soiled linen, soaking in a tub of water. I wrung the things out, my hands nearly numb with cold. I pumped water into the boiler and put it on the stove to heat. I scrubbed the diapers, put them in the boiler, and hung up the rest to dry. When

Joe came home, he finished hanging them up.

"I can't understand what happened to Ma. She said she would come over every day to help out."

"Ma and Mama were quarreling yesterday."

"Quarreling, what about?"

"I really don't know."

Joe found out when he went over to his mother's. "'Hannah wanted me to do all the washing and all the dirty work. All she wanted to do was take care of the baby. She can just do it all,' she told me,' Joe said.

"She went home, too, and left you without any help at all," Joe told his mother.

At about ten o'clock that evening, I began to get hoarse and by midnight, I had a bad case of the croup. Joe went to get Dr. Quinn. He was perplexed.

"Where on earth did she get such a cold? She was all right a couple of days ago." He gave me a spoonful of awful tasting medicine, and left some pills and a bottle of cough medicine.

"She had her hands in cold water and had to wash some clothes for the baby."

"I thought her mother was going to help out?"

Joe mumbled something about Mama having something to do.

"See that she stays in bed and takes her medicine. The baby will probably nurse some of this cold from her, so don't be surprised if she gets the sniffles, too." He closed his bag and shook his finger at me. "No more getting out of bed until I tell you."

We had learned our lesson: mainly, keep the two grandmothers apart.

Chapter Seven

It was 1900, and this year Mama's grandmother, old Granny Schwentzer, decided to move to Davenport. Mama had a family reunion for her. Uncle Willie brought Aunt Carey and their five children, Frank, Viola, Dora, Verona, and Olga. Granny Schwentzer was an immigrant from Germany, a couple of years after Uncle Willie had brought his family over. I was unprepared for Granny; instead of the tall, drab woman I had mentally pictured, she was a small, stooped, little woman with a hump in her back. She was very energetic, with sparkling black eyes. She had nodules on the top of her head, which her thinning hair could not hide. She also had lumps on her chin and forehead. She was gray-haired and quite deaf. You had to talk right into her ear to make her hear. Uncle Willie's family was all pretty well grown up and Aunt Carey was the same short blonde person I remembered, only older. Frank was seven foot, two inches tall, and when he walked through a door, he always had to duck to keep from bumping his head. Viola was tall, also, but only about five foot, eight inches. Dora and Olga were short and fat like their mother. Verona was thin and average height. It was an interesting day to get acquainted with the family again.

Old Ben was still paying Joe an apprentice's wage. We talked it over and decided we would be better off on a farm. We had not heard from Charles Kettleman since we had talked to him before we were married. Now Maybelle was to be a year old in March, and it was February. Joe decided to see if Kettleman still had an offer for him. As it turned out, Charles Kettleman was looking for a family to move into one of his farms to share crop.

"He will stock the place and we will get half the crop. He will furnish the machinery, but we have to pay for it out of our share, as we can afford it."

"Sounds like a good offer," I said.

"Do you think we can swing it?"

"We can try, Joe."

Maybelle was a little toddler, always right under our feet. We decided she needed a puppy to play with, but finding a puppy was harder than we thought. We were busy getting ready to move into the Kettleman farmhouse, and it was a busy time, so the puppy would have to wait.

The hay and grain were measured and appraised. The machinery was old and rusty. It all belonged to Kettleman, except for one hundred chickens and three horses, a cow and a calf, two sows, and our furniture, which all belonged to us. We started farming, owing Charles for the feed and seed, until we could raise a crop of our own.

The machinery kept breaking down. Joe worked from dawn until dusk, trying to keep everything working. He would come in at night, too tired to eat. I helped all I could, but with Maybelle, I was not able to do much.

"Joe, let's ask Granny Schwentzer to come and look after Maybelle, if she will. I can then give you a hand when you need it."

"Do you think she would?'

"We can ask her, she can't do more'n say no."

Granny was delighted when I asked her. "Sure, kinda, it will give me something to do," she said.

Joe and I worked all summer. He pitched hay up to me and I stacked it so it would balance on the rack and would not slide off when we took it to the barn. Then Joe stuck the hayfork in the hay, and I led the horse that pulled the hay up to the hay door in the mow.

I carried fresh water and a sandwich to him every morning and afternoon when he plowed corn. I waited for him under a big tree, while he carefully walked behind the plow, kicking a clod off a stalk of corn as he went and stopping to mop the sweat from his brow with a big red handkerchief. His clothes were white with dust as he dropped down beside me and rested after loosening the reins so the horses could drop their heads.

I shocked oats behind the binder, and after supper, Joe and I went out together and shocked what we could before dark.

I set eight broody hens with fifteen eggs under each old hen. Granny and Maybelle watered, fed them, and watched for the eggs to pip. When the twenty-eight days were up, they were ready to hatch. Mama had given me six goose eggs and one old hen was going to be the mother of some little goslings. When they finally hatched, we only had four; two of the eggs did not hatch, but we had a flock of little chickens, numbering one hundred twenty from eight setting hens. How happy Joe and I were to see a baby calf and eleven baby pigs. Molly's last-year calf was a yearling steer calf, and this year, she had a heifer calf, so we would have three head of our own.

With a cow to milk and a calf that had to be bucket fed until it could be weaned to grass, hogs to feed, and horses to take care of, it meant getting up in the morning by four o'clock and choring until six thirty before doing anything else. It was a busy summer, but a happy one.

We met our neighbors when we exchanged help during

the harvest. Joe learned how to operate the steam engine that drove the threshing machine that Mr. Kettleman owned. The threshing crew was made up of neighbors, usually a crew of twenty or more people: six to eight hayracks, usually four stackers taking turns, a couple of water boys, with Joe and Kettleman operating the thresher and engine. When it came to mealtime, a hungry crew would troop into the dining room of the family threshing that day. They really got to know who were the best cooks!

I found the healthy tan I had procured from the summer sun was becoming to me, especially with my long braid wound around my head, my greenish-blue eyes, and my flawless skin. I would swing myself around and around, admiring myself. Where is the tomboy I used to be? I smiled happily at myself.

The fall months were busy with storing vegetables and fruits. There were potatoes and apples to store in the cellar, along with carrots and turnips, as well as cabbage and pole beans to pick and lay out to dry. The chickens were culled and roosters were sold on the market.

The corn was drying and it soon was corn-picking time, a time of getting up before dawn and using a lantern to chore, then eating a hot breakfast Granny prepared. While I milked the cow, Joe harnessed the team and put the bang board on the wagon. Then I took care of the milk from the night before. Granny liked to make schmierkase [cottage cheese], so I carefully skimmed the cream and put it in a crock jar to save for butter making, so she could have the clabber that formed the milk into solids for the schmierkase. She only did this a couple of times a month, otherwise the clabber went to the hogs with their slop.

Getting ready to open the cornfield to pick corn was a new experience for me. Remembering Uncle Hans and Tante Lena picking corn, it seemed like an altogether different operation when I came home from school, ran out to the cornfield, climbed on the wagon, and dodged ears of corn, as they were thrown into the wagon. Now, I was actually using a corn pick that fit onto my right hand to rip open the shucks on the corn and throwing the ears into the wagon. They hit the bang board and dropped into the wagon box instead of going over the other side. With forty acres of corn to pick, it meant we had to be out there picking corn every day the weather permitted.

Thanksgiving was coming up fast. We already had some snow flurries and some pretty cold mornings. Joe said we always get bad weather a week before Thanksgiving and he wanted to get the corn in the crib before it turned inclement. We finished two weeks before the holiday.

For me, it was a rest. It seemed good to be able to sit down with Granny and listen to some of the stories she told about her life in Germany and what life was like after she came to America. Maybelle was eighteen months old. Granny had her trained to drink from a cup when she was a year old and it was not long before she was going to sleep on her own and I no longer had to nurse her. She was growing into a healthy, chubby little girl, who was learning to repeat words.

Joe went to Fairport and cut meat for Ben two days a week, which gave us some extra cash when we really needed it.

I had some days when I did not feel the best, but I just thought it was something I ate that did not agree with me, but when it continued I knew I must be pregnant again. When Granny heard me being sick one morning, she looked at me with a quizzical expression.

"Ju gonna be mama again, kinda?" she asked.

"I think so, Granny," I replied.

That night after we went to bed, I thought it was time I said something to Joe. "Honey, I'm going to have another baby."

"You're what?"

"I'm going to have a baby."

"How do you know? Who said so?"

"I know and Granny said so when she saw me getting sick this morning."

"Aw, you and Granny don't know what you're talking about," he laughed and took me in his arms.

"Yes we do, and it isn't funny."

"I know sweetheart, but it will be company for Maybelle."

"It will also be another doctor bill," I said.

"I know, we'll manage," he replied.

We invited Mama and Papa to spend Thanksgiving with us. I thought we would serve a couple of our fat roosters, but Ben gave Joe a turkey, and Joe dressed it at the market. I had never cooked a turkey, but Granny looked pleased and she cooked it to perfection, with an old-fashioned sage dressing. Mama brought a mincemeat pie and we had a feast. Mama could not believe I turned out to be such a good cook, and Granny would not take praise. When I said she made the meal, she insisted to Mama that I had done the cooking.

With the Christmas holiday only a month away, I tried to think what I could do for presents. "I'm afraid it will be the same old story as last year, no money for presents," I told Joe.

"I know, Marty, we need time to get on our feet and I'm afraid it's going to take a couple of years or so. We'll have to do the best we can. I don't need a present, I've got you and Maybelle and pretty soon we'll have a son–that's all I need."

"You don't know if I'll have a boy or not–maybe it's another girl."

"So, whatever, I'll have you and two babies."

I wondered how he really felt. I thought he was just trying to make me feel better.

I made an old sock into a rag doll for Maybelle. I made it

like Muggins, my old rag doll from Aunt Lena and Uncle Hans. I made some beanbags from bits of calico, and strung popcorn and colored beads and buttons for the tree. Mama sent clothes again, but she did get Maybelle a ball and teething ring. On Christmas morning, Joe took me by the hand and led me over to the window. There, standing by the gate, was a brand new surrey.

"Joe, what in the world! Where did that come from and who does that belong to?"

"It's ours."

"Ours? Where did you get the money?"

"Our family is too big for the buggy." I turned in time to see him wink at Granny. "Santa Claus brought it," he said.

"Granny, did you give Joe the money?" I asked after Joe went out.

"No, like Joe say, Santy bring it. You no ask questions. You like, nay?"

"Yes, but Granny, you shouldn't spend your money for us. We're in debt to you for all the help you are giving us," I protested.

"Na, na, we go to ju Mama for dinner. We ride in nice–what ju call it–surrey? Ju no tell your Mama I buy it?"

Chapter Eight

Spring came early. Granny and I put away the sewing and mending we had been catching up on, and started to plan our garden, saving goose eggs to hatch, and cleaning house.

Susan Rae was born May 30, a beautiful Memorial Day. I did not see the disappointment I thought I would when Joe saw we had another girl. Maybelle did not seem to mind that her Mama had a baby, she was happy sitting on Granny's lap.

Joe was busy planting corn and making hay, Granny and I were setting the brooding hens, and things were going very well, until we lost Blackie, one of our horses, in the midst of spring work. Blackie had a gash in his leg from barbed wire that Joe had plowed up from an old rusty fence line. We had not known there was any more wire there. Joe washed the gash and put turpentine on it to keep infection out, but Blackie got lockjaw, and we did not get a veterinary until it was too late to help him. We had to borrow money from Mr. Kettleman to buy another horse. The new horse we named Bruiser; our other horse's name is Mudder. Mudder and Blackie always worked well together, but it took Bruiser time to get used to work as part of a team and I think Mudder missed Blackie. Eventually, though, they got used to one another. I think it might have really been Joe getting used to Bruiser.

Joe planted twenty acres of oats and forty acres of corn. Seventy-five acres were cattle-grazing land and twenty acres were for hogs. Five acres was set aside for a fruit orchard, from which we had a variety of fruit from early summer to late fall.

Summer was busy but enjoyable. What a pleasure it was to see Granny teaching Maybelle some of the old German songs and trying to teach me to understand some of her language, as we planted garden vegetables and flowers. I decided we needed more ground for garden, so Joe plowed up a space alongside the cornfield, where I planted tomatoes, pickles, and pole beans.

Ted and Kelly came by one day and brought a little collie puppy. "Thought you might like to have a dog around," Ted told Joe. "Our old collie had a mess of pups and since they are old enough to wean, we need to get rid of a couple of the pups."

"How about it, Marty, do we need a dog?" asked Joe. Maybelle and Tad were already romping and playing with it.

"Yes, we thought about getting a dog, but we hadn't been able to find one."

"Well, you've got one now. His mother is a good stock dog, so I think her pups will be pretty good dogs," said Ted.

"Thanks, Ted, for thinking about us," I said.

"We think a lot of Shep, she's such a nice old dog," said Kelly. "Are those flowers on the fence sweet peas? I haven't seen them in years."

"Those are Granny's pride and joy. She loves sweet peas. She planted them and two days later we had a snow storm."

"It's a wonder they didn't freeze."

"No, they're very hardy. You can plant them in the fall

and they will come up in the spring," I told her. "Come in, we'll make some coffee. I think we still have some of Granny's oatmeal cookies."

"No, thanks, Marty, we have to go to Wilton Junction and we better get going or we'll be late getting chores done tonight."

"Well, stop again soon, and thanks again for the puppy'

'You're welcome. What are you going to name him?" asked Tad.

"I don't know yet, Tad. Do you have a good name for him?"

"I think Andy is a good name, Aunt Marty," said Tad.

"Why, that's a good name, Tad, how did you think of that?"

"I like that name, cause that's my middle name." We all laughed at that and Joe said that was a great name, so we will name him Andy.

Andy soon made himself at home and became a permanent member of the Mason family. Everywhere Maybelle and Susan went, there you would find Andy. He grew up that summer into a beautiful dark tan collie with white markings on his face and feet, and a white ring around his neck.

The spring months furnished us with some wild gooseberries and blackberries that grew in the timber where the cows grazed, and with spring fading into summer, the vegetables and fruit were ready for canning. And by threshing time in July, the heat and work were in full swing, so it was with great relief that there was a short reprieve from work when September came. It seemed so nice to turn the horses out to pasture and rest for a while. Only when we needed to go to town or had a trip to make were they herded into the barn to be harnessed again.

Soon corn picking was again just around the corner, and

with the first frost on October 10, the corn was drying and getting ready to be picked. I dreaded corn picking. It meant getting up early on cold mornings, getting the chores done, then going out to the cornfield where our gloves were soaked from the frost and my hands would nearly freeze. It was nice when the corn was picked and in the crib.

Thanksgiving came, and Granny spent the day with Willie and Carey in Davenport. Ma and Ann Mason were having all the family home, so we spent the day with them. Kelly, Ted, Teresa, John, and Helen their daughter, Joe and I, Maybelle and Susan.

Christmas we spent with Mama and Papa. Mama had some toys for the girls, and for Joe it was gloves as usual, but this year she gave me five yards of material to make dresses for the girls and a four-pound fruitcake,

With the New Year came the weekly Saturday night parties at our various neighbors. Granny was back home with us again, after spending Thanksgiving and Christmas with her kids.

After chores and supper, Joe hitched the team to the surrey, and Granny, Maybelle, Susan, Joe, and I climbed in and rode off to a neighborhood party. The dance was just starting when we got there. The music makers were tuning a fiddle and guitar, and half dozen kids were playing on the dance floor, where the host had dusted corn meal on the floor to make it slick. The dance space was a large kitchen floor. The stove had been moved to a corner, and tables and chairs moved to the front room, making enough space for six to ten couples to dance a waltz or fox trot and maybe a broom dance. One woman would dance with the broom until she saw a man dancing with whom she wanted to dance. She would tap his female partner on the back, hand her the broom, and take her partner. And that woman would dance with the broom, until she saw a man she wanted to dance with, but she must not give the broom back to the first woman to get her partner back. Such fun! We really enjoyed ourselves, especially when Granny would get out on the floor to dance a jig. Everyone laughed and shouted and clapped for her to continue. By 2 A.M., the music makers played "Home Sweet Home," and everyone said good night. Most men danced the last dance with their wife; Joe and I always waltzed together to the "go home" music.

January is a cold and snowy month, but we usually have a January thaw when the temperature moderates and it gets up to forty and fifty degrees. It was on Thursday and the temperature was zero; somehow, I did not feel like myself. I had a scary feeling in the pit of my stomach and I was restless all day. Granny and I were piecing a quilt. I was cutting the quilt patches and Granny was sewing them together. Maybelle and Susan were taking their afternoon nap. There was a rap on the door. I looked at Granny; she heard it too. I wondered who was coming to see us. It was Sam Glenney. I had not seen Sam for over ten years, probably longer; for a moment I did not know who he was.

"Hello, Marty, remember me, Sam?"

"Sam Glenney, how are you–my, I didn't know you for a minute. What brings you out here, Sam? Come in."

"Marty, your Papa is sick. Your Mama thinks he is bad sick. She thinks you had better come home to see him."

"Oh no! What's the matter with Papa?"

"I don't know. It could be a bad cold or the flu–your Mama don't know–but old Doc Werner came out to see him. I haven't talked to your Mama since he saw him."

"Joe is working for Ben today, so he won't be home until after five. Tell Mama I'll come as soon as I can, and thank you, Sam, for letting us know. Can I make you a cup of coffee before you go?"

"No thanks, Marty, I don't drink coffee. I hope your Papa gets better real soon."

"Thanks again, Sam." I closed the door as he went out and leaned against it. "Papa sick?" That scared, jittery feeling went through me.'

'Granny came out of the front room. "Who was at der door?" she asked. "What's der matter, kinda, ju look like ju cry?"

"That was Sam Glenney, a neighbor of Mama and Papa's. He said Papa is sick."

"So, so what is der matter mit du Papa?"

"Sam said he might have the flu. Mama wants me to come home and see him. Mama wouldnt want me to come unless he is very sick."

"Nau, nau, don't cross bridge."

"Don't cross bridge? What do you mean, don't cross bridge?"

"Means don't cross bridge before there is a bridge. Don't worry until there is something to worry about."

But I did worry. Mama would not send someone to get me, if it was not bad.

It was after five o'clock when Joe got home. Granny had supper ready and while Joe washed up for supper, I told him about Papa. He took the towel off the hook and wiped his face before he looked at me.

"You worried?"

"Yes, honey. Can we go to Mama's in the morning?"

"Yeh, I should be cutting meat for the Saturday trade. Ben will just have to do it himself if I don't get back in time."

After the dishes were done, I sat down by Granny and she tried to interest me in the quilt, but I could not concentrate on anything but Papa. Granny got the girls ready for bed, finally, and told me I had better get some rest, if we were going to leave early.

"Don't worry about Maybelle and Susan," she said. "I take gute care of dem. Ju stay wit Mama and Papa as long as dey need ju."

"Granny, I love you," I said, giving her a big hug. I realized I did not ever thank her enough for what she does for us.

We arose at four o'clock in the morning and got ready to go. Joe hitched Fanny to the buggy and we took off for Wilton Junction. We wanted to catch the train to Blue Grass, and it went through town at about seven in the morning. We arrived at Wilton Junction fifteen minutes after six and I stayed at the station while Joe put Fanny in the livery stable.

We arrived at Blue Grass at nine thirty, and again I stayed at the station while Joe rented a horse and buggy from the livery stable to drive to Mama and Papa's.

Mama met me at the door. I had never seen her in such a state of depression before. Instantly, I thought Papa must be very sick. I put my arms around her. "Mama, how is Papa?"

"Ju Papa is sick, bad sick," she said, wiping the tears from her eyes.

"What does the doctor say?" I asked her.

"He say apoplexy. He not get better, he not work, he not use his arms. He no can eat, he no can talk, he no can tell when I touch him. He can't feel nudding. Doctor say, hospital, but he say it do no gute, he not get better, he say maybe he live a week, maybe not. What I do without Heinrich?"

I tightened my arms around her waist, and led her to a chair. I had never seen Mama so nervous and helpless. She got up and went to the bedroom. I followed her in and saw Papa lying in a curled position, his eyes closed. It looked like he was sleeping.

"He got up day before yesterday, he say he haf headache, and he go out and do chores. When he eat breakfast, he say he not feel gute and he go to bed. I try to wake him up for dinner. I no can wake him. I go out and ring the bell, I ring and ring, and soon Sam Glenney come to see what is wrong. He get doctor, and then he go tell ju," said Mama. "Sarah

Clausmann and Elsie Glenney stay by me last night. Marty–Marty what I going to do?" I did not know what to do or say to my mother.

"Mama, we have to let Pete and Aunt Lena and Uncle Hans know"

Joe came in from taking care of the horse. He immediately sensed it was bad news. He took Mama's hand and patted it. "How's Papa?" he asked, looking at me. I shook my head.

"Papa's very bad...he's paralyzed...the doctor told Mama he won't get better. He can die."

It suddenly hit me–Papa is going to die. I started to cry, a feeling of guilt, love, and longing engulfed me, a strange and scary feeling. A feeling that I experienced when Martha Glenney died and when I had opened my trunk, and now the same sensation when Papa is so sick.

Joe put his arms around me and said, "You'd better stay with your Mama, I will go back home and let Granny and Ma know–then I'll come back and see what I can do."

"Oh Joe, I love you so much. I don't know who is doing chores."

"George Clausmann du der chores last night und Sam did dem dis morning," Mama said. "Elsie is coming back today and Sarah said she would be back, too. One of der Glenney boys will be back tonight to do der chores."

Joe was leaving when Mr. Clausmann drove in. He had Sarah and Elsie with him. "How are you, George?" said Joe. "Remember me, Joe Mason?"

"Of course, good to see you, Joe."

"Good morning, ladies," said Joe.

"Good morning," said Mrs. Clausmann. "So sorry about Heinrich."

"Yes," said Joe, "Heinrich is not that old. I think he is only sixty-two or sixty-three."

“Too bad,” said Mrs. Glenney.

“I have to go back home and take care of some business,” said Joe. “I’ll be back as soon as I can.”

Elsie, Sarah, and George came in, and I was amazed to see the way Elsie had aged over the last ten years since Mate had died. I did not know Sarah very well. Connie Clausmann never had much to do with the kids at school, she was more of a teacher’s pet, so I never had much to do with the Clausmanns except if there was something special at school; otherwise, the only one I saw was Mr. Clausmann. Papa and Mr. Clausmann were good friends. Sometimes Papa would herd a cow over to the Clausmann farm and leave her there a couple of days. When he took Molly over there one day, I asked him why Molly had to go to Mr. Clausmann. Papa told me there was better grass over there for Molly to eat. It was a long time before I knew it was because Papa did not own a bull.

Mama greeted the two women, and they asked if Heinrich had woken up.

“No,” said Mama.

“Hannah, do you mind if I go in to see Heinrich?” asked George.

“No, komm,” Mama led the way and Mr. Clausmann went in. He was gone only a few minutes when he came out holding his cap in his hand and a sad look on his face. Mama poured some coffee and we all sat at the table. Sarah had brought coffee kuchen and cut slices from it to have with the coffee.

“Are you going to stay with your Mama?” asked Elsie. “Who is taking care of your little ones, Marty?”

“Granny Schwentzer is staying with us, and she is taking care of Maybelle and Susan,” I told her. “I’ll be with Mama as long as she needs me.”

“That’s good. Your Mama really needs you.”

"Joe will be back tomorrow," I said.

"Is there anything I can do to help you, Hannah?" asked Mr. Clausmann.

"I don't think so, George. Elsie's boys are going to do the chores," said Mama. "I haf to let Peter know and Lena and Hans. We haf to send wire tomorrow. When Joe comes back, he can do it for me."

The neighbors left soon afterward, and I was alone with Mama and Papa. It was a long afternoon, and the evening dragged slowly. I do not think Mama had slept since Papa had the stroke. She was restless, going to and from Papa's room. I could see she was tired. I tried to get her to lie down and rest, but she just could not relax. I finally coaxed her to eat some stew Pearl Cleggar, one of the neighbors, sent over. I persuaded her to lie down beside Papa. She dozed off, and I laid down on the sofa, thinking I could rest with Mama sleeping beside Papa. I closed my eyes and lay there, wondering what Mama will do without Papa. I think I also dozed off–I am not sure what happened–but I felt a gust of air brush past me. I awoke instantly, and looked for Mama, because that is what it felt like, someone in a hurry had brushed past me. I jumped up, and went to the kitchen. Mama was not there. I hurried to Mama and Papa's room. Mama was lying beside Papa, just the way she had climbed in bed beside him. Suddenly, I was overcome by that same feeling of excitement and fear that enveloped me when I opened the lid of my trunk, and that had come over me at the hotel the night I had slept in the room on the third floor. I must have choked out a scream or an audible gasp, because Mama was awake instantly.

"What is, Marty?" she asked, her voice wavering.

"It's all right, Mama, I thought you woke up," I said.

"Ju scream, "Papa." Is Heinrich wake up?"

"No, Mama, go back to sleep. I'm sorry, I didn't mean to wake you."

"I no can sleep," she said, getting up. "What time is?"

I looked at the clock in the front room. It was six thirty. We had slept all night. I went to the door and saw pink streaks of sun lighting up the sky.

"It's six thirty, Mama," I said. "I'll make some coffee and get some breakfast ready."

"Is early yet. Is fire in du stove?"

"I'll start the fire. There's still some coals in the firebox. All I need is some cobs to start it burning."

"There's cobs on the porch."

I soon had a fire burning in the cook stove and it was warming up in the kitchen.

Mama was up by the time I had finished. She came in and got a basin of warm water from the reservoir, and picked up a washcloth and towel. "I wash him. Maybe he wake up."

I followed her into the bedroom. She set the basin on a table near the bed and pulled back the quilt. She picked up his hand and began moaning, then laid his hand down and put her hand to his cheek. When she turned and looked at me, there were tears in her eyes.

"I tink he not liv, no, no, Heinrich, he die, I tink he die." She started moaning again, and her face turned pale. She stopped and I thought she was going to fall. I wanted to scream, but all I could utter was "Mama, Mama," so I thought about it. I knew I was not prepared for it either. I walked to the window. There was a spring wagon and team at the hitching post. It must be one of the Glenneys. I grabbed my coat and ran to the barn. Gibson was just coming out.

"Tom, Tom," I screamed as I ran toward him.

"I'm not Tom, I'm Gib . . . what's the matter, Marty?"

"Papa died! I don't know what to do . . . Mama . . .she is crying."

"Oh, I'm sorry . . . you need someone here with you. As soon as I milk, I'll go get Mom. Calm down, you'll be all right."

"Joe will be here this morning sometime," I said. "But Gib, I'm scared. I don't want to stay here alone with Mama."

"I'll go get Mom now, I can milk when I come back. Go in the house, I won't be gone long."

I walked slowly back to the house. Mama was still in the chair, tears running down her cheeks.

"Elsie Glenney is coming over and Joe will be here after awhile." She did not seem to hear me. I went to the kitchen and poured us a cup of coffee. I went back and took her by the hand. "Come, we'll have a cup of coffee, Mama."

She got up, but pulled her hand away and went to the bedroom. She opened the door and went in. She was in there a moment or two and she came out. She acted like she was in a daze. I took her hand again.

"Come, Mama, Mrs. Glenney will be here pretty soon." We sat down at the table and I poured some cream in her coffee and urged her to drink. My coffee had cooled by the time I tasted it and I poured myself a new cup.

It was after nine o'clock when Roy and Elsie Glenney got there. Gib did not come with them. Elsie said he had to get ready to go back to the Navy, where he is stationed, and his shore leave would be up on Friday and this was Tuesday. He had a couple of friends to see before he left. She also told us Tom would be home from the Army on leave before long.

"Is Sam in the service, too?"

"No, Sam is deferred to help on the farm," she told me.

"Gib said he did not get the milking done. I better go out and do that, Hannah," said Roy.

"Ja, du pail is in der butry. Danke [thanks], ist so nice ju do that for uns. We only milk two now, der rest be dry."

There was a knock on the door. Doctor Werner opened

the door and walked in. "Good day, Hannah," he said to Mama. To Mrs. Glenney and I, "Good morning, ladies."

"Doctor," Mama got up. "Doctor, Heinrich, he die this morning."

Doctor Werner went immediately into the bedroom. Mama followed him. I went too, but I stood outside the open door. He checked Papa with his fingers for a pulse, and turned and came back out.

"Yes," he said, "probably sometime in the night." He talked to Mama for a little while, patted her on the shoulder, and turned to me. "I'll send the undertaker out from Blue Grass."

Joe got back a little before noon. I was so glad to see him. "Papa passed away last night. Doctor Werner was here this morning. How's Maybelle and Susan? Did you tell Granny what happened?"

"Slow down, Marty, one question at a time. I'm sorry your Papa died. Sweetheart, the kids are fine, so is Granny, and yes, I told her what happened."

"The undertaker is supposed to come this afternoon. Oh, Joe, what will happen now? Mama can't live here by herself. What is she going to do without Papa?"

"Joe, will ju go to town und send a wire to Lena and Hans and Peter?" asked Mama.

"Sure Hannah, I better go do that."

"Wait 'til der undertaker here. Maybe he haf to do something else." Mama was calmed down and getting herself under control.

I looked around to find something to fix to eat and Mama said, "In der smokehouse is ham and bacon."

I went to the smokehouse and found hams and bacon hanging from hooks. The acrid smell of smoke prevailed. Papa had been smoking the meat. He must have butchered three or four hogs, not long ago, and was curing the meat.

There was no way I could get one of those big hams off the hook and carry it to the house. I saw some sausage links hanging around, so I took six links of sausage.

I fixed the sausage, fried some potatoes, and brought some canned vegetables and fruit from the cellar. I was hungry. I had not eaten very much since we got here. Joe ate a good meal, too, but Mama only ate a dish of plums, as did Elsie.

It was two o'clock before the undertaker arrived. He had another man with him. They went into the bedroom and closed the door after saying a few words to Mama. She nodded in agreement. They were in with Papa a long time. When they came out, the smell of formaldehyde was heavy in the room. They talked to Mama again and left.

"What did they say, Mama?" I asked.

"They just tell me they bring coffin pretty soon, and I get Papa's suit, so they can dress him. They say I komm and look at coffin. I tell them just plain, I no can pay a lot. Joe can do it for me."

Joe left to do Mama's errands for her right away.

I busied myself doing little things. I washed the dishes and swept the floor. I asked Mama about the chickens, and she told me to feed them and take warm water out to the chicken house. She seemed to be doing all right. The tears had stopped and she seemed to have squared her shoulders for a burden she knew was hers. Roy Glenney came, and he and Elsie left. They said they would be back tomorrow.

Joe got back about five o'clock, and shortly after, the undertaker came, bringing the coffin. By six, the coffin was in the front room by the window and Papa was in it, wearing his Sunday suit. He looked like he was sleeping. I could not believe this was the last time I would see Papa. That scared, sad feeling was still with me when I looked at him.

We spent a long night, the three of us, alone with Papa. Mama talked to Joe about a graveyard plot. She did not know what to tell the undertaker and she had to let him know tomorrow. He thought Blue Grass, but Mama said she would talk to Hans first, but he said he had to know before then.

"Papa liked Wilton Junction, so tink we put Heinrich in graveyard in Wilton Junction."

Joe made arrangements for a lot in Wilton Junction and to get the grave opened. The funeral would be Saturday. Ma Mason and Ann came and stayed. Neighbors were coming and going all day on Friday. Friday evening, Sarah and George Clausmann and Elsie and Roy Glenney stayed all night for the wake.

Papa was buried on Saturday, January 26, in Wilton Junction.

Chapter Nine

Spring weather was late this year. It was the end of April before Joe got the oats planted and disked, and the garden and truck patch plowed and harrowed. When the weather finally settled, life became busy–I could plant the garden and Joe could plant corn and Granny and the girls could be outside and watch the little red baby pigs in the pigpen. She would also give the girls some chicken feed so they could not only watch the chickens but feed them as well–and then chase after them. We traded ganders with our neighbors, Henry and Emma Peters, a middle-aged couple with three kids, Ethel, Priscilla, and John. Henry was a tall strong man with a contagious smile; I never saw him without the smile and a warm greeting. Emma was short and heavyset, a good-natured person, always ready to help whenever there was a need.

The gander we named Sergeant, a young goose from last year's hatch, and by trading the males we could make sure the hen eggs would be fertile and the goslings not crippled. Aunt Lena had said the gander should come from another flock, so it would not be too close a relation to the hens. It did not make much sense to me, but if Aunt Lena said it, I knew it must be right.

With the passing days, I realized I must be pregnant again. I had a couple of little upsets, but I did not think too much about it until I realized my period time had long passed since the middle of March, and it was now the last of May. Susan was two years old. I dreaded to tell Joe, and I did not know what Granny was going to say with the prospect of another baby facing us. She had her hands full with Maybelle and Susan, and although she never said so, I could see she was tired and she always slept after she put the girls down for a nap.

I started taking over some of the chores she had been doing; at age seventy-five, she had to start slowing down. Somehow, we had gotten into the habit of expecting too much of Granny. She just naturally started the cooking and was always washing dishes and sweeping. Both Aunt Lena and Mama were Granny's daughters. I could believe that Tante Lena was, but Mama's personality was so much different, it was hard to believe she was Granny's daughter.

The summer was hard work, but also a pleasant time. In the evening, Joe, Granny, Maybelle, Susan, and I would have a picnic lunch along the creek. The girls would try to catch a fish with homemade fishing poles or go wading in a shallow place, or pick up rocks and snail shells. When it rained or we did not feel like having a picnic, we sat on the porch and enjoyed the evening. Joe was always ready to show the girls something special, like woolly caterpillars and garden spiders, or to do something fun, like catch a big grasshopper, dig earthworms for bait, and catch fireflies.

I was putting on weight. For the last two years, I had noticed I was getting heavier. I must have weighed twenty-five pounds more than when Joe and I were married, and by my sixth month, I was really showing my pregnancy. Joe told me, "You are just a good armful."

It was the beginning of my eighth month and the middle of October. Joe was plowing out potatoes with the sulky. He had pulled the wagon to the field. I was picking them up to carry them by the bucketful and place them in the wagon. We worked most of the day and wagon was nearly full. Dark clouds were gathering in the west and Joe wanted to get them in the cellar before they got wet, so he pulled the wagon up by the cellar door and then went to do the chores. I started unloading, even though my back ached so bad I could hardly straighten up. I had filled a basket and was about to pick it up when I felt warm fluid run down my legs. Alarmed, I sat down and wondered what to do. Granny was in the kitchen. I could hear her rattling the pans and talking to the girls. Joe was at the barn. I tried to stand up, but the pressure was too great, and it started a contraction. "My God," I thought, "I'm going to have the baby out here and it's too early. I'm not supposed to have it yet." I got on my hands and knees and started crawling toward the door.

"Granny, Granny!" I shouted. The sound that emitted from my lips was a hoarse whisper. My throat was constricted with fright, and as deaf as Granny was, I knew she could not hear me. It seemed an age before she opened the door and started toward the well.

Then she saw me. "Marty, Marty, what's der matter mit ju . . . ju got pain?" I nodded. Granny tried to help me to my feet, but I could not stand. She ran toward the barn.

"Joe, Joe, come quick. Marty ist sick mit der baby"

Then Joe was at my side, gathering me in his strong arms. He carried me to the bedroom. "I'll get the doctor," he said.

"No, no," I moaned, "there isn't time."

"I don't know what to do." His face was pale.

Granny came into the room with a pan of hot water and an old sheet over her arm, one I had saved to tear into bandages if anyone got hurt.

"Go out, get the doctor," she told Joe. To me, she said, "Don't be afraid, kinda, I help lots of babies get born."

"But Granny, I am afraid, it isn't time for the baby yet."

"Na, na, ju be all right."

I was crying, as contraction after contraction gripped me, and the blood vessels in my neck convulsed–then I felt the baby slip out.

Granny took a scissors from the pan of water and worked busily, then she was holding the baby upside down and patting it sharply on its bottom. There was no sound, so she put her hand under its neck and shoulders and with her other hand firmly grasping its feet, she pressed them forward into its stomach, then back, forward again, and back, until after several attempts, it finally let out a weak cry.

"Tank God," I heard Granny mutter to herself.

The baby was another girl, thin, tiny, and bluish-red. Granny laid her beside me, and I pressed the tiny form against my breast to keep her warm.

Granny had the bed changed and was dressing the baby when Joe returned with Dr. Werner. He looked the baby over and examined me.

"Everything's all right. You don't need me . . . Granny, you did an excellent job. The baby will need a lot of special care . . . she'll probably be touch and go for awhile."

We named this little girl Dorothy Jean, after Granny. Joe dubbed her Dot. She was a sick child from the beginning, and she cried and fussed a lot. Large black and blue spots appeared on her stomach, arms, and legs from time to time. I mentioned them to Granny one day.

"I tink du kinda get worms. We fix her some medicine," she said.

She brought in a pumpkin and scooped out the seeds. Then she peeled the seeds and saved the kernels. When she had a half cupful, she crushed them and let them soak. This concoction she poured into one of Joe's corn cake tobacco sacks, which she had washed and boiled to make it good and clean. Every day, she would try to get the baby to suck on the sack to extract some of her medicine. Dot did not respond to the pumpkin seed tea. We took her to Dr. Werner.

"Perhaps the spots are due to ruptured capillaries bleeding into her tissues and clotting. She will probably outgrow it."

With a sick child, I was pretty well tied down. Thanksgiving, Mama came and brought food. I found it hard to be thankful with a sick baby and no way to help her.

Granny took care of Maybelle, Susan, and the house. I took care of Dot, some nights holding her and trying to comfort her all night.

Joe was busy fixing machinery and choring.

The parties were starting again. I urged Joe to go and take Granny. She still liked to square dance. Joe filled in as a square dance caller.

First couple out to the couple on the right,
The lady around the lady and the gent al lo,
The lady around the gent and the gent don't go,
Four hands around and around you go,
Break with a do-si-do and promenade.

Usually, he would sing it to the tune of "Turkey in the Straw." I tried to tell myself that I did not mind, particularly, when Joe came home with the stench of liquor on his breath.

Day by day, I brought Dot through the winter without a cold or even a sniffle. The snow had piled up over the winter and by spring there was two feet of it on the level and drifts up to six feet high in sheltered places and around the buildings. Then all of a sudden it was warm, the snow began to melt, and a heavy rain fell. The creek that ran through our farm was a raging torrent, sweeping away our fences, the soil, and everything in its path with a mighty destructive force.

Joe hastily threw up a temporary fence to keep the livestock from wandering. We had oats to plant and plowing to do. A permanent fence would have to wait until the spring work was done. But after the seeding came the hay crop, then corn plowing, oats binding and shocking, a second crop of hay. It was the middle of September before Joe pulled the separator into the shed.

It was a shimmering Indian summer, shiny wisps of cobwebs floated in the gentle breeze, spiraling downward, only to be picked up by the wind and hurled skyward, the sun touching them with gold. They lightly brushed my cheek as I gathered vegetables from the truck garden. Joe was over by the creek making the fence. I had been working about an hour. I glanced over to where Joe was working–he was busy stretching the wire tight and stapling it to the post. As my gaze wandered across the meadow, I saw a woman. She was dressed in black, with a black sunbonnet on her head. She was walking toward the creek, where Joe was making fence. She walked with such ease, she seemed almost to float along, and thinking it might be a neighbor, I called to her. She did not hear me, so I called again.

Joe looked up. "Who you hollerin' at?" he asked.

I glanced back to where I had seen the woman. She had disappeared; puzzled, I wondered how she got out of sight so quickly. I decided she had walked down over the bank by the creek. I went over to Joe. To my amazement, the bank of the creek sheared off the water's edge, so she could not possibly have walked over the bank without going into the water.

"Did you see where she went?" I asked.

"Did I see where who went?"

"That woman . . . didn't you see her walking along the bank? She wasn't over one hundred feet from you."

"I didn't see anybody. You must have imagined it."

It bothered me. I had seen a woman in a long black dress and when I looked away, she disappeared. I forgot about the woman when I got back to the house. Dot was running a fever. Her eyes were dull and she had two blotches on her abdomen, which was swollen and distended.

"Get the doctor," I told Joe.

Doctor Werner shook his head when he saw her. "She is a very sick child," he told me. "We better make arrangements to get her to the hospital." He sat by her bed examining her. He got up and talked to Joe a few minutes and left.

Maybelle and Susan slept. Granny and Joe was quiet and troubled. I could not sit still. I walked from room to room, then returned to Dot to smooth her hair from her hot forehead.

"What did the doctor say when he was talking to you?" I asked Joe.

"He said she has a blood disease–an incurable blood disease–she's very sick."

I walked out on the porch. The cool night air bathed my face as I looked up, beseeching God to ease my child's pain. The stars seemed so near, like they had been hung there for a special purpose. As I turned to go inside, I saw a star streak across the sky and drop earthward. Joe came to my side. With his arm around me, we saw our baby gasp and labor for her last breath.

"No, no, she can't die," I sobbed. With tears streaming down Joe's face, he led me away. The clock was striking three.

Granny took Dot's death hard, but even in her grief, she tried to comfort us. I blamed Joe. If I had not worked so hard, she might not have been premature.

Word soon spread around the neighborhood. Friends came and did the chores, brought food, and sat with us through the wake. The small grave left a scar in the smooth green cemetery near Papa. It also left a deep scar in our hearts.

The small garments in the bureau drawer were all it took to make my grief almost unbearable. Joe only came into the house to eat and sleep. I did not realize he needed comfort as badly as I did.

Going through the closet one day, a glow in the darkness attracted my attention. The glow was coming from the trunk. I pulled it out and packed Dot's clothes in it. I found myself opening the trunk often in the days that followed, taking out the white celluloid ring Dot had cut her first tooth on. I could see the marks on it, and the little sweater Kelly had knit for her, and my heart broke all over again. Granny came and helped me to my feet. "Come, Marty, we haf cup of coffee," and with gentle persuasion she led me away.

The days that followed were a daze of picking things up and laying them down and hardly knowing what I was doing. I had periods of deep depression and tears would come often. Joe came in and tried to comfort me, and in my state of mind, I thought he did not care about Dot. But even though he smoked his pipe and hummed the same tune as he went about his work outside, the slump in his shoulders and the sadness on his face told a different story: the days she had been so sick had taken their toll on him as well.

Granny tried to interest me in Maybelle and Susan, and would often have the girls do something special like help her bake cookies and make something special for dinner, so they could show me what they did and make me feel better.

Chapter Ten

Ted and Kelly moved to a farm about two miles from us. Tad started school with Maybelle. Susan was lonely with her sister gone all day and she demanded more attention from me. Slowly the ache in my heart eased.

I went out and helped with the chores once more. A quiet peace enveloped me as I helped carry corn from the crib, counted out eight ears for each horse, and put them in their small feed box. I followed Joe to the hayloft to hunt for a nest of eggs a hen might have hidden. Joe was up on a high crossbeam that held the hay; he took my hand and pulled me up beside him and into his arms. With the contented sound of the animals below, we sustained our love for one another.

The first snow came two weeks before Thanksgiving and stayed all winter, piling up drifts with every storm. It covered fences and roads. Everything was a great white wilderness. We chored early on winter days; the sound of milk squirting in a pail always brought the Maltese mother cat with her young family, and they waited patiently until the cows were milked and we filled their pan with warm milk.

Suddenly, it was spring again, and time to set the broody

hens and to make a garden. Along one end of the garden was a grape arbor and behind the arbor was a coppice.

I worked all day with my plants and seeds. After supper, I went out to pull weeds and encourage the tender shoots to grow. I was engrossed with stirring the soil and when I looked up it was dark; when I looked down again, I could hardly see the row. Gradually, a scared feeling went through me. I looked toward the thicket. It seemed something was watching and holding me with a hypnotic stare. I tore my eyes away from the thicket. I was so weak I could hardly move my legs as I slowly, step by step, backed away. I finally gathered enough strength to turn and stumble to the house.

"What's the matter with you? You're as white as a sheet," asked Joe.

"I don't know, there was something by the grape thicket. I couldn't see anything. I was hoeing and when I looked up, it was dark. Something was holding me–I mean, it seemed something was holding me. It took all my strength to get away from it–I mean, from there."

"Just your imagination. You're afraid of the dark," he teased, knocking the ashes from his pipe.

"I'm not afraid of the dark and you know it." I went to a drawer, took out a towel, wet one corner, and sat down to rub my face. Andy growled low in his throat. I listened. "The dog heard something," I said, as he started to bark.

Joe went to the door. Someone was coming up the lane on horseback, his lantern swinging with the motion of the horse. Joe lit our lantern and I followed him out to meet whoever it might be. It was Tom Riley, our neighbor.

"Ted Miller's boy fell out of the mow," said Tom. "He landed on the handle of a pitch fork. The boy's in a bad way."

"Oh, mercy, not Tad!" I said.

"Yep, he was playing in the loft and jumped on a pile of hay Ted had just thrown down for the stock. He left the fork sticking in the hay, and when the boy jumped, the handle went into his belly. Happened about an hour ago."

Later, as we neared Ted's farm, I was thinking of Dot and what her death had meant to us. I hoped Tad was not too badly hurt. We turned into the farmyard and drove up to the hitching post. Ted came from the shadows, tears running down his cheeks. "Tad died a few minutes ago,' he said.

Doctor Werner came out of the house. "I'm sorry, Ted. I did all I could for him. He was hemorrhaging, and the wound to his belly injured his insides so bad . . . ," his words trailing off. He gripped Ted's arm for an instant, got in his rig, and drove away.

Kelly seemed calm when I went in. She spoke to me and talked about the accident. "He was playing in the barn. He shouldn't have been out there. It was getting dark. He jumped from the mow, when Ted was ready to come in. He was conscious when Ted carried him in. He said to me, 'Don't worry Mom, it don't hurt.' He was unconscious when Dr. Werner got here. He was bleeding inside." She stopped talking and just sat beside the small form of Tad, covered with a sheet. She started sobbing, uncontrollable sobs. I could not think of anything to say, so I just put my arm around her to comfort her.

Thinking of what happened to Tad, I wondered if the scared feeling I had earlier in the garden was a premonition.

After the funeral, Kelly said, "Marty, I'm going to have a baby. I'm about four months along." I was curious as to how could she hold up so well.

It was shortly after this when I found I also was with child again. When I told Joe, he said in a resigned voice, "If we have another, I hope it's a boy this time."

The summer drew to a close and Susan started school. Maybelle began presenting us with a problem about going. She and Susan walked by themselves, now that Tad was gone. She seemed upset and often cried without apparent reason.

She had only asked once about Dot. I explained the best I could. “God loves little children and wants Dot in heaven with the angels.”

“But Mama, I didn’t see heaven.”

“I know, Maybelle. It is something you will understand when you get older.”

“Mama, will God take me and Susan to heaven?”

“No, Maybelle, God takes little children who are sick or get hurt and can’t get well. You and Susan are well.”

I recalled the talk with her when she was particularly unhappy one day. “Maybelle don’t you feel well?” She shook her head and started to cry. I lifted her to my lap. “Tell Mama about it.”

She looked at my face, with tears streaming from her beautiful brown eyes. “Did God take Tad to heaven?” she asked.

“Yes, dear, he took Tad to heaven,” I answered.

“Was Tad sick?” she asked.

“No, he wasn’t sick, he got hurt very bad.”

“Will he take me away if I get hurt?”

“You must be careful and not get hurt.”

“I'm afraid to go to heaven.”

“Don't be afraid, sweetheart, nothing is going to hurt you and Susan. Go get your book. Mama will read you a story.”

After the story, she seemed happier. But I still worried about her, so I talked with Miss Elsie, the teacher at Sharon, where they were going to school, and told her of Maybelle’s fears. Miss Elsie was a tall, thin woman with dark brown wispy hair that escaped from the hairpins and combs meant to hold her hair in place. She was always pushing it back from her face. She had dark eyes and thin lips, but her voice was soft and kindly. Joe called Miss Elsie an old maid.

“Why do you say she is an old maid?” I asked him.

"She's not married. She must be at least thirty."

" doesn't mean she's an old maid," I told him.

She told me she would watch Maybelle and let us know if there were changes in her schoolwork.

In August, Kelly gave birth to twins, Lawrence and Lorna.

Our little Katherine was born in October. She was a healthy baby and grew fast, but she always seemed to have a cold. We had to watch her closely, because it seemed like the least little sniffles and she would get the croup.

I hovered over Kathy, like a hen with one chick, at the first sign of a cold. Susan came down with the whooping cough in February, and two weeks later, Maybelle and Kathy both had it. Granny and I sat by Kathy in shifts and by some miracle pulled her through it. Maybelle did not have it so bad–she only whooped a couple of times, but Kathy whooped every time she coughed. I was so worried about Kathy that I felt I had been through a mill. Several times Joe had said, "Come to bed. Granny can handle the baby. If she needs you, she will call you." But I could not go to bed. I dozed in a chair and jumped when I heard Kathy start to whoop.

Joe was going to Wilton Junction frequently. I did not realize we were growing apart until one day Joe accused me of thinking too much about the kids and not having time for anything else.

"When I asked him what he was going to town for, he said, "I went to see Ma. I'm tired just sitting around listening to your problems with the kids. When it's time to go to bed, you still have things to do, and by the time you come to bed, I'm asleep. How many times have we went to bed together?"

That shook me. I knew he was right and come to think of it, for the last three months, we had not really been lovers more than three or four times. I vowed to myself that I would give more time to Joe. I felt going to see his Ma was not the only reason for going to Fairport–it was such a long way.

We had frequently seen rats all summer and winter. Hoards of them had moved from the board pile and buildings into the barn and cellar. We could hear them gnawing at the floor, trying to get in the house. Andy would get one once in awhile and drag it out from under the porch. Joe would see one running across the yard at night, when the moon was bright, and would get the old twelve-gauge shotgun.

Early in April, I set some hens in the empty corncrib, putting fifteen eggs under each one. Eighteen days passed, and in three days, the eggs would start to hatch. I always fed the hens in the morning and again in the evening, waiting until they were through eating and gone back to their nest. Then I carefully cleaned the rest of the feed from the floor, so it would not attract the rats.

We had been in bed several hours when Andy woke us. He was barking, and now and then would growl.

"What do you think is the matter with him?" I asked Joe.

"I dunno, probably sees his shadow," said Joe, pulling on his pants.

I threw a coat over my nightgown and followed him. Everything seemed quiet and peaceful. Still Andy was growling low in his throat. Joe told him to shut up and lay down. He crawled back under the porch.

At breakfast, Joe remarked, "I wonder what got into that fool dog last night."

"I don't know. He sure made a fuss," I said, pouring some cream in my coffee and stirring it. "Maybe he saw a coon or possum."

"Maybe," agreed Joe.

I went about my morning chores, picking up the bucket of oats I had soaked the night before to give to the setting hens. I shall never forget the carnage I saw when I opened the door. The hens were all off the nests and scattered about, four of them with their necks chewed off, the other three so badly bitten that Joe had to kill them. Most of the eggs had been carried away. The rest were broken. The hundred chicks I had looked forward to hatching were all destroyed in a single night. I was so heartsick that I cried all day.

"I don't know what to do about the rats. It just seems to be a bad year for them," said Joe.

Joe fixed the oat bin so it would be rat proof, and I set some more hens.

Several days later, Kathy had a cold. She was running a slight fever. "It's probably her teeth," I told Granny. Her temperature had risen by the time I put her to bed. I went to the closet for my nightgown. I could see my old trunk over to one side. It loomed in the darkness with a white glow around it. It frightened me. This was the second time I had noticed the trunk when it seemed to have a light around it. I closed the closet and got in bed with Joe.

"You know, dear," I said to him, "it seems to have some kind of luminous finish."

"What has a luminous finish?"

"My old trunk. Sometimes it seems to have a light shining all around it."

"There you go with that imagination of yours, again."

"Joe, I get so mad at you–it's not my imagination! If you don't believe me, go look for yourself. The closet is dark, but you can see the trunk, there's a light all around it."

"All right, so it has luminous paint."

I was restless a long time before I dropped off to sleep. I suddenly awoke from a nightmare, more frightened than I had ever been. It seemed I was sitting on the bank of a river; on the other side, was a meadow of wild flowers, and sitting among the flowers, was a woman in a long black dress and sunbonnet. Beside her was a little girl and the woman was twining flowers in her hair. The little girl was Dot. I tried desperately to get across the water to them, but the water looked black and bottomless. Just as I was about to fling myself into the stream, I awoke.

I quickly got out of bed and went to Kathy. She was burning with fever and coughing a dry, raspy hoarseness. I woke Joe. "We better get Dr. Werner."

"Wait 'til morning. She's just got a cold."

By morning, she was not any better. "Get Dr. Werner," I pleaded. Joe rode into town after breakfast. He thought I was unduly worried because we had lost one child.

Granny greased Kathy's chest with turpentine and goose grease, and covered it with a wool flannel cloth. I bathed her face with cool water to break her fever.

Doctor Werner got there just before noon. He listened to her lungs and what he said struck panic in my heart: "I'm afraid the child has pneumonia."

"Pneumonia, what is dat?" asked Granny.

"Lung fever," replied Dr. Werner.

I lifted Kathy from her bed and sat with her on my lap. Doctor Werner left some medicine and said, "I'll be back this evening."

I sat through the afternoon, holding tightly to my child. Granny brought me some food, but I could not eat–it stuck in my throat.

Doctor Werner came back about six. He listened to her lungs again, and shook his head. "We have to hope her heart holds out, and she makes it through the night," the doctor said. He was with us when Kathy died. I was holding her when her breathing stopped. I screamed. Doctor Werner took her from me and worked over her, trying to get her heart started again. I ran out to the porch moaning, and ran back in again. Joe was standing by the bed and dropped to his knees; sobbing, I dropped beside him.

Doctor Werner said, "I'm sorry folks, she just wasn't strong enough to handle it."

I do not know how we made it through the next few hours. Doctor Werner gave me a pill, and told Granny it would help calm me down. Joe would not take a pill. The doctor asked Granny if she needed one. Granny was in the rocking chair by the window in the front room. She was rocking back and forth. Her hands gripping the arms of the chair were trembling, her face set in a stoic expression, her eyes staring.

We went to Wilton Junction and arranged for Kathy's funeral in a daze. The little coffin stood between the windows in our parlor. It was the same spot where Dot's had stood scarcely two years ago.

Soon neighbors and friends were coming in and trying to comfort us and help us, bringing food and flowers.

The lights were dim in the parlor. I sat in the dining room where I could look through the double doors and see Kathy's casket. I could not sit for long, walking from the parlor to the dining room, and back to the parlor. I stood looking at Kathy, trying to imprint her image in my mind, when I saw a slight movement outside the window and glanced toward it. It was dark, and I did not see anything more, but my eyes kept wandering to the window. Then I saw them–long gray forms of rats! They were on the windowsill outside, their sharp noses poked against the glass. Rats, trying to get at my baby. I remember screaming over and over, and pounding on the glass, then darkness. I came to on the leather couch in the dining room. Joe was bathing my face. I struggled away from him and sat by the casket, guarding my baby all night, even though the men told me they had taken care of the ugly creatures.

Now, there was another mound in the cemetery, and Kathy's clothes were put with Dot's in the old trunk.

I was a bunch of frenzied nerves, never resting as long as I could keep going. I did not want to think. I was selfish in my grief, not knowing how Joe must be suffering. He was always doing something, humming a discordant tune and smoking his pipe. I thought how heartless he was, never realizing this was Joe's way to keep from losing control.

Chapter Eleven

Maybelle and Susan started back to school in the fall after their summer vacation, but they had only been in school a month when Maybelle came home crying with an earache. I looked in her ear, it was red and swollen.

"Probably her glands," said Joe. He blew warm smoke in her ear trying to ease the pain. I kept her home from school the next day. Sue cried about going to school alone, so I let her stay home, too. Maybelle's ear did not seem to be any better, and when I looked at it again, the ear lobe stuck straight out from her head and had a large swollen mass behind her ear.

"Better ju take her to der doctor," said Granny. "She got a beelin."

"What's a beelin?" I asked.

"It's a swelling mit puss in it. Der doctor will haf to cut it out."

We took Maybelle to Dr. Werner that afternoon. He examined her ear and took her temperature. It was 104 degrees. "We must get her to the hospital," he said. "She has mastoid." That was all I needed to convince me there was no hope for Maybelle-no one went to the hospital unless they were going to die.

Doctor Werner, realizing my fear, told me, "Maybelle's only chance is to take her where there is a specialist on ear diseases. She is very sick, and if anyone can help her, Dr. Kornish can. Try not to worry too much, and don't frighten the child."

It was four o'clock before the train left to take us to Iowa City, and it was two minutes until six when we reached the hospital. Maybelle was taken into an examining room, and Joe and I waited until the doctor finished with her. We sat in a waiting area for nearly two hours before an attendant told us we could see her. She was in bed, in a room by herself. When she saw her dad and me, she started crying and wanted to go home.

Time passed slowly for Joe and me. Maybelle was operated on at eight o'clock the next morning. She was in the operating room for six hours. The time grew endless; every time we saw a doctor come toward us, I was sure he was going to tell us bad news, but he only walked by. We continued to wait. Finally, Dr. Kornish came to us in the waiting room. He was smiling as he shook hands with Joe.

"Your daughter came through the operation fine . . . don't be alarmed when you see her, Mrs. Mason. She had a close call and it will be a few days before she's out of the woods, barring any complications," he said, patting my shoulder. "We scraped the bone, and removed the gland. We need to get more lab reports back. The first test came back positive for tuberculosis. The reason for the removal of the gland was the mastoid mass, which could have gone to the brain. She's young and healthy, otherwise. You may go in and see her."

Maybelle's head and neck were swathed in bandages, with just her eyes, nose, and mouth set in a pasty white face. She was still under anesthetic. A nurse sat beside her, listening to her breathing and heart rates, and recording them on a card. Occasionally, she spoke to her and with her fingers lifted her eyelid, trying to arouse her.

"Let me try," I told her, she nodded and stepped back.

"Maybelle, Maybelle, honey, it's Mommy . . . open your eyes for Mommy." She moved, opened her eyes, and closed them again.

"Good, she is doing very good," the nurse said. Well, this had not been so bad. My first experience with a hospital–I thought they were a last resort and anyone going to a hospital was going to die.

Maybelle was in the hospital eleven days. We had a grand celebration when we brought her home. Granny fixed her a kettle of dumplings, cooked in blackberry juice, sugar, and a cinnamon stick. It was Maybelle's favorite dessert.

Life was soon back to normal at the Mason farm. Soon school was out and Uncle Willis decided there was no place like the farm for his kids to spend the summer, so Aunt Carrie packed their clothes and they came to spend the summer with their Grandma. Granny grumbled now and then, but they were her grandchildren, so she did not say very much, but it was a strain on her as well as myself. We baked bread every other day, and as soon as the fresh hot loaves came out of the oven, it seemed they vanished. Good thing Joe always exchanged wheat for flour at the Durant mill, so we always had plenty of flour to make bread.

Joe tolerated the situation for Granny's sake, but I knew he did not much like our three cousins around all summer. He gave Tom chores to do. Tom was fifteen, a very tall fellow, six feet and five inches, and when he came in the house, he always ducked for fear of hitting his head on the top of the doorsill. Tom was pretty much a sissy, growing up in a family of girls. When Granny would tell one of the girls to do something, Tom would untie Granny's apron, tie it around his waist, grab a broom, and start sweeping. Lucy and Dorie would head for the creek; they did not like Granny giving them jobs to do. One morning, Granny caught them before they could get away and she took them to the garden to pick peas. When the peas were picked, she set them down under a tree in the yard to shell the peas for the canner. The next week it was green beans, and eventually she kept them busy pulling weeds when there were no vegetables ready. Granny knew what she was doing–she was deftly trying to get them homesick, all the while telling them she was teaching them how to keep house, how to save food for winter. When they protested, Granny added manners and social skills. They had to learn how to be helpful when they were guests in someone's home. It worked for the girls–the second week they were ready, and when Uncle Will came, they insisted on going home. Tom did not want to go home; he was happy helping Joe and picking on Granny. Joe thought Tom should help milk the cows, so I took Tom out to Molly one morning and showed him how to talk to a cow.

"First, you pat the cow on her right side and say, 'so bossy, so bossy,' so she knows you're there. Then you take the stool, sit down beside her, and take hold of one of her teats. Then you squeeze, loosen, and squeeze again, without taking your hand off her teat." I showed him how it was done. "Now you do it."

Tom took the stool and patted Molly; she turned her head and looked at him. Tom jumped up. "No, Tom, sit still," I told him.

"She doesn't like me," he said.

"She's all right, Tom, she just knew it wasn't me. Sit down and she'll be all right." He gingerly sat back down on the stool and reached for the cow's udder. Molly whisked her tail in his face. Up jumped Tom.

"She doesn't like me, Marty."

"You just have to act like you know what you're doing . . she's trying to bluff you," I laughed. "Now sit down and don't pay any attention to Molly."

He picked up the stool, patted Molly, said "so bossy," and sat back down on the stool. This time he took a hold of

Molly's teat and squeezed it–nothing came out.

"Loosen your fingers, then squeeze again," I told him. This time he got a stream of milk. Molly just chewed her cud and paid no attention to him. After two or three more times he became more confident and I told him to do it with both hands. After two more lessons, he was able to milk Molly, and since our cows were not stanchioned, we could milk them anywhere in the barnyard.

The hogs had their own pen, so there were no animals except the cows in the barn lot; the other occupants were the chickens, ducks, and Mr. Sergeant and his goose hens. One of the goose hens laid eggs in an old barrel that Joe had put out by the barn. Mister Sergeant took up his job as guard when the hen got ready to set on the eggs. While the hen was on the nest, anywhere near her was off limits to anyone, be it a cow, a human, or even an old rooster. Mister Sergeant would go after the interloper with his beak wide open, *th-th-thing* and flapping his wings. He could really hit you with just like Mr. Wicket when I was a kid. I still remember the whipping Mr. Wicket gave me when I got too close. Tom was leery of Sergeant. I had told him to stay away from the old gander and he never went into the barn lot until the geese went to the creek.

Tom forgot about Sergeant one evening at milking time, and when he took the pail and went to milk Molly, he did not think about anything except the cow, who was only about thirty feet from the barrel, where the goose hen was setting. Mister Sergeant was making love with the other two goose hens and not on guard, until Tom sat down to milk Molly. He was nearly finished when Mr. Sergeant came back and saw him. Instantly, his feathers ruffled and with his beak wide open, *th-th-thing*, wings flapping, he started toward Molly and Tom. Molly was not going to tangle with that gander. She put her head down, kicked up her hoofs, putting one of them squarely in the milk bucket, and upset Tom off the stool, the milk slopping all over. Away Molly went to the other side of the barn lot. Poor Tom, the gander was after him, but he rolled over, got up, left the pail, and started after Molly. Joe was over by the hog pen and saw what happened. He ran over, got between Tom and Sergeant, and picked up the pail, trying to keep from laughing. He brought Tom in the kitchen, dripping milk from his pants.

"What happened?" both Granny and I asked, practically in the same breath.

"I was milking Molly, and Sergeant was close by and I didn't see him. I lost all the milk–Molly put her leg in the bucket and spilled it all,"said Tom. "The bucket was half full too. I fell off the stool and the milk got all over me."

Joe was laughing, "You should have been there, Marty. Molly reminded me of the time you tried to ride her."

Tom seemed to be near tears, but when he saw Joe laughing about it, he started laughing too. Tom went home two weeks before school started, and we really missed him.

Maybelle and Susan made the most out of what time was left before school started and were either fishing in the creek, or out with Joe in the barn and playing in the haymow.

Granny was busy sewing; she made dresses for the girls for school. I was pregnant again, almost three months along. It seemed like I was always tired and listless. Even though I had not told her, Granny sensed what was wrong and encouraged me to rest.

Chapter Twelve

Baby Lonnie was my fifth child, this time a boy. He was a blue baby, with a heart defect. My health had been poor all through this pregnancy, and my attitude was worse. I blamed Joe for getting me pregnant again.

When Dr. Werner told us we could not expect to have Lonnie very long, I blamed myself and believed it was God's punishment on me. Joe never answered my angry outbursts. He just walked away. He had wanted a boy and now that he had one, death was waiting to claim him. In my own blind grief, I could not see that Joe was grieving too. Every day Lonnie lived, I tried to store up his baby sweetness; when he smiled, I treasured each one. At the hospital, the doctors did not give us any hope and we brought him home.

Granny never interfered in Joe and my quarrels, and she never took sides. She spent her time piecing quilts.

This day, February 15, Granny sent me to get the quilting frames from the storeroom where we had moved the trunk. As I opened the door, a strong breeze seemed to be coming from the inside, even though there were no windows in the room. Then I saw her! The woman in black sitting on the old trunk. I did not cry out–I saw her only for a moment, then she was gone. I backed slowly out of the room, forgetting the frames I had come after. I was so weak, I could hardly walk down the stairs.

"Did ju bring der quilting frames?" asked Granny.

"No, Joe will have to get them for you, I couldn't reach them," I lied.

"I thought dey were right in front."

I did not say anything more. If I told Granny, she might say something to Joe and he would say I imagined it. I was restless all day and could not get it off my mind. Maybelle and Susan came in from school and threw their books on the table.

"Granny, is there anything to eat?" asked Susan.

"Ja, we save pancakes from breakfast," she answered.

Maybelle beat Sue to the cupboard, holding the plate over her head until she got to the table for fear Sue would get more than her share. They sprinkled sugar on them and rolled them up. Taking them in their hands and a couple more for Andy, they made for the back door and out toward the barn.

"Maybelle, Susan, change your dresses and get your chores done."

"Yes, Ma," they answered.

I went to gather eggs from the barn and help Joe with the milking. The woman in black receded to the back of my mind. Why was I so upset about that woman? The first time, Joe said I imagined it, and I thought I probably did. The other time I saw her, it was a dream, so why should I get upset? Did I imagine I saw her this time?

At supper, Maybelle and Sue kept up a running conversation with Granny. Joe was quiet.

Granny and I did the dishes, and then I put Lonnie to bed. Joe sat on the porch in the late evening dusk. I went out and sat beside him, resting my head on his shoulder. Far off in the distance, we could hear the plaintive call of a whip-poor-will, as the thin crescent of moon was about to disappear behind the horizon and leave the sky dark and speckled with stars. Joe sat solidly, sucking on his pipe. He seemed to be far away in his thoughts, the small muscle in his thin cheek twitching as he gazed toward the creek, the night sounds of the frogs and crickets unheard.

"Sweetheart, what are you thinking about?"

"Nothing."

"Joe, can't we move away from here? We've had nothing but bad luck here."

"I've been thinking about renting a place of our own. We'll barely have enough to get started with, when we get settled up with Charlie."

"Yes, but what we have will be ours. Maybe we can get closer to school, so the kids won't have to walk so far."

"It don't hurt them to walk, remember how far we had to go?"

"Yeh."

Getting ready for bed, I felt better. Maybe we could soon get away from this place with the bad luck and rats that inhabited it.

I went in to check Lonnie. He was asleep. His face looked pallid, and his lips were blue. He often looked pale like this. I kissed my fingertips and pressed them against his tiny lips. He was only ten months old.

I slept soundly, and awakened as a sunbeam came through the tree branches outside our window. Joe was up. I had not heard him. It must have been five o'clock. I dressed, went to the kitchen, and set the coffeepot on. The fire was going. Joe was probably out choring. I mixed the pancake batter and set the table, then went to see if Lonnie was awake.

He was lying very still, and I thought he was asleep. I

pulled up on the iron bedside and let it slide down. I felt to see if he was wet. He did not move. Alarmed, I put my hand on his face–he was not breathing. He was dead, passed to God's heavenly care, along with Dot and Kathy. My mind went blank. The next thing I realized was Granny trying to take Lonnie from my arms. I was sitting in our rocking chair, rocking my baby, his little form clasped tightly against me. Joe was shaking me by the shoulders.

"Marty, Marty, what happened?"

"He died! He died before I came in to take care of him, he died in the night, Joe, without anyone with him." I rocked and rocked. Granny put Lonnie back in his bed, and I rocked dry-eyed, a lump in my chest. Granny brought me a cup of coffee, but my throat was so tight I could not swallow.

"Cry, kinda, ju must cry."

Doctor Werner came and gave me a shot. I was not aware of it when they came and took Lonnie. I still sat dry-eyed.

I moved through Lonnie's funeral in a daze. It was only when I saw the open grave that I realized they were burying my baby and began to cry. It started with a sob that felt like the lump in my breast had burst and I cried for hours.

When I was putting Lonnie's clothes in the trunk, a strange feeling came over me as I thought about the woman in black who I saw sitting on it. This was the third time I had seen this woman–was it my imagination as Joe had always said? No! It was not my imagination. I saw her–I am sure I saw her–the same woman each time, dressed in black. She must be the angel of death.

Uncle Hans and Aunt Lena came from Fenton to Lonnie's funeral. Aunt Lena did not look well, though she tried to console Joe and me. They stayed a couple of nights with Mama, and then went home. Granny mentioned several times that Lena did not look well. In April 1908, Aunt Lena passed away of a heart attack. It was a sad spring for us, two funerals only weeks apart, baby Lonnie on February 14 and my beloved Tante on April 10, Granny's daughter and my Aunt Lena, who was more than a mother to me.

Granny left us now, to keep house for Hans. We missed Granny; she left a void in our life. I was lost without her counseling. Maybelle and Susan missed her too. Granny had kept their days as normal as possible, sending them to school each morning and soothing their days as much as she could through the funeral. They spent two nights of Lonnie's wake with Ted, Kate, and the twins.

Joe seemed thin and pale. I had not noticed it before, but several days after the funeral he said, "Marty, I don't know what we are going to do about our bills. We owe Dr. Werner more than six hundred dollars. We sold two hogs to pay the last hospital bill for Lonnie and Dot. The funeral bills–it's gonna to cost up to over a thousand dollars. I just don't know where we are going to get the money."

"I hate to ask her, but maybe Mama could help us, if you ask her."

"I don't want to ask your mother. We'll just have to get along and see what we can do."

Chapter Thirteen

It was a beautiful fall day on September 19, 1908, when I gave birth to Elizabeth Ann, another strong, healthy girl. Joe did not say much, he just looked at her, that little muscle twitching in his cheek. If he was disappointed, he did not show it, as he bent over the bed and kissed me.

"Got to get busy and clean the barn before corn husking starts and got to get the wagon ready–and I have to go get your mother to help you for a couple of days."

"Dear, are you disappointed it wasn't another boy this time? I know how much you have missed Lonnie, and honey, I miss him too. Even though she's a beautiful baby, it doesn't mean we are forgetting Lonnie. I'll never forget my little boy."

He shrugged his shoulders and went out. My eyes filled with tears and for some unknown reason, I started sobbing. Maybelle came in. "Mama, what's the matter? Can we see our new sister?"

Susan came in. "Can I hold her?"

"Be careful girls . . . Susan . . . you wait until Mama or Grandma can help you, when she gets here."

"Why does Maybelle get to do everything?" Susan whined.

"Maybelle is stronger than you."

"But I'm almost eight and I'm strong too."

"Why don't you girls change your clothes and put on your play clothes, so you don't get your school dresses dirty?"

Maybelle laid the baby on the bed beside me and went out. Susan lagged behind, unwilling to follow Maybelle.

"Go on, Susan, change your clothes and get your chores done." Susan's chores after school were to pick up a bucket of corncobs from the hog pen and put them on the porch, and help Maybelle feed the chickens, get the cows to milk, and fill the reservoir on the cook stove, so there would be hot water for dishes and cleaning. Her face screwed into a pout and she went out. Later I could hear Joe in the kitchen with the girls, and it sounded like they were trying to get supper.

"Maybelle," I called. She stuck her head around the door. "Get a jar of canned meat from the cellar and some potatoes, get a jar of beans and some canned apples, and bring them up for supper."

"Dad has peeled potatoes, Mama, and he has some meat in the skillet."

"You're big enough to get supper. Don't you remember what Granny taught you about helping in the kitchen?"

"I remember, but Susie's big enough to help, too."

"Well, you girls should work together. Sue can set the table." Maybelle was gone before I could say more.

"Sue, you're supposed to set the table, Mama said so," she yelled.

When they brought my supper, Sue was carrying a glass with a bouquet of asters. She brought them to me, then set them on the dresser where I could see them and enjoy my supper of fried side meat, a boiled potato with milksop gravy, and some grapes from the arbor, which Maybelle proudly presented to me. Joe was smoking his pipe and humming, carrying a cup of coffee and a slice of bread with butter and jelly. He set the coffee and bread on the dresser and pulled a stool up to the side of the bed to put the plate on. I could not help but think of Granny's fruit dumplings with buttermilk soup that she made for me when Lonnie was born.

Joe went to get Mama early the next morning, after seeing the girls were ready for school. Mama got settled in and then gave Elizabeth a bath. She brought me a washcloth and towel with a pan of water and soap.

Monday was warm and sunshiny with a gentle breeze. I could see Mama out the window. She was hanging diapers on the clothesline. I wondered what Joe was doing. Mama came in to see if I wanted anything and put the baby in my arms so I could nurse her.

"Where's Joe, Mama?"

"He go somewhere on horseback."

"That's odd, he always tells me if he goes away."

"He no tell me where he go."

"Maybe he's checking something in the field."

Joe did not return until late in the afternoon and when he came in, he was smoking his pipe and humming.

"Where have you been?" I asked.

"Oh, you missed me, huh?" taking his pipe and tapping it on his leg.

"Yes, where have you been all day?"

"I rode over to Kettleman's . . . it soon will be settle up time. I needed to see if we agree on everything."

"Do we?"

"Yeah, he allowed for the fences I had to build after the flood and the two weeks of threshing and taking care of the steam engine; for the belts on the separator; for the extra threshing jobs and when he took off the hundred dollars pasture rent. He still owes me, but we won't settle up until after corn picking. He also told me his brother Fred's farm is going to be for rent next year. The people who rent it are going to have a sale and sell everything, even household stuff. Sounds like they are going to move out of Iowa."

"Do you think we'll come out all right? I'm surprised he's paying for the fences, that's been a couple of years ago."

"I mentioned it to him last year, but he said he forgot it, and besides, he said keeping up the fences was part of the contract. But I didn't think buying the wire was part of it, and that's what he's going to pay for. How's our baby doing?"

"She's fine. I just fed her before you came in. Maybelle and Sue got home from school a while ago. Mama sent them out to do their chores."

"I better get mine done, too." Mama came in as Joe was leaving.

"Kinda, you wan me to set bread start?"

"Yes, I always set it the night before and make bread in the morning."

"I cook kettle of mush and make some smoked ham for supper."

"Sounds good. Send one of the girls to the cellar to get a jar of plums, too."

The two girls came in. They had herded the cows to the barnyard to be milked and had the rest of their chores finished. I heard Mama scolding; it sounded like one of them had spilled something. "See, ju swine, ju make floor dirty," she said in a loud voice. "Now, ju clean up der mess."

"Maybelle spilled it," Susan was quick to reply.

"But you pushed me and it splashed out of the bucket . . Susan pushed me, Grandma."

"I no care who dun it, clean it up." Mama's voice sounded like she had the bumps showing again. I almost felt that old home feeling of being a kid again.

"When ju get done, ju wash up for supper . . . ju Papa will be done mit milking." Maybelle and Susan must have done what Mama told them, for I heard no more.

Mama and Susan brought me a bowl of mush with sugar and sweet cream, skimmed from last night's milk, two slices of bread spread with drippings from the skillet Mama had fried the pork in, and a cup of coffee with some more of that sweet cream in it.

"Thank you, Mama and Susan, for making me fat." It was true, I was two hundred pounds after Lonnie was born and I know I am fatter now.

After supper, Joe sat with me and lit up his pipe. "I think I'll go talk to Fred Kettleman about his farm that's going to be for rent next year. What do you think?"

"You know I'm all for moving out of this place–we've had nothing but bad luck here."

"It's not the place we live in that gives us bad luck, honey, it's just circumstances . . . something that happens and you don't know why–it just happens."

"We've lived here almost twelve years and I think it's time we tried it on our own and not on shares."

"I think I'll ride into town tomorrow and talk to him."

"Joe, be sure and close the chicken house before it gets too late," I told him, as he was going out.

I could hear dishes rattling in the kitchen, and I supposed Mama and the girls were washing them, but when Susan came in later, she told me with a long face, "Grandma made me wipe dishes."

"Didn't Maybelle help?"

"No, Grandma washed them and I wiped them."

'What was Maybelle doing?"

"She got to sweep. I never get to do any good jobs."

"Maybe you can change tomorrow, and you can sweep

and Maybelle can wipe," I cajoled her.

Beth was a good baby. She never cried or fussed very often, and when I fed her she slept well, waking up only once. Joe picked her up and put her in my arms, and then put her back in her bed. Joe was up early the next morning and had chores done by seven o'clock. Then he took off for Wilton Junction to talk to Fred. When he returned about noon, he seemed pretty confident when he told me he had gone with Fred to look the farm over and for Fred to think about it and he had gone down and talked it over with his mother.

So it was that Joe rented the farm on a cash basis and we began moving to a new place on March 1, about twenty miles away. We were better off than we had hoped to be when we settled up with Charlie. We had ten brood sows and a boar, six milk cows, two heifers, two steers, over one hundred chickens, three goose hens and a gander, and five horses.

The last two weeks of February had been warmer than usual. By the first of March, the roads were mud and sticky clay. Ted Miller and Tom Riley were helping us move. Ted had the bed, cook stove, dishes, and lamps on his wagon along with everything from the cellar and smokehouse. I drove the spring wagon with the coops of chickens and chicken feed, and Sergeant and his hens and feed. Elizabeth was bundled up in a quilt and I had Joe's sheep-lined coat on. Andy was under the seat. It was a hard trip. Ted had to stop often to let the horses rest for a time; the mud was axle deep. I took these opportune times to nurse Beth, so she would not get fussy. Nursing her was no easy matter with the baby in a quilt and me in a sheep-lined coat. It took some doing to get baby and breast together; once we made contact, she held on.

We reached our destination near nightfall. Tom and Ted stayed long enough to set up the stoves, unload the furniture, and stable my team. They started back when I assured them that I could manage. I found the lamps and lit them. Tom had put the chickens in the hen house. I knew I had to feed and water them before I did anything else, or I would not have the courage to go out. Beth was asleep, so I took the lantern and went to tend the chickens and horses. Large grotesque shadows played around me as I went from the hen house to the barn. I found that the men had fed the horses. By the time I was ready to go in the house, it was dark. I could not get to the door fast enough to get inside and close out the vast darkness, even though I had not been out over ten minutes. Beth was still asleep. I fixed myself some food, and sat munching on some bread and cold ham. I called Andy in. I wondered how Maybelle and Susan were going to get along driving the cows, and if Joe would take Susan in the wagon and just let Maybelle ride old Nell, our saddle horse. They were going to stay there and get an early start the next morning. I did not think Susan was quite the type to ride the horse, but that was right down Maybelle's alley.

I picked up the lamp and carried it into the bedroom, where the men had put the parts to the bed. The headboard was leaning against the wall. The rails were on the floor nearby. I put them together by holding the foot of the bed with one hand and fastening the rail with the other, only to find the slot for one rail was split and would have to be nailed. Well, Joe would have to do that when he got here. I spied an old wooden candy bucket that had been left there. I set the bucket under the broken slot, letting the weight of the rail rest on it. I put the slats in, tugged the spring onto them, and managed to get the tick on it along with the rest of the bedding. I put Beth in bed.

The strange house and dark rooms were making me uneasy. In fact, I was scared. A lone woman with a helpless baby, a mile from the nearest neighbor. I began to hear strange noises. I called Andy. A cow lowed off in the distance. Andy began to howl with a low pathetic wail. My fears increased when I spotted my old wooden trunk near the bedroom door. Somehow, I feared it. "Marty, I told myself, "don't loose control, or what happens to Beth."

I went to the kitchen and found a large butcher knife and a hammer. Turning the light low, I crawled into bed with Beth, putting my weapons beside me.

I was very tired and soon dozed off. Suddenly, it seemed as if somebody or something raised the bed from underneath and let it down with a crash to the floor. I was so scared I could not utter a sound. Cautiously, with my eyes glued to the foot of the bed, I reached for the knife with one hand and grabbed the hammer with the other. I quietly sat up, the knife and hammer suspended in midair, ready to strike whoever might stick his head out from under the bed. I sat motionless, my arms aching from the strain. Finally, common sense came to my rescue. I relaxed and lay back, and finally went to sleep. When I awoke, it was already daylight; the sun was peeking through the east window. I looked around and slowly the episode with the bed came back. I soon realized one side of the bed was down on the floor. I got up and saw that the candy bucket had collapsed and the bed rail was down.

Beth was waking up and beginning to fuss. I went to the kitchen where everything was piled up and found the sack containing her diapers I had left there the night before. I changed her and nursed her; she fell back to sleep for a bit. I started the kitchen cook stove and put some paper and kindling in the heater. Thank goodness Ted had thought to bring in some wood. I soon had the house warm and Beth on a quilt on the floor by the stove. Then I had some breakfast: warmed-up ham from last night, bread, and apple butter. I fed Beth some applesauce. I sorted some beans and put them on the stove to cook with ham, and made some coffee, so I would have something hot for Joe and the girls when they arrived. I busied myself with unpacking dishes, pots, and pans. "Where is the clock?" I wondered. I had no idea what time it was. I went to the door and looked out. The sun was getting pretty high, so it must have been close to noon. Two wagons were coming from the east, but I did not see anything of the cows or the girls. I wondered where they were . . . did one of the wagons belong to Joe? I went in and saw that Beth was asleep on the floor, so I went out again and watched the wagons until I could see they were Tom Riley and Ted. There was no sign of Joe, Maybelle, and Susan. I could hear squealing hogs and decided Tom had the hogs. Ted had furniture, so I knew Joe was still with the girls. Tom turned in the lane and took the hogs to the barn, waited for Ted to catch up, and together they unloaded the animals in the barn. Then they came in and unloaded the furniture from Ted's wagon. They set the table up for me and I gave them a bowl of beans, bread, and some hot coffee. They were laughing and kidding one another, and were soon on the way again. Ted said they were bringing another load today and said Joe was having quite a time with the cows.

"Susan wouldn't ride the gray," said Ted. The gray was old Bill, an old horse that behaved well. "So she's riding with Joe in the wagon. We'll be back later with another load."

As they started, Ted spotted the cows coming down the hill, so he and Tom waited by the lane so the cows would come in and not continue up the road. Maybelle was doing a good job keeping them together. Ted helped her get them through the gate into the pasture by the cow barn, and Joe drove in, old Bill tied to the end gate. Susan jumped off the wagon and came to the house.

"Didn't you want to ride Bill?" I asked.

"Daddy didn't want me to."

"Why not?"

"He thought I couldn't do it, so he made me ride in the wagon."

"That was better, you could keep warm that way."

"But I can ride a horse."

"I know you can, honey. Come in the house, we'll see if Beth is awake." She skipped to the house, forgetting to be unhappy and began playing with Beth.

"Mama, will Maybelle and me have to go to a new school tomorrow?"

"Not tomorrow, honey."

"When can we go to school?"

"You and Maybelle will have to care for Beth while I get things unpacked. I think you can start at your new school on Monday. Daddy will have to take you for a while, 'til you get used to the road and the way to go. It's going to be quite a piece to walk. It's Thursday, honey, and there's only one day left this week, so it will be better to start school the first day of the week. That way, you have time to explore and see everything before you have to go to school."

"What are we going to explore?"

"The house. We'll find where you're going to sleep. There's three rooms upstairs. We have a special summerhouse where we can cook this summer. There's a barn and some other buildings you can explore. We have two wells, a pump by the porch and the windmill out by the barn. There's a brook that runs down by the creek that flows through the meadow." Maybelle came in as we were talking.

"Gee, Mom, how did you see all that already?" she asked.

"Daddy told me, before we decided to move here," I told her. "How did you get along herding the cows?"

"Oh, it was a snap," she said, snapping her fingers at me.

"Good. What's Dad got on the wagon?"

"Rocking chair, couch, cupboard–I don't know what else." Joe was taking some things off the wagon and putting them in the shed.

"Joe, there's food ready," I called to him.

In the days that followed, we got everything unpacked and the furniture in place. We really had time to see the place as home. The creek south of the barn wound off in a southerly direction to meet the road, where there were beautiful steel spans that bridged it. Our house sat on a hillside looking to the east and north–you could see for miles up the valley to neighboring farms. There was a huge garden just a few yards from the house, with a fancy woven fence. A chicken house set on a knoll; a grain bin and corncrib were just below it. A fenced pen and hog house was just east of the barn with a cattle shed beyond. The windmill pumped water to the large galvanized tank for watering the stock. Becoming settled, the girls starting a new school, and retrieving the few belongings left at the other place all went smoothly. A piano was still in the front room, and we were expecting to hear from the people who had moved so they would take it out. Joe finally went to Fred Kettleman and told him we needed to get the piano out of the house. He told Joe, "The people tried to sell it during their sale, but didn't get a bid on it, so whoever rented the place could have it. If you don't want it, I'll try to get it out."

Maybelle and Susan, however, had been thumping on it every now and then. They wanted the piano to stay. Joe agreed with the girls, so we became the owners of the piano, an upright with a black finish and white ivories tinged with yellow. It sounded pretty good; it was not too far out of tune for an old instrument.

We soon settled into another spring of planting, tilling, and meeting some of our neighbors. There were Dave and Louise Murdock and their children, Dave Jr., Irene, and William, whom they called Bill. They lived up the hill to the northeast, and Arthur and Ethel Grimes lived to the west, with one child, Betty. Farther to the west were George and Bessie Haley with Jake and Jonathon, twin boys, aged nine. Dave Murdock was a heavyset man who must have weighed three hundred and fifty pounds. When he sat in a buggy, he had to sit in the middle of the seat to keep the buggy level, otherwise, it was so lopsided, it looked like it would upset and it made the wheel scrape the side of the buggy. Dave had a booming laugh and his way of being comfortable was a pair of bib overalls with the sides unbuttoned and the legs short. They were almost to his ankles and he was always barefoot in his shoes. On the other hand, Louise was a slender woman, a neat person with two braids of dark brown hair hanging down her back. Irene seemed like she would take after her mother and Dave Jr. seemed that way as well, but Bill seemed like he would be like his dad, because he was tall and big boned. They were a delightful family, always ready to lend a hand to anyone needing it and always ready to socialize whenever a person needed a friend to talk.

Chapter Fourteen

Beth was sturdy and was able to pull herself up to a chair and stand. In July, I found I was expecting another baby. When I told Joe, he said, "Don't tell me you're hatchin' another egg." He just sat, that muscle twitching in his cheek. I was hurt. I was sick from the beginning. I gained too much weight and retained fluid, my face was bloated, and I had an unhealthy color. Doctor Werner warned Joe about my having any more babies when we went to see him.

"She is having the children too close together–she needs rest. She isn't in the best of health. I can't tell you that she will come through this easily. I'll need to see her in another month." In the buggy going home, Joe seemed nervous and did not say much.

"What do you think of Dr. Werner's new car?" I asked.

"He says it gets him where he wants to go."

"Do you think he can really go fast?"

"They say these new cars can go thirty miles in an hour."

He made no further effort to talk and I sat quietly the rest of the way home. Joe unhooked the horse, took him to the barn, and started chores.

Sue had peeled potatoes and we started making supper. Maybelle went out to start her chores. When she came in, I told her to tell her dad supper was ready. He did not come in and Maybelle said she could not find him at the barn. I thought he was in the mow or at the cow barn, so we waited. I sent Sue to the cellar for some milk. When she came up, she said, "Mama, Daddy's down there, I think he's sick." He had been all right when we came home from town. I went down. Joe was sitting on a bucket near the potato bin, his head in his hands. When I approached him, I realized he was drunk, a whiskey bottle between his legs on the floor.

"Joe, you're drunk." I shook his arm, and could feel my face flush with anger. "Come on up to supper," I snapped.

"Lem'me alone" he said.

"Just look at you–you're so drunk–you can't stand up."

"Go-way!" He raised his arm and pushed me, and staggered to his feet.

"Come on, if you don't want to eat, you can go to bed."

"Don't want to go to bed, s'no use goin' to bed, you're too fat!" He staggered up the cellar steps and went toward the barn. I was so angry, I did not try to stop him. The girls and I ate our supper–the girls did the dishes. By nine o'clock, Joe still had not come in. I went to the barn but I could not find him. My anger began to subside. That had not been my Joe talking, it was the whiskey. If he had been sober he would not say such things to me. I waited up all night listening for his footsteps. He did not come. I got breakfast for the girls and told them their dad had to go away for a couple of days, hoping my lie was not too evident on my face, but I was not fooling them. They knew their father was drunk and had run off, and there was no use trying to say anything different. I busied myself with chores and the house all morning. I fixed the girls and myself lunch at noon, but I could not eat. I went out and worked in the garden. Beth was missing her dad; he usually came in the door leading to the summer kitchen and she was always there to meet him. I knew they were wondering when he would come home. Maybelle asked, "Mom, why does Dad get drunk and go away?"

"I don't know, honey, sometimes things just get to pressing on your mind and you just have to get away by yourself and think things through. He'll be back tonight or tomorrow."

Joe left on Thursday night. On Friday morning when we got up, the hogs were out of the pen, running loose in the yard. I told the girls to open the gate and chase them back in the hog lot. When they opened the gate, the rest of the hogs came out. Maybelle and Susan worked for an hour or more trying to get the hogs back. The stubborn animals would not go in. I told Susan to go up to the Murdocks' and ask if Bill or Dave would come and help them, because I was not able to help much. Maybelle and I continued to try to get them in, and finally, when Bill and Dave helped, we had them all in except one big old sow. I finally set Andy on the stubborn hog. The day was hot, and as Andy would bite at her legs, the sow would turn the other way. She started toward the creek with Andy at her heels. The hog plunged into the water and there she died, before Dave and Bill could get her out. The two boys buried her in the pasture alongside the creek.

Joe came home that afternoon, kind of shame-faced. He went about fixing the fence without any explanation as to where he had been. I knew he had been to the city again.

Maybelle was quiet and did not say anything against her dad, but Susan was quick to condemn him. "Why does he get drunk and make such a fool of himself?"

"It's none of your business, Sue," warned Maybelle. After the girls went to bed, I tried to talk to him. All I could get out of him was a few grunts. I could see he did not want to talk about it.

"Susan is getting so sensitive about what people think. Where have you been? I've been worried sick about you. This morning the hogs were all out, I'm not able to cope with it."

"Maybelle's old enough to help, so is Susan."

"But it's a man's work, we lost a good hog today."

"Lost one, how?"

"We couldn't get her in, we just about run our legs off. I set the dog on her, then she ran into the creek and drowned. Dave and Bill buried her in the pasture."

"That's a fool thing to do, run a hog in this heat. Hogs don't have sweat glands–they get overheated. She didn't drown, you run her to death. That's forty dollars you buried." He got up, went into the bedroom, and slammed the door.

After that, there seemed to be a wall between us that I could not penetrate. We quarreled often, mostly at night after the children were in bed.

Joe was teaching Maybelle to handle the machinery and horses. She took to farming, and he taught her like he would have trained a son. Susan was more feminine and liked to fuss with food and the house. It worked out well. Joe had help in the fields and I had Susan and Beth in the house.

It had been one of those hot, muggy days and I had just finished the work in the kitchen. I went out and joined Joe and girls on the porch. It was a beautiful evening; after the heat of the day, a cool breeze had sprung up from the south. Maybelle and Sue were playing tag and Beth was toddling around, trying to get in their game, too. I sat down on the step and Joe said, "There's a light down yonder by the creek."

Looking toward the bridge, I could see a campfire and people moving through the flickering light. "I wonder who it is?" Then, as if in answer to my question, the soft strains of music floated up on the evening breeze. Someone was playing a violin, softly at first, then the music started weaving a spell. It held me entranced, as the notes drifted out over the meadow and wafted up the valley. The soft sweet notes seemed to suggest a lover wooing his lady. Gradually, the music grew louder, as if in anger he had struck her, then louder and louder as the music rose to a shriek as she crumbled in his arms, dying from his saber. The notes dropped to a throbbing tremble as he sobbed for his lost love. The music stopped. Enthralled at the imaginary sight of naked emotions, there were tears in my eyes. Never in my life had I heard such music, and I doubted I ever would again.

We sat there for a while under the spell the music created. Then Joe arose and took my arm, helping me to my feet. The intensity of musical drama had stirred him, too. Strange as it seems, our differences were forgotten in silent mutual consent.

"It's probably a gypsy caravan camping for the night," said Joe. "Better get the girls in. Gypsies are noted for stealing, and that includes child stealing."

I called the girls in and washed Beth up and put her to bed. Maybelle and Susan stayed up to have some fresh baked bread and milk.

We had barely finished breakfast the next morning when someone knocked. Standing on the porch was an old woman dressed in a swingy skirt of the brightest orange and a dazzling blue shirt. She had a scarlet scarf wound around her head and long earrings dangling to her shoulders.

"Hello, madam,' she said. "We are a poor people, but me I see the future for maybe two," she held up two fingers, "fat hens?"

"Well, I don't know. I'll have to ask my husband." I walked past her and looked toward the barn for a glimpse of Joe. Instead, I saw an odd little man. His legs were thin, and his tight pant legs made them look almost scrawny. His body was fat and shaped like an egg. His head was set atop a long, thin neck. He was coming out of the barn with a hen in each hand, their heads dangling toward the ground. When he walked his feet turned in. He put me in the mind of a big turkey. I went toward him, then realizing the woman had not moved, I turned and said, "Come on." I did not want her in my kitchen when my back was turned. She came obediently.

"Who gave you the chickens?" I asked the man.

He mumbled some unintelligent thing. The woman quickly seized my hand.

"Aw, Madame, now your fortune. See, the lifeline goes on and on. You have a big, big heart. You 'ave children and I see your coming baby-he is a boy, a big husky boy." Stepping back and looking me over with a clever scrutiny, "I see," she stopped, an odd look on her face, then she went on, "yes, I see you 'ave trouble. Don't worry, you will triumph over trouble." Before I could collect my wits, they were off toward the creek. Joe came out of the corncrib.

"What did you do, give them some chickens?"

"No, I thought you did. I think I have just been fast-talked out of two old hens."

We both laughed when I told him how I had been flimflammed. We named the old man "Turkey Legs." They camped by the creek for a week, but they did not get any more free chickens. Old Turkey Legs traded Joe a horse for eggs and vegetables and ten dollars. We really could not afford the ten dollars, but we could use another horse and the horse looked in pretty good shape for as old as he was. Joe thought he could be twelve or fifteen years old. Even though we did not trust them, they left special memories. Joe said old Turkey Legs could filch you out of your eyeteeth when you were not watching him.

The musician, who played the tempestuous music, was a swarthy lad of about fifteen. He came and sat on the porch one evening and played for us. Joe gave the young lad two dollars and he acted very pleased. The gypsy caravan made the summer bright and colorful. I watched them leave with sadness. We had enjoyed the music, the maidens in gaily hued dresses, dancing barefoot in the cool grass; the young swains who sang in a tongue foreign to us, but with soft, beautiful tones. They were content to roam, these gypsies, free from bondage of home, their worldly goods in wagons, their stock driven along in a group. Now, they were moving to another camping place. The dapple-gray horse we named Gypsy and Maybelle staked her claim to him.

My health did not get any better. The days passed slowly. Maybelle and Susan were back in school, and soon it was corn-picking time. I wondered how Joe was going to get it all picked by Thanksgiving, having to do it alone. He started picking the middle of October, getting up at five o'clock and getting to the field by seven. He could pick about sixty bushels a day. That amounted to about an acre a day, except on a clay knoll, where the corn did not amount to much and the ears were a lot of nubbins. Then he was lucky if he got thirty bushel a day. We were thankful there was not too much of this kind of corn.

Maybelle did most of the chores when she came home from school, so her dad could scoop the corn into the crib. Susan was slow–she dawdled when her sister wanted her to help. When Maybelle had the chores done, Susan would run to Joe and tell him she herself had fed the pigs and then helped Maybelle feed the horses and put hay in the stanchion for the cows.

Thanksgiving was a quiet day. Joe killed two roosters, which I cleaned and fried. I made two mincemeat pies from the supply of mincemeat we had left from last year's canning. The girls were enjoying three days' vacation for the holiday. Joe had finished picking corn about ten days before, so it was just Ma Mason, Ann, and us for the holiday. Ma stayed for the weekend and Ann went home. Ma said she could not leave her boyfriend that long.

"Boyfriend! I didn't know she had a boyfriend."

"A fella from Buffalo, his name is Barton, Jess Barton. They're talking about getting married," Ma said.

The weekend was a time of catching up on all that had

been happening in Fairport. We really had not seen much of Joe's mother and sister since we had moved. Joe would ride over once in awhile to see them, but I only saw them on special occasions, and the girls hardly knew them as their Grandma Mason and Aunt Ann.

Ma was concerned about Joe. "He's getting so thin," she said. "Marty, you don't look so good either. I know it's been a hard time for you and Joe, losing three babies and all."

"I know, Ma," I said. "We've had some heavy expenses and it's a worry for us, and now with another baby on the way . . . ," my voice trailed off.

"You shouldn't have so many babies. I don't think I have seen you since you and Joe were married that you haven't been pregnant. Beth's only eighteen months old and you are almost ready to have another child. I know it's none of my business, but I'm only thinking about your health. Did you ever think that might be the reason your babies get sick? You don't have enough strength to build up your body."

"I know you're right, Ma, but I don't know what I can do about it."

"Tell Joe, be careful."

"He is, it just happens." It was getting embarrassing. I wanted to get off the subject–after all, I hardly knew this woman who was getting so personal, even if she was Joe's mother.

With Thanksgiving over, I needed to think about Christmas. I had not been able to save much egg and cream money. There were not too many hens laying since it was getting cold weather, and there was not too much cream. We were using a good bit of milk with three kids and me drinking it. I made butter whenever I had saved enough cream. I had to make do with what I had. I had planted Job's tears last spring, and there was a good supply of tears on the bushes that grew about eighteen inches high and bloomed in the spring. When the flowers dried up, they left small seeds shaped like teardrops. I pulled the seeds off and colored them by using whatever I could find that would change the color of the gray seed. These I strung on heavy thread. I made necklaces for Maybelle and Susan, and for Beth I made a stuffed doll, with Joe's old Rockford socks. I added tablets and pencils, and made dresses for all three girls. Joe and I did not exchange gifts–there was not enough money for that. The joy and satisfaction we had watching the kids enjoy their gifts was enough.

The New Year came in windy with snow blowing through the bright sunlight that would come and go with the clouds. It was 1911. I hoped it would be a happier year. My baby was about due; we thought it would be about the middle of the month. I would be glad when it was over. My belly was so large–I had never been that big with the other children.

One evening, several days later, I was sitting at the table after supper. I was sorting some soup beans for the next day's meal. I was facing the door leading upstairs; it was late, Joe and the girls had already gone to bed. I heard the latch of the stair door lift, and I looked up expecting to see either Maybelle or Susan. Instead, as the door slowly opened, it revealed the black angel on the stairs. Slowly, the door shut again. As I watched, fascinated, the latch lifted and dropped back into place. I sat there, unable to move, my eyes staring at the door. "I'm going to die," I thought. I moved like a wooden statue as I got up and went to the bedroom where Joe's familiar figure filled one side of the bed. Lying next to him, I shook with a chill of despair and fright.

With the coming of daylight, I was a little calmer. This was something I could not tell Joe, something I must face. I had a talk with Maybelle–she was old enough to know that babies were not dropped down the chimney by storks.

"Maybelle," I told her, "Mama hasn't been very well. Sometimes girls your age are called upon to raise their sisters and brothers. If you should have to do this, honey, remember all the things I have taught you."

"Mama, don't talk like that. You scare me."

"I don't want to scare you, honey. You and Sue and Beth must get your education, and if something should happen that I can't see to it, then you must. Your daddy won't be able to see to everything, and you must help."

"Mama, why do you talk like you're going to die?"

"I'm sorry, dear, but you're a young woman now, and if something should happen to me, you'd have to be the lady of the house."

"Well, you needn't worry, Mama. I can take care of things, and Sue and Beth, too, although Sue sometimes won't do as I say."

"Well, you have to remember, Sue is getting pretty big, too."

Three days later, I knew my time had come. I had contractions all day and by evening they were about fifteen minutes apart. Joe went to the Murdock's; they had a telephone. He asked Louise to call Dr. Werner. Louise came back with Joe. "I thought I might be of some help, Marty," she said, cheerfully.

With a calm deftness, she padded my bed, and put the kettle on for hot water. She shooed the girls off to bed, telling them to go to sleep, and when they awoke in the morning, they would have a little sister or brother. She took Beth and went upstairs, but Maybelle lingered. If she was going to be the lady of the house, nobody was telling her to go to bed.

Doctor Werner drove up in his new car. It had not taken him very long. He came in through the kitchen, stomping the snow from his boots on the braided rug in front of the door. He brought a gust of cold air with him as he swung his overcoat from his shoulders and unfastened the muffler about his neck. Louise took them from him and hung them on a hook on the back of the door. He warmed his hands over the cook stove.

"How does the machine work in the snow?" asked Joe.

"I've worn out two pair of chains–been stuck more times than I care to think about."

"Can't beat the old team of mares, can you?"

"They're a little more dependable in the deep snow and mud, but when the going's good, the car gets me there in good time. It sure shortens up the road. How's Marty doing?"

"Pains are the same, about every fifteen minutes."

Doctor Werner came into the bedroom. He said a few words to me while he rolled up his sleeves, but I was too concerned with my coming ordeal to make sense of what he was saying. He examined me and went back to the kitchen. I heard him talking to Joe and Louise in a low voice. I thought, "He doesn't need to keep it from me, I saw the death angel."

He sat beside me, and when I had a contraction he worked with his rubber-gloved hand, stretching and pulling, until I begged him to let me rest. Gradually, the contractions got worse. They were closer together until I thought I could not stand anymore. I begged for relief, but he said, "Soon, Marty, I need your help now." I was only half-conscious and I heard him say to Joe, "I hope I won't have to take this baby in pieces." Then there was the cloying smell of chloroform. With Joe holding tightly to my hand, I receded to a world of darkness, suspended without pain. I came out of the blissful peace to a turbulent room filled with the odor of anesthetic and a frenzied Joe.

"That baby is a calf," I heard Dr. Werner say. "Everything came out at once. She collapsed too suddenly. We need heat. Get the lids off the stove, anything hot." Again, I slipped back into that dark world of rest. I knew when I awoke that the baby was dead. What surprised me was that I was still alive. Doctor Werner said it was the largest baby he had ever delivered, a boy weighing fifteen pounds. If the baby had been alive, it would have been a record. It weighed as much as a four month old.

Joe arranged with the funeral director to have another grave dug. Ted made a pine box and Kate lined it with cotton and soft flannel diapers. They laid baby John in it. Joe, his mother, Kate, and Ted laid the baby in the grave beside Dot.

I recovered slowly, always tired and cross. Louise ran down the hill to my house, every other day or so, always bringing me something, trying to make me feel better. Her chicken soup was delicious and her cookies disappeared too soon. Beth loved them, and when the girls came home from school, they finished them off. "Louise," I protested, "you shouldn't."

Life slowly got back to normal in our household. Louise was always popping in and out, making sure I did not stay depressed. She got Maybelle, Susan, Beth, and Irene busy making valentines. She spent several weekends with me, while the girls worked with flour and water, making paste, and cutting out hearts.

I noticed that Maybelle was always interested in what Dave was doing on those weekends. She made a special valentine just for him, and when she did not receive one from him, I could see she felt bad. I really should not have asked her if he gave her one, because I could see she was about ready to cry.

Valentines were not the only thing Louise was good at. She made beautiful crepe paper roses. She came down one afternoon and showed me how to make them. They looked so real when she stretched the petals in the center to make them look that way. I really got involved.

Chapter Fifteen

The first time I realized our house was haunted was the night Maybelle stayed out too late. Before going to bed, I had locked all the doors just to make sure she would have to wake me to get in. Then I went to bed. I slept through until morning. My first thought when I awoke was, "Maybelle didn't come home last night." I got up and went to her room. She was safely asleep in her bed.

I went about getting breakfast started. Joe came in. "Joe, did you get up and let Maybelle in last night?"

"No, can't she get in by herself?"

"I told her to be in by ten thirty. It was after eleven when I went to bed. I locked all the doors to make sure she would have to wake us up to get in."

"I think she has been with Dave too much, lately."

"It isn't only Dave. There's Bill and Irene, Jake and Jonathon, and there's Betty Grimes. The whole gang is together every night."

"What are you tryin' to prove, lockin' her out?"

"She always tells me she's in by her curfew time, but this is the third time I know for sure she didn't come home on time."

I called the girls for breakfast, and a little later Sue came down. "Sue, did you get up and unlock the door for Maybelle last night?"

"No, why?"

"I'm just wondering. Maybelle came down and sat for breakfast.

"Don't you girls believe in getting your face and hands wet?"

"Oh, sorry Mama," said Maybelle. "Gee Dad, you oughta see Gypsy perform. I can make her dance, kneel, and even shake hands."

"What time did you get home?" asked Joe.

"It wasn't very late. I guess it was a little after ten thirty, though."

"It was after eleven thirty," I said. "I was up until after eleven. By the way, how did you get in the house?"

"I came in the front door."

"Do you have a key?"

"No."

"I locked the doors before I went to bed."

"You missed the front door, it wasn't even shut tight."

"Aren't you afraid to put Gypsy in the barn so late at night? It's so dark," said Sue.

"Dave rode home with me. He put Gypsy in her stall."

"Maybelle, I want you to be in by ten thirty, and that doesn't mean eleven or eleven thirty. Do you understand?" said Joe.

"Yes, Dad."

"One more thing. Let's make this only twice a week from now on. If you want to be with that gang, they'll have to come over here."

"Aw, Dad, we just go riding. All the kids do."

"Twice a week, Maybelle."

I was hardly aware of their argument; I was still puzzled about the front door. Perhaps I did not get it locked securely. I would make sure next time.

On Saturday night, Ethel and Arthur Grimes were having a dance. I baked a cake to take for lunch. Joe and the girls were in the surrey, and I picked up the cake and went out. This time, I tried the door several times after I had locked it. It was secure.

People came from miles around. George and Bessie Haley and their twins, and Jim and June Potter were there, along with the Kirbys, who lived east of the Murdocks.

The men got together in a card game. Occasionally, Joe got up and called a square dance. The sun was coming up by the time the party broke up.

"Why don't you folks come back after chores? We'll finish our pitch game," said Art.

"We might do that," said Joe.

I got out of the carriage by the front gate. I carried Beth; she was asleep. Without any hesitation, Maybelle pushed the door open. It was not locked.

When Joe came in, I told him, "The front door was open again."

"You should have locked it."

"I did. I made sure it was locked. I tried it several times to be sure."

"You didn't have it shut tight, or something."

"The next time you can lock it," I told him.

We went to sleep until after six o'clock, then went out to do the chores. We returned to the Grimes. The Haleys and the Potters were there, too. After dinner, the women washed the dishes and sat in the parlor; the men played cards. Our conversation lagged as we sat there, half asleep.

Out in the yard, the kids were shouting and laughing. Then they began parading single file into the kitchen, Maybelle in the lead. Holding her dress tail was Dave and holding his shirttail Betty, then came Jonathon, Irene, Jake, and at the tail end, Arty Potter. They were shouting at the top of their lungs.

Chase that possum,
Chase that coon,
Chase that pretty girl,
Around the room.

From the kitchen, to the sitting room, to the bedroom, and back to the kitchen, round and round they went, until about the fourth time around Ethel picked up a fly swatter. On their next trip through, she gave Dave a good swat, she missed Irene, and got Jonathon next. With an extra good swing she got Jake, who let go of Irene's dress tail and howled, covering his seat with his hands. Next time around she got another good shot at Dave.

"Ouch, damn it, that hurts," he made a quick motion to get the swatter, but Ethel was too quick for him.

They decided right then they had better go elsewhere, and soon we saw them parading down the road toward the Haleys', still holding shirttails and chanting, "chase that possum...."

We enjoyed the summer, and in late July, the gypsies returned to camp again along our creek. Turkey Legs came to the house to make a trade for the staples the tribe needed. The old gypsy woman came, too.

I talked to the gypsy woman one day and told her about the strange things that had happened over the years. I told her of my old trunk and how it glowed in the dark, for now there was always a strange effulgence about it.

"Madam is endowed with a clairvoyance. How did you

come by the trunk?"

"It belonged to my father. He died when I was five years old. Mama packed all my clothes in it when she sent me from England to America to live with my aunt and uncle. That was right after my father's death."

"You brought the spirit with you. It resides in your trunk."

"But why am I the only one who sees the black angel?"

"Aw, yes, Madam, you have great powers to see into the spiritual world. This, too, you brought from England, a great gift of your ancestors."

"I can't say I have appreciated the gift."

"But they are friendly spirits. The phantom in black you see only when death has already claimed a loved one."

"But that terrible experience I had in the haunted room at the hotel when I was a girl. That was no friendly spirit."

"No, Madam, that one was evil."

I told Joe about my talk with the old gypsy. He laughed. "That's just foolish nonsense. Gypsies are noted for their claim of seeing into the future. That's how they make a living, when they can get suckers like you. What did you pay her?"

"Nothing, we just talked."

"Didn't she offer to look into your future and tell you where all this gibberish nonsense would lead you?"

"No."

"Well, that's the way they usually work. She'll be back."

"Explain why we can't keep the front door locked."

"There's a logical explanation for it. I'll put a new lock on it."

Now I feared the trunk more than ever. "What should I ever do with it?" I wondered. I decided it would never be opened again. As much as I wanted to believe Joe, still too many things pointed to discarnate spirits.

In December, I found I was two months pregnant again. It was normal. I did not have bad days and I was not feeling so depressed. Christmas was pleasant, even though there was not much money for gifts. Sue was in the fourth grade and Maybelle was in the fifth grade. Beth had started to school in September. She would be seven years old in March. So I had quiet days, enjoying the spring with Joe, and setting hens so we would have baby chicks by Easter. On March 28, the eggs started to hatch. That was Beth's birthday, and when she came home from school, I told her we had baby chicks.

"Oh Mom, can they be my chicks?"

"They are our chicks, honey. They belong to everybody, but it you want to, you can feed them when they get a couple of days old."

Easter was the seventh of April, an early date for Easter and a cold day. It did not warm up until the middle of May, our wedding anniversary; sixteen years of marriage on the eighteenth.

With school out, the girls helped me plant the garden. Sue and Beth were not much help; they liked to play in the dirt, but they did not do much helping.

At 2:00 A.M., Wednesday, June 4, my eighth child was born. It was a normal birth, nothing like little John, when Dr. Werner had to use forceps to pull him out and use stitches to sew me up.

Lori was an eight-pound baby girl. She was active and grew fast.

Maybelle had heard enough about the door, and now Dave always came to the door with her. Joe changed the lock, but that did not help much. Maybelle could get in, but the door was locked when we got up in the morning. I accused them of using the back door instead of the front door. She replied, "You can ask Dave. He walked with me up to the front door–it was open." So now we had another mystery. The door was open for Maybelle to get in, but was locked afterwards. Joe was troubled about the door. He did not say much about it, but I saw him examining the lock. I did not mention any more about it, but it was always in the back of my mind.

Mama decided to sell the farm and asked Joe to help her get ready for the sale. He spent a couple of weeks lining up machinery, tools, and visiting with Oliver Loberman, the auctioneer who was also a real estate broker. He helped Mama decide what household items she was going to ship to Fenton. Pete by this time had married a woman from Guttenberg, Iowa. They lived in Fenton. He owned a blacksmith shop. Mama had made arrangements to ship the few things she wanted to keep to them until she could get a place to live and get settled.

The sale was set for February 8, and a large crowd of neighbors, friends, and other interested people showed up that day. George and Sarah Claussmann bought Mama's farm. George had been farming the place since Papa died. Mama stayed with us for a week before leaving for her new home. After Mama left, I had a strange lonely feeling, as if something was missing from my life. I did not sleep well, and that was the same feeling I had when I first opened my old trunk, when I started making baby clothes for Maybelle, before she was born.

I awoke one night from a sound sleep; it seemed I heard Granny calling me, "Kinda, kinda." A shadow on the wall moved. Startled, I sat up. The black angel moved into the closet. I started shaking.

"Marty, what's the matter?"

I started crying. "Joe, something's the matter with Granny. I heard her calling me."

"Nonsense, you were dreaming."

I did not say anything about the woman in black. He

would just laugh at me, disgusted like.

"I don't think I was dreaming. Something's wrong Joe, I know it."

He put his arms around me and drew me close. "Go back to sleep. Everything's all right."

Gradually, I settled down, but not to sleep. I kept hearing those words in my mind, "Kinda, kinda," and that shadow of the woman I feared.

I got up as the sky was turning pink in the south, signaling the rising sun. As the morning passed, "Kinda, kinda," echoed in the back of my mind as I went about getting breakfast and the kids off to school. It brought back so many memories of the years Granny had lived with us. I made a pot of vegetable soup and fixed a sandwich for Joe and me for lunch. I was thinking about an afternoon when Granny was teaching me how to crochet: carefully showing me how to manipulate the thread over my fingers and give it just the right tension, for the stitches to be the right size throughout the doily I was trying to make; and showing me how to put five or six stitches on a quilting needle and pull it through the quilt, leaving stitches small and even, and making different patterns with the stitches.

I was stirring up a cake for supper when I heard Louise come in the door. "Marty, I have a message for you to call the telephone operator at Wilton Junction. You have a telegram. I knew in an instant the telegram was from Mama and Uncle Hans.

Joe came in the opposite door. "Hello, neighbor, what's up?" he asked, looking at her.

The fear I felt must have shown in my face.

"What's goin'on?"

"I've just had a call from the telephone operator at Wilton Junction. She is asking for either you or Marty to call her–she has a telegram for you."

Joe looked startled when he glanced at me. He tried to look calm. "I'll go with Louise, honey, and get the message. It's probably something about the sale that your mother forgot about. Don't worry."

Joe was gone nearly an hour and I walked the floor, back and forth. I knew the telegram was bad news. When he came in, I saw at a glance that the news was bad. "It's Granny, isn't it?" I asked.

Dorothy Schwentzer passed away, Wednesday morning at 3:15 A.M., from pneumonia, body to arrive Davenport, Thursday morning. These cold words were hard to believe. Our beloved grandma was dead.

The next three days were a mixture of grief, of remembering, of trying to tell the girls. Mama, Pete and his wife Greta, and Uncle Hans was arriving on Thursday. The funeral was to be Friday at 2 P.M.; her grave was to be in Memorial Cemetery in Davenport. Everyone left on Saturday morning. It was a good thing the girls were home from school; they helped me cope.

Somehow, over the winter and spring, things were changing. Maybelle started going out with Buck Potter and Dave Murdock transferred his attention to Susan, which caused some friction between the two girls. Maybelle was seeing Buck, but she did not want to give up Dave. Susan fell headlong in love with Dave when he started paying attention to her.

Joe was talking about President Wilson, hoping he would keep us out of the war that was going on overseas. Germany was attacking France. Mexico was trying to get involved with Germany, wanting the return of their lost territory from Texas, Arizona, and New Mexico.

I was three months pregnant. With summer, it was garden and canning time again. By the time threshing was over, it was good to be able to relax. The old swimming hole in the creek was a popular place to go and cool off. Dave Murdock was a frequent visitor to that hole. One Sunday, we had a neighborhood picnic. Everyone was splashing around in the creek but Dave. Joe asked him why he was not coming in and getting wet, but he refused. Beth caught a big frog and was playing with it, chasing the boys, who pretended to be scared. After everyone had eaten, they gradually packed up. Art, Dave, Jim, and Joe went to the house, and when everyone else got there, we found them playing cards at the dining room table. Dave was sitting with his back to me, the bib of his overalls gaping open. I could see his bare fat belly. Beth was carrying her frog. I do not know why I did it, but I could not resist. I picked up the frog and let it slip down inside Dave's overalls. It landed squarely on his bare belly. Dave jumped to his feet, nearly knocking the table over, shaking his pants, trying to get the frog out. The other fellows thought he had lost his mind. When he finally got the overalls off and saw it was a frog, he was calmer–he thought it was a snake. No one had seen me drop the frog down his pants. When Dave dropped his pants, he exposed a pair of underwear with Kewpie dolls embroidered on them. The men had a good laugh at Dave's embarrassment. If anyone suspected I had done it, they never let on and I never confessed, not even to Joe.

In October, we had a telephone installed and a line run into the house, so we were able to call our neighbors and friends as well as businesses or emergency personnel. We did not have to bother Dave and Louise when we needed to call someone. The telephone really made a difference. If anyone who was on the line had an emergency and needed help, all that person needed to do was ring ten short rings, which would ring into everyone's home and help was on the way, as soon as you let them know who you were and what kind of help you needed. If only one person was needed, he or she would speak into the phone and tell the person he or she would be there as soon as possible. If more than one person were needed, several would answer the call. We were on line 566, and our phone number was 666 on 566, which meant if the phone rang three long rings it was our call. Number six was a long ring and numbers five through one were short rings, so 661 would be two long rings and one short ring, or 665 was 2 longs and 5 shorts, or 616 was 1 long, l short, 1 long. The telephone was a plaything for Maybelle. She knew the Potters' ring, and every time they had a call, she ran to the phone to listen. She was always calling Irene, Betty, or some of the other kids. Finally, the neighbors got tired of the kids on the phone all the time and we put a stop to her using the phone to call her friends.

Lori was only a little over one year old and already I was six months along. I was pretty heavy and my pregnancy was not evident to anyone but me. I had been feeling movements for about a month. I had not told Joe. I knew I should tell him, but I dreaded it. We were just getting caught up on our bills and he was talking about getting a car. I just kept putting it off.

The peaches in the orchard were getting ripe and I told the girls to pick them for me when they came home after school, but they put it off until I got tired of asking and waiting. I decided to go out and pick them myself. Lori was napping, so I picked what I could reach from the ground and then put my foot into the crotch of the tree, took a hold of two upper branches, and pulled myself up where I could reach the fruit. I had a milk pail full, so I took them inside and peeled them. I had four quarts when I got through. When I got up from the chair, I felt something sticky between my legs. Alarmed, I went to the bedroom and checked. My bloomers were all sticky with blood. Panic surged through me–what had gone wrong? I got a washbasin with a washcloth and water and cleaned up, hoping this was just a minor incident. I went back to the kitchen and put a pot of water on the stove. I put three cups of sugar and a teaspoon of salt in when it started to boil. I dropped the peaches in and boiled them until they were tender, then ladled them into jars that had been boiling in hot water and were now clean and sterilized.

I went back to the bedroom and checked. The clean

bloomers I had changed into had a couple of spots, but I thought it was just some blood that I had not wiped away. I was scared. Why had I not told Joe I was pregnant? I worried all afternoon. Was I going to lose this baby? What is Joe going to say when I tell him? Should I tell him about the blood? I knew I should not climb when I was pregnant. I decided we would not go to sleep tonight until I told him.

When the girls got home from school, I scolded them for not getting the peaches picked for me. Maybelle said she told Sue to do it. Sue said she did not hear her and why didn't she do it? "You can climb better than I can," she told her sister.

Lori was fussing, so I put her on my lap and rocked her.

"That will do–get your chores done," I told them.

I knew climbing a tree had been a foolish thing for me to do. I had not given it a thought when I did it. Now I was afraid.

I scrubbed some potatoes and put them in a kettle to boil. Then I scrambled some eggs, and opened jars of corn and applesauce–that was supper. All the time those sensations of fear and excitement–or was it dread and panic?–went through me.

Joe sensed something was wrong. "Marty, what's the matter?"

"I guess I'm just tired. I picked some peaches and had to climb up in the tree to get them." Maybelle and Susan quietly got up from the table.

"You were picking peaches and climbing trees in your condition?" Joe asked incredulously. Beth followed her sisters.

Startled, I asked, "What condition?"

"Don't tell me we're not going to have another kid. I've known for a couple of months that you're pregnant."

"Why didn't you tell me?"

"I was waiting for you to tell me."

"I'm bleeding! I knew better than to climb. I just didn't think when I did it."

"You're bleeding? Very much?"

"Not very much, but I think I should tell Dr. Werner."

"You had better call him."

"And tell him over the telephone? Everyone on the line could be listening."

"Tell him to stop by as soon as possible." Joe seemed anxious about it. "Do it now."

"Then call his house?"

I called his office first. There was no one there, so I asked the operator to ring his house. The doctor's daughter answered the phone. She told me he was out on a call, then asked if she could take a message.

"Will you tell him to come to Joe Mason's as soon as possible?"

"I'll tell him as soon as he comes in," she said.

"Thank you."

Waiting for the doctor to show up, Joe was smoking his pipe and rattling the daily paper, Beth was thumping on the piano, Maybelle and Sue were clanging the dishes, and Lori in her high chair was banging a spoon. I was so jittery I could not sit still. The telephone rang–three long rings. It was our ring. Maybelle ran to answer it.

"It's for you, Dad," she said.

Joe took the receiver and I heard him say, "Yeah, Doc, it's Marty, she's not feeling good. I think you should come and take a look at her." There was a pause. "No, I'd really feel better if you saw her now." There was another pause, "Good," he said, hanging up the phone. "He'll be here in about an hour."

"I'm not having any more trouble," I said.

"Better be safe than sorry," he answered.

I went to the bedroom and changed into my nightgown. It was nearly nine o'clock when Dr. Werner arrived. The girls were in bed. He came in without knocking.

"What's happening?" he asked looking from me to Joe.

"Marty is afraid she is having a miscarriage."

He looked at me. "How far along are you?"

"About seven months."

"Seven months! Why haven't I known this before now?"

"She didn't even tell me," said Joe.

Doctor Werner wrinkled his brow and looked at me. "What's happening?"

"I climbed up in the tree to pick some peaches, and I started bleeding."

"You had better lie down so I can examine you." The exam lasted only a couple of minutes. When he was through, he straightened up.

"You have a little seepage from your womb. How much blood did you lose?"

"Not very much," I said.

"How much is not very much?" he asked. "Do you have the soiled pants?"

"No, I soaked them and rinsed them out."

"Have you had any more blood loss?"

"No."

"I think we had better take you off your feet. We don't want the baby arriving too early. Stay in bed for at least two weeks and I will see you again tomorrow. In the meantime, if you lose any more blood, you'll have to go to the hospital right away." He picked up his hat and left.

Oh no! How am I going to manage with Lori just the age to be getting into mischief and the three other girls in school, lunches to pack, and meals to get? My head was spinning.

"How am I going to stay in bed?" I asked Joe. "The girls are in school, Lori really gets around and is always getting into things." I sat up, fighting back tears that were flooding my eyes.

"We'll get along. You need to take care of yourself. I can help with Lori and getting the meals. The girls are old enough to keep things going until you get back on your feet again. Don't worry, you stay right there in bed until Doc tells you to get up."

I lay back down and turned my head to the wall, letting the tears run down my face. Joe went out and soon I could smell the smoke from his pipe. I pictured him blowing smoke rings, as he often did when he was just sitting, his thoughts on some problem that was bothering him.

I do not know when he came to bed, because I awoke hours later from a nightmare. The trunk that Joe had placed over in one corner of the room was sitting at the top of the stairs. The lid was open. There was blood all around it and a baby lying in the blood with long blond hair covering its face. I sat up. My God, what a terrible dream.

"What's the matter?" Joe sat up too.

"I just had a terrible dream."

"What did you dream about?"

"I dreamed my trunk was open and there was blood all around it."

"Well, it was just a dream. You were just dreaming about what you were doing yesterday and it was on your mind when you went to sleep."

"There was a baby lying in the blood, and the trunk was sitting at the top of the stairs."

"Honey, go back to sleep, it was just a dream."

"I can't get it out of my mind, it scares me"

"It was just a dream," he repeated. "Now go back to sleep."

I laid there for a long time with the vivid picture of a baby lying in blood. Finally, I dozed off only to wake up with a start. I thought I heard a baby cry. Joe was not in bed. I got up and went into the front room. He was sitting with his head in his hands, his elbows resting on his knees.

"What's the matter, Joe?" I asked, putting my arm around his shoulder.

"Couldn't sleep. What are you doing up? You're supposed to stay in bed."

"I missed you and I thought I heard Lori crying."

"She's not crying. You just imagined it–now get back in bed."

"Are you coming back to bed?"

"Naw, I think I'll stay up. It's about five o'clock, I can get the chores done before it's time for the girls to go to school."

I went back and laid down, but I did not go to sleep. I kept listening for the sounds of kids upstairs, or Joe coming and going from chores, and of dishes clattering in the kitchen. Somebody was getting breakfast. Finally, Maybelle, Sue, and Beth were ready for school and waving good-bye as they looked in. Joe, with a cup of coffee and a couple of pieces of French toast sprinkled with sugar, came in and sat on the edge of the bed, putting the French toast in my lap and holding my coffee for me until I finished eating.

"Well, that wasn't so bad," he said.

"Did you feed and water the chickens?"

"Not yet, I'll do that next."

"Did you feed Andy?"

"No, I'll feed him, too."

"Is Lori still asleep?"

"Yep."

"You better go up and see if she's awake, or she'll try to get up and fall down the stairs."

"I think she can manage the steps."

"She gets up the steps, but I don't let her try to come down by herself."

"Quit worrying."

"I'm not worrying. I'm just reminding you so you won't forget."

The days dragged slowly, with nothing to keep my hands busy. Lori was in and out, and crawling up on the bed and down again. I thought this cannot go on. Doctor Werner came about one o'clock.

"Well, how's things going?" he asked, examining me.

"Doctor," I said, "I can't stay in bed, there's too much to do with Lori here and the other girls in school. I just can't . . . Joe's trying to help, but I know things are not getting done."

"Marty, I realize things don't get done when a mother can't take care of her family, but you will have to stay off your feet or you might lose your baby. Isn't there someone who can come out and help you?"

"No . . . can I just sit in a chair instead of lying down all the time?"

"You know you wouldn't stay in a chair if you see something you think you need to do–first thing, you would be up and doing things and forget to sit."

"I promise, I'll sit."

"No going outside to feed chickens or milk cows, no going to the garden, don't even go to the privy–use your combinet–and no climbing stairs," he added.

"I promise."

"If I have to come as an emergency, you'll have to go to the hospital," he warned. "I don't want you on your feet, cooking or cleaning, I want you to lay or sit. Let me know how things go, Joe."

"I'll make her behave," Joe walked to the door with him and they chatted briefly about the weather. It looked like we were due for a thunderstorm. The doctor did not want to stay too long. He might have to put chains on the car to get up the hill and out to the main road, and putting on chains was not his favorite activity. Louise came in the back door as the doctor was leaving.

"Who's sick?" she wanted to know.

"Nobody," I said.

"Wasn't that Dr. Werner?"

"Yeah, he was here to see me, but I'm not sick."

"It's really none of my business, but was that a social call?" The inflection in her voice said why is he here, there has to be a reason.

"No, sit down," I said, pulling a chair up to the table and indicating she should do the same. "He's afraid I might lose my baby."

"How come?"

"Oh, I did something foolish. I climbed up in the peach tree and picked some peaches to can and that was the wrong thing for me to do. Pulling myself up, opened my uterus and I started to bleed. Now, he wants me to stay off my feet until my baby comes, which will be almost two months yet."

"What's the matter with Maybelle, Susan, and Beth? They surely can do that."

"I did tell them to pick them for me, but you know kids, it goes in one ear and out the other, so I decided to do it myself. I should have told Joe to pick them, but he's been real busy."

"Did you get them all picked? I can send the boys down to help."

"No, no, there"s not too many left to pick and Joe can shake them down. The limbs on the tree are too flimsy to hold a ladder."

"Well, don't you be climbing around in trees again."

"I won't."

"I brought some crepe paper. I thought we might visit and make some roses this afternoon."

"Good. I need something to do to take my mind off being house bound."

"Do you need anything done that I can help with?"

"No, Sue has made bread before and it will be good for her to practice. Maybelle can help with the cooking. Sue will be twelve in May, and Maybelle will soon be fifteen. It's time they learn how to keep house, and they're really pretty good at cooking."

We worked all afternoon with the crepe paper and when we were through, we had more than a dozen red and yellow roses. I was getting pretty adept at making them. When Louise left, I continued, and tried to make a pattern for peas and daisies.

Chapter Sixteen

September passed slowly, but the days of Indian summer were welcome, with warm days getting shorter and cool evenings turning a large red sun into a huge ball of fire sinking below the trees, coloring clouds a beautiful pink. Sometimes, the sky was clear, and other times the sun set behind a dark cloud that showed cracks of yellow, orange, and pink–an artist's delight.

My two weeks of being tied down were over and I was thankful to get back to normal days again. Joe opened the cornfield the first week in October and started cribbing on the fifteenth. When I told him I was going to help, he insisted I stay in the house and let the girls do the chores I had always helped with.

Halloween was just two days away. Maybelle and Susan had been acting very mysterious.

"What are you kids up to?" I asked. They looked at one another.

Sue said, "We're going...."

Maybelle interrupted. "...Nothing Mom," giving Sue a disgusted look.

“Where are you going, Sue?” I asked, ignoring Maybelle.

“We’re going outside,” she said, hesitatingly. “The gang’s coming over and we’re going to play ball.”

“Oh,” I said, “who is the gang?”

“Dave, Bill, Irene, Betty, Jake, and Jonathon.”

“The Haley twins? Don’t they live pretty far away to come down here? That's almost two miles.”

“Yeah, but they have a two-wheel cart and they hitch their pony to it.”

“Is that who drives that bay pony and cart?”

I had seen the pony and cart several times on the road. The pony had a white mane and tail, a beautiful animal, and two boys were always driving it.

I did not think any more about it then, except to wonder why Maybelle did not want me to know. Five o’clock came and I realized no one had showed up. It was almost suppertime.

“What happened to your ball game, Maybelle?” I asked.

“I guess their folks made them stay home. It’s Saturday, and I know Dave and Bill have to help with corn picking, and I suppose Jake and Jonathon do too, when it isn’t a school day.”

Well that sounded reasonable, although Saturday was usually “go to town day,” and the whole family goes.

Monday was Halloween and Mabel Fitzpatrick, the teacher, had a party and program planned at school. Since my baby was due any time, I asked Louise if the girls could go with them. Joe did not feel much like going to the school program after a day of corn picking, and as usual she was very obliging. I had spent most of the day making popcorn balls and decorated pumpkin cookies to send along with the girls, and they were more than happy to go with our neighbors. The program was supposed to last from 6:30 to 7:30, but the girls were still not home by 8:30 and I called Louise.

She told me the kids were outside, thinking of pranks to play on our neighbors. The Haley twins were out there too, and so was Betty Grimes.

"Will you tell those youngsters of mine to get their hides home?"

"The Grimes drove to school, they picked us up, and we all went in one rig, so I expect the girls will ride home with them."

I did not think any more about them and I worked on a doily I was crocheting. Joe was reading the paper, and finally got up and knocked the ashes out of his pipe.

"I think I'll go to bed," he said, stretching and yawning.

I looked at the clock. It said 10:15. Where in the world are the girls? I wondered. I went to the phone and called Louise, she answered sleepily.

"Were you asleep?" I asked.

"Yes, I've been in bed for an hour or more...what's the matter, Marty?"

"The girls aren't home."

"They left here right after you called me."

"They didn't come home."

"Maybe they went with the Grimes and the kids are fooling around."

"Is Irene home?"

"Yes, she's in bed, but Dave and Bill rode along with Arthur and Ethel. I told them to get home by eleven. They were going out Halloweening. I told them they could soap windows, but not to damage anybody's property or do anything to cause the neighbors any trouble. The Gates twins were with them too. I'll bet your girls went along with them and will have to walk home."

"Well, Joe will deal with them tomorrow. Sorry I woke you up."

"That's all right…don't be too hard on the kids, they're only young once."

"They're getting old enough to get some responsibility. Thanks for everything."

"You're welcome. Don't worry, I'm sure they'll be home soon."

I went to the door and looked out. It was so dark, I wondered how they could see anything. I walked around the room, fluffing the pillows on the couch, picking up, rearranging things on the piano, and going to the door every few minutes. Finally, I heard voices and laughing. Dave, Bill, and the girls were coming down the road. It was 11:45. I blew out the lamp and sat in the dark, waiting for them to come in. Sue opened the door very quietly. Beth and Maybelle stepped inside, and Maybelle closed the door very quietly. I waited until they were about to the kitchen door before I spoke in a loud voice.

"WHERE HAVE YOU KIDS BEEN, MAYBELLE, SUE?"

"We were just walking and talking and having fun," said Maybelle nervously. "You scared me."

What kind of fun?" I ignored her scared feeling.

"We soaped some windows."

"Where did you get the soap and whose windows?"

"Jake and Jonathon and Dave and Bill had soap," said Maybelle.

"You girls with a bunch of boys?"

"Well, Betty was with us, too," she said.

"Whose windows did you soap?"

"Haleys."

"Who else?"

"Just theirs."

“What else did you do?”

“We didn't do anything–we watched the boys.”

“What did they do?”

“Nothing much.”

“You were watching them do nothing?”

“Well, they didn't do very much.”

“Tell me what you were watching them do”

“They pushed over the Sheldons’ toilet,” said Sue.

“What else?”

“They tied the Haleys’ goat to Sheldons’ gate by their garden.”

“The Haleys and the Sheldons? Why did you kids pick on those poor old people? George Sheldon won’t be able to get their toilet back up and George Haley won’t know where his goat is. Your Dad is going to deal with you when I tell him what you kids did tonight. You better get to bed or you’ll never get up in time for school."

Beth had already sneaked upstairs. Sue and Maybelle jostled one another trying to get through the stair door.

Joe was asleep when I crawled into bed and I did not wake him up. After all, it was not such a big thing, after I got to thinking about it. They really had not harmed anything.

I woke up at six, but I did not get up right away; it was six thirty when I finally got breakfast. I gave the girls corn flakes, fixed their sandwiches for school lunch, and they hurried away before their Dad came in from chores. When I told Joe what the kids had done, he said, “It wasn’t our kids that pushed the shit house over, but I’ll get Dave and see if we can set it back up again. Old George wouldn’t be able to do it, everybody knows that. The Haleys owns goats, so they’ll know where the goat belongs." I was not surprised when Joe grinned and shook his head. “Them damn kids, you never know what they’re going to do next.”

"Honey, how would you like it if some kids came here and pushed our toilet over?"

"I guess I would cuss a little, but I would set it up again."

"I'm not so sure the girls were watching. I'll bet they were pushing too."

"Probably. Call the Murdocks and ask Dave to help."

Later in the day, I saw Joe go east toward the Sheldons, riding Bill, a coil of rope on his saddle horn, and Andy tagging along. I took Lori's hand and walked out to the garden; we picked some tomatoes for supper. I noticed there was a row of beets I needed to take care of. Pickled beets will taste good when the snow flies.

I went back to the house when I felt a spasm in my back. Oh, oh, I'm going to have the baby. I hope Joe comes back soon. I gave Lori some milk and a cookie, and waited for another contraction. Joe was gone more than two hours. I waited anxiously, and finally saw him coming, but I had not felt any more spasms or contractions. I relaxed. It must have been my imagination. The girls came in from school, changed their clothes, and went outside. I got supper ready. Beth set the table. Sue and Maybelle squabbled about washing dishes when we were through eating. Joe told them to stop fighting: Maybelle wash, Susan wipe.

I had a contraction about ten o'clock and I knew for sure it was the baby about to arrive. Joe was getting ready for bed.

"Honey," I told him, "I'm ready to have this baby."

"So am I," he said.

"No, I mean really, I'm having contractions. I had one this afternoon. Now I just had another."

"Why didn't you say something if you had one this afternoon?"

"Because I wasn't sure."

"We better call Doc."

"And Louise," I said.

Joe called the doctor first, then Louise.

"Did Louise say she would come when you had the baby?"

"Yes, I told her I was going to get Minnie Gates, but she said she would come and help out. We can keep Maybelle home from school until I get back on my feet again. Louise is such a good friend. Whenever I need anything, she is always right here to help. My pains are getting closer together," I told Joe. "It's only been about five minutes since I had the last one."

"Well, I hope Louise comes right soon."

"I hope the doctor gets here."

Another baby girl was born at 11:45, November 1, about two hours after Louise got there and about an hour after the doctor arrived. Joe, the doctor, and Louise had a gabfest while they were waiting to welcome a baby we named Bessie Jane. Later, I asked Joe what they were talking about, and he said they were discussing political rumors and the war overseas.

We kept Maybelle home from school for the next few days, and between her and Louise, things went smoothly. Bessie was a good baby and hardly ever cried. Sue and Beth made quite a fuss when they had to go to school without Maybelle. I built up Sue's confidence when I told her she would have to take care of her little sister and see that she got to school all right, and that she was the boss of Beth. I did not realize that was the wrong thing to say. She decided she was her sister's boss at school, too, and it got her in trouble with Miss Fitzpatrick. She spent ten minutes sitting in a corner with her face to the wall. We got a note from the teacher telling us that Sue was misbehaving. She had slapped her sister twice and the third time she was punished. Sue handed me the note when she got home and started crying.

"What were you doing that the teacher had to

punish you?"

"I tried to make Beth clean her shoes when she went in the school house. Miss Fitzpatrick always makes us clean our feet. Beth made a face at me and I slapped her."

"Did you talk nice or did you yell at her?"

"I just told her, her shoes were still dirty."

"That wasn't your job–the teacher should tell her."

"You told me I was her boss."

"But honey, the teacher is boss at school."

"How can I be her boss, then, if you're the boss here at home?"

Oh, oh, I thought. I used the wrong choice of words; it should have been responsible instead of boss.

We went to Fairport for Thanksgiving with Joe's family, who gathered at Ma Mason's for the holiday. Teresa, John, and their daughter, Helen, were there from Texas, so Helen has to meet all her cousins. We still missed Tad Miller very much. The Miller twins were there and our family of five girls and Ann's husband, whom they had never met. It was a great reunion.

Winter came in with a blizzard and when Christmas Day arrived, roads were clogged with snowdrifts. The snow was so deep the cattle could not roam in the cornfields where the corn was picked. They munched hay, remaining near the cow barn, where there was shelter.

Chapter Seventeen

The New Year dawned bright, sunny, and cold with a strong wind blowing the snow. School vacation extended into the second week of January before the roads were passable and school opened. It was a relief to have the girls back in school-the bickering and fighting and piano thumping was more than I could stand. Louise came over one afternoon with her crafts and we had a peaceful afternoon with the kids playing in the snow, making a snowman.

Winter finally passed into spring and the flooding was bad. The creek that was normally just an ordinary stream with water rippling over the rocks in the creek bed became a roaring, tumbling mass of water that rose to depths of fifteen to twenty feet. It covered half of our garden and was only a few feet from the house. The barns were surrounded and the animals crowded into the barn lot. Joe opened the fence to the timber, so there would be room for them.

The high water only lasted a short time, but the mud and debris it left was quite a mess. It was the last week of April before the ground was dry enough to plow the garden. School dismissed for the summer.

Bessie was cross and had a bout with croup. I kept the

teakettle on the stove so the steam would keep the air moist. I rubbed her chest with mentholated gel. I was worried, and tried to remember what Dr. Werner had told us to do when the kids got the croup or a bad cold. It seemed that Bessie had a worse case of the croup than I could remember the other kids having. Her face was flushed and she felt so hot that we decided we should call the doctor. When he answered the telephone, I told him I thought she had a high temperature, so he decided he had better see her. He arrived about an hour later.

"Well, the little one isn't feeling well. Has she been coughing?" he asked.

"Yes, she has a fever."

"Are the other girls coughing?"

"Sue and Beth have been coughing. Beth sounds croupy.

"Have the girls had whooping cough?"

"Maybelle and Sue have had it, but Beth and Lori haven't."

"Her temperature is 101 degrees," he added.

"Do you think she has whooping cough?"

"I don't know, I hope not. It's hard on babies . . . and serious, too. There's not much you can do for them . . . it just has to run its course."

"Do you mean Bessie can die from it?"

"Well, children less than three years old can't handle it very well. I'll leave some cough syrup. Give her a half teaspoon when she gets to coughing. Call me if she gets worse."

Around nine o'clock, she seemed more feverish and fussy. I picked her up and tried to nurse her; the milk came out of the corner of her mouth. It seemed she could not swallow very well and she began to cry.

"We better call the doctor again, Joe," I said.

He took her from me and tried to quiet her, walking

around the room and patting her on her back. She did not want her Dad, though, she wanted me. I was about to take her, but I heard a knock on the back door. I wondered who it was–people usually used the front door. Louise was about the only one who used the back door, except for our family. Louise always knocked, and then opened the door and came in. When Louise did not come in, I went to the door. Someone was walking around the house, a dark figure. I could not make out who it was. Puzzled, I thought whoever it was, was coming to the front door, and I went to open it. There was nobody there, either, and I did not see the person who had walked around the house from the back.

"I wonder who's fooling around outside," I said. "Whoever it is, didn't come to the front door."

"You're hearing things again, Marty. You better get the doc on the telephone."

I unhooked the receiver and rang for the operator. When I put the receiver to my ear, someone was talking. I hung up and waited for a minute or so, then listened on the receiver again. They were still talking.

"Someone is using the line," I told Joe.

"Tell them to hang up, you need the telephone."

"I hate to do that."

"Do it," he commanded, in a voice that sounded angry and scared.

I unhooked the receiver and talked into the mouthpiece, "Excuse me, this is Marty Mason. Our baby Bessie is very sick and I need to call the doctor."

"Of course you can have the line. I was just talking to a friend, this is Martha Sheldon. We'll hang up, Marty."

I waited a minute. When I tried again the line was clear and I asked the operator to ring Dr. Werner for me. Doctor Werner's daughter answered the phone. "My father just went out for something. I'll tell him as soon as he gets back that you need him."

"Thank you," I said, and hung up the receiver.

The telephone rang as soon as I hung up. Martha must have been listening. "I'm sorry about your baby being sick. What's ailing her?"

"We think she has a bad case of croup, but Doc says it could be whooping cough, but he wasn't sure."

"Have you been steaming her?" she asked.

"Yes, but it doesn't seem to help."

"Well, the doctor should be there soon. Let me know if I can do anything for you."

"Thank you, Martha, we're just waiting for the doctor."

"Marty! Marty! Bessie's choking," Joe came toward me.

I hung up and took Bessie from him. She did not seem to be able to breathe and it was as if she were going into a convulsion.

"JOE, JOE, SHE'S DYING," I screamed. He came, took her, and tried to pat her back to help her breathe.

Doctor Werner came in and took her from him. He laid her over his arm and put his fingers in her mouth to look at her throat. He gave her back to Joe and took something out of his bag, a syringe with medicine in it, which he sprayed in her throat.

"No, no, my baby is dying," I sobbed, walking from the kitchen to the bedroom, and to the front room again.

Doctor Werner worked over her, but she still kept getting coughing attacks. He looked at Joe and me and said, "We better get her to the hospital as soon as possible-it's her only chance." He told Joe to bring the baby.

I called up the stairs to Maybelle. "We're taking Bessie to the hospital. Maybelle, Susan take care of Lori. We'll be back as soon as we can."

Maybelle came running down the stairs.

"Take care of things, Maybelle," I said.

She was crying, and Susan came down, rubbing her eyes, but I was already out to the car, and did not hear their screams. The ride to the hospital was a nightmare. Bessie was gurgling, but then seemed to quiet down and lay in my arms limp. She seemed to be asleep. Doc parked the car a short way from the door, took Bessie from me, and hurried inside, leaving Joe and me to follow. Inside, the nurse led us to a waiting area. I could not sit. I walked back and forth. Joe stood by a window and looked out over the rooftops, the muscle in his cheek twitching. We could hear children crying. We waited a long time, nearly an hour, before Dr. Werner and another doctor came out. Doctor Werner introduced the other doctor. "This is Dr. Whatson. Doctor, this is Marty and Joe Mason, the child's parents." Doctor Whatson shook hands with Joe, and took my hand and patted it.

"You have a very sick baby. She has the type of croup that we don't see very often and we don't know what causes it. A thick layer of membrane builds up in her throat. She isn't strong enough or old enough to expel it, and it threatens to choke her. We have a medicine that can help clear it out, but it's too strong for a child this age. If we give her this drug it would be too strong for her heart and it might kill her. We are just going to have to remove the tough membrane by suction and we don't know what's going to happen. We will do the very best we can to bring her through this. I'm so sorry. I know how this is affecting you, but like I say, we will do the very best we can. She will be here 'til we get this cleared up and to make sure it doesn't start again. I would suggest you stay here until we get her out of danger. We should know in the morning."

"Don't worry, doctor, we won't leave," said Joe.

"Can we see her?"

"I'll see," said Dr. Whatson, and he went back to Bessie.

"You can take a peek at her, but the doctors are working

with her so you cannot stay in the room," he told us when he returned. A nurse came and walked us to a lift that took us to an upper floor. Two doctors were in the room and two nurses were helping. They had Bessie lying on a table. One of the doctors had a tube in her mouth and was squeezing a tube at the top. I felt like screaming–she was lying so still with her little head turned upward and that tube in her throat. I thought she must be unconscious, such a tiny person; she was not quite six months old. The nurse took me by arm and urged me along with her, telling Joe we should go back to the waiting room and wait for the doctor to come and talk to us. We had barely gotten to see Bessie and we had to leave. In the waiting room, I sat and cried, envisioning my baby lying on that table with just a diaper on, a doctor manipulating a tube in her throat. I thought for sure my baby would die. I walked back and forth until I was completely exhausted. Joe tried to comfort me, but I could tell he needed me as well. A woman dressed in a blue hospital gown offered us coffee. It was the blackest and the strongest coffee I ever tasted.

The sun was climbing above the treetops when the doctor finally came to talk to us. It was the same doctor who was working over Bessie. He shook hands with Joe and put his arm around my shoulder.

"Your baby is having a difficult time trying to breathe. She has laryngotracheobronchitis and it has gone into pneumonia. We are doing everything we can for her. It doesn't look good. There is only so much you can do for a baby. They just can't survive as much stress as it puts on them."

A nurse and the woman in the blue hospital gown came to the waiting room. The nurse took the doctor aside and they left in a hurry. I sensed it was Bessie and I ran after them, but the blue-gowned woman caught me and said the doctor wanted me to wait right where I was, and she led me to a seat and sat down with me. "My name is Lola," she said.

Joe asked, "Where are they going?"

"Doctor Whatson needs to check on something."

"Our baby?" Joe's voice sounded worried.

"I don't know."

"I want to see my baby," I told the woman, standing up.

"I'm sure someone will come and let you know how she is. Please sit down Mrs. Mason."

Joe came over and sat beside me. We waited a long time–it must have been three quarters of an hour. He was getting anxious and I was crying.

Lola got up. "You stay right here and I'll see what's going on," she said.

Lola didn't come back; instead, Dr. Whatson came back, an expression on his face that immediately told us he had bad news. Joe put his arm around me and I sobbed on his shoulder.

Doctor Whatson said, "I'm sorry folks, we did everything we could . . her heart just didn't hold out. She died and we couldn't do anything for her."

I screamed, "NO! NO!" and pounded on Joe's chest. He took my hands and held them until I settled down. I felt weak. I could hardly move. A nurse came in with a cup of water and a pill to calm me down.

Arrangements were made to take us home in a hospital car. It was late afternoon before we could leave. Another car from the funeral parlor came to take Bessie to Wilton Junction.

Maybelle and Sue were in the kitchen. Beth and Lori were playing on the porch.

"Where's Bessie?" asked Sue.

"We couldn't bring Bessie home because she died," Joe told the girls.

"Why did she die?" asked Maybelle, crying. "Was she sick?"

"Where is she?" Sue started crying too. Beth and Lori came in from the porch.

"What's the matter, Sue?" Beth asked her sister.

"Mama and Dad didn't bring Bessie home. They said Bessie died," answered Maybelle. "They left her at the hospital."

"No, Maybelle, Bessie is in Wilton Junction at the funeral parlor." I put my arms around her and let her cry on my shoulder. Sue came over and put her arm around my neck, crying on my other shoulder. Maybelle had been fifteen years old in March and Sue would be nine in May. Maybelle could remember Kathy, Dorothy, and Lonnie. Sue said she remembered Lonnie, too, but she was barely two and a half years old when he died, so I do not think she really remembered him well. Maybelle was six when Kathy was born but she seems to remember her, so Maybelle and Sue really felt the impact of Bessie's death, and they both tried to comfort me. With two babies at home, Beth was barely three and Lori eighteen months, and just losing my six-month-old baby, I could endure no more. I shrugged the two girls off my shoulders, stumbled out the door, and collapsed on the porch. I lay there sobbing until Joe and Sue came out and tried to lift me to my feet. I could hardly walk, and they almost dragged me into the kitchen and sat me in a chair. Beth climbed up on my lap and Lori tried to get on my lap, too. She stood at my knee, crying. Somehow, I found the strength to put Beth down and pick Lori up and cuddle her. It seemed to calm me as I rocked back and forth on the chair to quiet her crying. Maybelle tried to take Beth and interest her in something besides her seeing Lori on my lap.

I do not know what happened, but a quiet, serene calm enveloped me. I put Lori and Beth to bed, then went back down the stairs to help get the kitchen back in order. I straightened up the front room where the girls had been playing.

Joe had gone out to finish the chores that Maybelle and Sue had not done. It was bedtime, but I kept finding things to do. I could not face that little iron baby bed with the rail that I could pull up to make sure the baby would not fall out of bed; the little celluloid rattle with the tooth marks from tiny teeth that Kelly had given Lonnie and he had not gotten to play with before he died–Elizabeth had cut her teeth on it and Lori had often taken it away from Bessie when I had given it to her to play with. Finally, I sat down in the rocker that I always rocked the kids in and fell asleep. I awoke in bed, Joe sitting on the edge of the bed, fully dressed, holding his head in his hands. Slowly everything was coming back to me. I tugged on Joe's arm; he took his hands away from his face. He looked like he had not slept–his eyes were red and bloodshot, and his hair was rumpled.

"You better get dressed, Marty," he said. "We have to make arrangements at the funeral parlor."

For the first time, I noticed his hair was getting gray at the temples; his voice sounded like his throat was sore. He stood up and tried to help me out of bed, but I wanted his arms around me, I needed his comforting shoulder. I could not think; I did not know what to do. I just held on to Joe, dry-eyed, my mind slowly turning the events of yesterday over and over. The knock on the back door–who was that person I saw walking around the corner of the house–the death angel–was that the answer?

"Marty, you better get dressed. I'll put the coffee on and get the kids up." Joe brought me back to the present.

"We need to call Ma and your mother," he said.

The telephone rang three long rings, our call. Maybelle ran to answer it. "Mama, it's Mrs. Sheldon," she said, handing me the receiver.

"Marty, how is your baby doing this morning?" I did not answer; I just gave the phone to Joe.

"Martha, Marty can't talk right now, we lost Bessie–she

died yesterday afternoon at the hospital. We're getting ready to go to the funeral parlor in Wilton Junction. It was a bronchial pneumonia, but it had to do with a different kind of croup . . . the doctor had a big long name for it," he told her. "Well, I thought I would ask Dave Murdock, but thank you, we will be grateful."

When Joe hung up the receiver he said, "George and Martha are going to take us to Wilton Junction. Martha said they are sorry and wanted to know if there was anything they could do and said they would be glad to take us–she asked what Bessie died from."

The trip to Wilton Junction was quiet. George did most of the talking about last year's crop. The little pink dress and baby booties on my lap brought on the tears again as I smoothed them out.

Martha just squeezed my hand and said, "I'm so sorry."

We parked in the back of the funeral home. George and Martha waited for us in the Studebaker.

Mister Simpson, the funeral director, met us at the door and showed us to his office. The room was furnished with armchairs around a long narrow table. He pulled out a chair. "Sit down here, Mrs. Mason," he said, after shaking hands with both of us. "And Mr. Mason, sit beside your wife," he indicated another chair. He sat down on the side of the table opposite us. He opened a large heavy book with pictures of coffins in it. He turned the book around so we could see them right side up. We chose a light pink casket with white satin lining. How different from the other funerals for Kathy, Dorothy, Lonnie, and John. We went to the basement where he showed us rough boxes. The coffin was made of light metal and wood and the rough box was a hard wood treated with a substance that would keep it from deteriorating. I do not know how I managed to stay calm until we were back in the car and on our way home. Martha took my hand and patted it.

"Marty, are you feeling all right?" she asked.

"I feel nothing. I should be crying. I've lost my baby girl but I can't cry, Martha. I just feel nothing but numbness and I'm tired . . . just so tired."

"You've been through a very hard time. I can understand your need to rest."

"I haven't remembered you very well. You left right after school was out. What year was it that you went to work in Fairport and left Yankee Hollow?"

"I was only fifteen years old then–that's a good fourteen years ago or more. It was in 1897."

"George and I moved to where we live now about thirteen years ago. It's a smaller place and not as much farm ground. George can't handle the work on a big place anymore."

"Mama doesn't live at Yankee Hollow anymore either. She sold the farm three years after Papa died and moved to Fenton. My Aunt Lena and Uncle Hans lived there, but Aunt Lena died and Mama went to keep house for Uncle Hans."

"I didn't know it was you, Johanna's girl, that married Joe Mason, until I was visiting with Mrs. Glenney and we were talking about old neighbors. She mentioned that Johanna's girl had married Henry Mason's boy."

George was turning into the lane to our house. "Martha, George, thank you for taking us. Will you come in and have some coffee?"

"No, we need to get home and you're very welcome. Let us know if you need anything–we'll be back this evening."

Louise met us at the door and put her arms around me. "I'm so sorry, Marty," she said, releasing me and putting her arms around Joe.

"I didn't know the baby was sick until I heard Joe talking to Martha on the telephone this morning, and by the time I got around, you had already left for Wilton Junction. I knew the girls had colds, but I didn't know the baby was sick."

"It just happened so fast. Yesterday morning she was playing and laughing, and about four o'clock she started to sound croupy. By nine o'clock, she had a fever of one hundred and one degrees, couldn't nurse, and was coughing very hard. When Dr. Werner got here, he immediately wanted to take her to the hospital, so we were at the hospital until last evening. Our little Bessie died about ten o'clock yesterday morning, but it was about five o'clock when we got here. We came home in a hospital car. Bessie is at Simpson's in Wilton. Her funeral is tomorrow at two o'clock. They will bring her home this afternoon and we will have her at home until the funeral."

Simpson's brought Bessie at four o'clock and set the coffin across the corner, opposite the door. Friends had started coming in the afternoon and the room was full of flowers. Mister Simpson and his wife arranged the flowers until it looked like Bessie was lying in a garden of iris, tulips, carnations, and daisies. Maybelle and Sue started crying when they saw their baby sister. Beth and Lori were quiet. Joe was sitting at the kitchen table, leaning his head on his arms. Jim Clagger and Clay Hemper came in and sat down by Joe, and Pearl and Stella sat with me near Bessie, good neighbors offering comfort, love, food, and help.

Louise and Minnie Gates made sure there was coffee and food, and Dave and his son Bill did the chores.

Jim and Pearl, as well as Stella and Clay, stayed through the night. I sat and reflected on a small family lying in the cemetery. Bessie was the fifth child we lost. My heart was crying out to God, "Why, why?" I was restless and walked from my chair to Bessie and out to the porch. Faint streaks of dawn were appearing in the east, and in the west long streaks of lightning and the distant sound of thunder of an approaching storm.

Joe came out and put his arms around me. I laid my head on his shoulder and we stood silently, comforting one another. After awhile, Pearl and Jim came out.

"Looks like we might get some rain," said Jim.

"Yes, it does," said Joe, releasing me. "I hope it doesn't rain too much."

"It looks like it might go to the north . . . maybe we won't get much . . . we don't need slippery roads today." But even as Jim spoke, it started to rain and a breeze came up, blowing the rain through the screen. It became chilly as the raindrops got us damp, so we went inside. Stella had some coffee made and she set out a pan of coffee kuchen that she had brought. Dave and Bill came in to get the milk pails and start chores, so they had coffee, too. As the morning progressed, the rain stopped and the sun peaked through the clouds. By ten o'clock, the clouds had cleared and the sun was shining brightly. Ma, Kate, and Ted came by noon, and Mama and Hans arrived shortly after.

Mama put her arms around me. "What happen Marty?" I started to cry.

"I don't know, Mama, she got sick. It started with the croup and then it got in her throat. Then she couldn't swallow and she was getting pneumonia, too. I don't know, the doctor had another name for it, but I can't remember it. I only know my baby is dead," I sobbed.

Ann and Jim came. Ann gave me a hug. "Marty, I'm so sorry," she said. I could see Ann was going to have a baby–she must have been at least seven months along.

"When will you have your baby?" I asked.

"In July, the doctor says."

Maybelle and Susan kept Beth and Lori upstairs and got them ready to go with us to the cemetery, but Louise took charge of them.

"I'll take care of Beth and Lori," she said. "They wouldn't understand what's going on."

We rode to the cemetery with Ann and Jim, following the hearse. Ted, Kate, Ma, Maybelle, and Sue followed us. Mama and Hans didn't go with us, but waited at home.

As I watched baby Bessie being lowered into her grave, I vowed to myself that I would not have another baby. Thirty-two years old and I had given birth nine times and only had four living children. Why was God giving us babies, just to claim them again, when less than a year old? Mama and Hans stayed two days, but they thought they should be getting back home, and I was not very good company. I had crying spells and did not feel like visiting. Slowly the days passed. Our wedding anniversary was coming up. I did not remember telling Louise when our anniversary was, but she came down the hill carrying an anniversary cake decorated with colored frosting and a big eighteen years printed on it. I had not given our special day a thought, but that was Louise, she had to cheer us up somehow.

Chapter Eighteen

Newspapers were headlining the conflict overseas. France, Britain, Russia, Italy, and other allies were being invaded by Germany, Austria, Hungary, Turkey, and Bulgaria. The two sides were battling one another and we were hoping the new president, Woodrow Wilson, would keep us from getting involved. It was a long way off. I did not think about it much and Joe never mentioned it either.

The weather was warming up. The oats were planted. The garden was coming up and needed hoeing-same old rut every spring. One of the goose hens was sitting on eggs that would hatch in about a week, and as usual, Sergeant was on guard. I loaded the incubator and turned the eggs every other day. They would be hatching in about two weeks. I stayed outside in the garden as much as I could. Sue was good at doing the cooking and the housekeeping. Maybelle spent the summer following her Dad and learning how to farm. Beth and Lori were like Topsy of *Uncle Tom;s Cabin*–they just grew.

By the time school started in September, I was pregnant again. My vow to not have another baby was something I could not seem to avoid; the baby was due in February. Beth started to school. Maybelle had changed. She was going to parties with Buck Potter and Sue was going with Dave Murdock. Buck and Dave had frequent spats at school. Dave was jealous of Buck because his father let him drive the family car while Big Dave would not let Dave Jr. or Billie drive theirs.

Joe was president of the school board. After the teacher complained several times, he finally called a meeting and discussed it with the board. It was decided Joe would talk to the boys and their fathers. Joe was not too happy with the idea, and when Fred Potter took Buck out of school, he felt bad that Fred had made that decision. Joe felt like our neighbor was not punishing the boy, but doing just what the kid wanted. When Joe protested taking him out of school, he said he needed the boy on the farm and he had enough schooling.

Maybelle decided she wanted to quit school, too, but she was in her last year of grade school and we insisted that she graduate from the eighth grade. If she did not want to go to high school, we would not insist, because she would have to go to Tipton, which was ten miles away and the school bus only went out five miles in the surrounding area of Tipton. Kids that went to country schools had to meet the bus or stay the school week in town.

Dave Jr. was punished by having to sweep and clean the schoolroom, stoke the fire, and do whatever else to help the teacher until school let out in the spring.

Beth was turning into a pesky brat at school. Sue was constantly coming home with complaints of Beth having to sit in the coatroom because she had scratched or pinched one of the boys, usually Gail Potter, Buck's younger brother who was in the third grade. When I questioned Maybelle, she said it was not all Beth's fault, because the boys pulled Beth's hair and teased her. She was just fighting back and she got caught at it, while the boys teased her and did not let the teacher see them do it.

Buck and Maybelle were still going out together. Buck

reminded me a lot of Joe when he was about his age: tall, skinny, and always teasing. Buck picked on Lori and Beth, chasing them and telling them he was going to kiss them. The girls were always trying to outrun him when he jumped on his dapple-gray pony and chased them, both of them screaming at the top of their lungs.

Maybelle was putting on weight. Her height was five foot four inches and she weighed one hundred and fifteen pounds. Her hair was light brown and her eyes were brown, too. Her arms and legs were muscular. She was always lifting buckets of feed and pitching hay, things she did to help her Dad with chores. Sue was tall and skinny, more like I was at that age. She weighed about a hundred pounds with dark hair and brown eyes. Beth had brown eyes, Lori had blue eyes, the color of mine. Their dispositions were entirely different; Lori was quiet and got along with the other girls, even though Beth was always picking on her. Lori ignored her and went to Maybelle for protection. Beth would complain to me that Maybelle was picking on her. Thus the fall passed into winter and the holidays. School activities and house parties were in full swing; we enjoyed neighborly card parties and house dances. The front door still gave us problems, but we just did not worry about it anymore.

February 2 dawned sunny and cold, and with it the birth of a baby boy, a husky baby with lusty lungs and brown shiny bright eyes. Joe was as happy as I had ever seen him. He had another boy and this one seemed to be healthy. We named him Frederick Jonathon. He grew into an inquisitive toddler, always getting into mischief; the girls spoiled him with attention until he got into their trinkets and messed with their makeup.

Now that we had a son, Joe talked about buying the farm and going on our own. "No more putting out cash for extra feed and pasture rent . . . we work all year and get only half of what we work for," he said.

"I don't know, dear, we don't have money enough to buy

the farm. We would have to borrow–and besides, I thought we were going to buy a car. All our neighbors and friends have cars. We really need one."

"I know, we're gonna get one. There are used cars on the market and I have been thinking about getting one."

"Joe, I have two hundred dollars saved from the cream, eggs, and chickens. Can't we buy a new one?" I could still picture the brand new surrey that Grandma had given us some fifteen years ago, and the dilapidated thing it was to ride in now. He did not say anything. He just turned, took his tobacco bag out of his pocket, and stuffed tobacco in the pipe he had been holding in his teeth, scratched a match across his thigh to light it, and walked out the door humming. Well, I thought to myself, he will just forget it. Sometimes I got so depressed, it seemed Joe no longer cared. It was just humdrum days one after another; we did not seem to be any further ahead than we were eighteen years ago.

We would be celebrating our nineteenth anniversary in May, and my thirty-third birthday in July. Work and worry and grief seemed to be all we ever had. Somehow, I would forget we had five healthy kids, each other, and a pretty good living. True, we had lost five children, and when Memorial Day comes around we feel grief and futility as we decorate five small graves. I shook my head and slapped myself. Marty, snap out of it, I would say to myself. Then I would busy myself with cleaning the house and getting some mending done, mending that had been shoved to one side in a drawer, waiting for us to get in a mood to sew on buttons and darn socks.

It was about ten o'clock when Joe went out. He did not come in for lunch. I wondered where he was. The telephone rang three long rings and I went to answer it. It was the local operator with a message to call a long-distance operator, who connected me with a Fenton operator, and she connected me to Mama.

"Marty, Hans ist dead," she said. "He die dis morning."

"Oh no! What happened?" I asked.

"His heart ist sick, ist fail, we bury him Thursday," she said in her broken English. "I call, I tink du vant to komm?"

"I don't know. I would have to talk to Joe . . . he's outside somewhere. We will come if we can," I told her, wondering if we really could and thinking I would probably have to go on the train by myself. When I hung up the phone, I went out to tell Joe, but I could not find him; he was not in the barn and our saddle horse was gone. He had not said anything about going away. He was probably checking fences. It was late afternoon when a new car turned into our lane. Joe was driving it. I ran out to meet him. He was grinning from ear to ear.

"Did you buy that–where's our horse? Where did you get that–is that ours?"

"Slow down, honey, one question at a time. No, I haven't bought it and I got it in Durant. Our horse is at Ma's. I went to see Ma, and Ted was there. We were talking and I told him I wanted to buy a car, so he said he would take me to Durant–he knew a car dealer over there."

"Where did you get the money?"

"I haven't paid for it yet, we have to go to the bank. The dealer said I could try it out and if you like it, we can pay him tomorrow. It's not brand new–it's a demonstrator–one he has been showing to people and letting them drive. He took me for a ride and told me to drive it home. If you like it, we can make a deal."

"Honey, Uncle Hans died. Mama called me. She says he will be buried Thursday. I would like to go to the funeral, but we didn't get to Aunt Lena's, and we would have to go on the train."

"Oh no, I'm sorry about your Uncle Hans. What happened to him?"

"He must have had a heart attack."

"I don't know how we can go. Tomorrow is Wednesday. I have to take this car back and get Gypsy from Ma's."

"We would have to take the train tomorrow," I said.

"I don't think we can make the arrangements in time. I think we would have to change trains somewhere to get to northwest Iowa. We are on the Rock Island lines from here," he said.

"I guess we might as well forget about going. We really shouldn't leave the girls alone and Jonathon is still just a baby–he's only eighteen months, you know, and he's always in to something. I don't think we can leave him that long and expect the girls to take care of him–besides, I don't think it's a good thing to leave the girls alone that long, either," I said.

"The girls are able to take care of themselves."

"Honey, you know they would have their boyfriends here. They wouldn't mind Beth, Lori, and Jonny. I'll send Mama a telegram and ask her to get some flowers for us. Honey, I hate it that we can't go."

'I told myself, "It's all right. I'll always remember Aunt Lena and Uncle Hans as my second mother and father." But my heart was heavy when I thought about the years I spent with them, and how I could not be at either one's funeral to say good-bye to the two that meant more to me than my real mother.

"Do you want to take a ride in the car and see how you like it?" he asked.

"I suppose so," I said.

We drove around the square about four miles and I really enjoyed the ride.

"I think this would be a good car to have," I told him.

The next day he took Maybelle with him so she could

ride Gypsy home and he returned the car. When he returned, we owned a new Ford.

Chapter Nineteen

World War I was declared in April 1919. Jonathon was three years old and I was pregnant again. Buck Potter was the first in our neighborhood to be drafted into the Army. Dave went next and finally Arty. Joe was too old for the draft; since we were in farming, he would not have to go anyway. Our old house resounded with the tunes of "Over There," "K-K-Katy," and "Keep the Home Fires Burning." Maybelle and Sue wrote to the boys. The flu was bad that year, and Joe came down with it just before the birth of our eleventh child. He had worried that I would get it, then he came down with it the night Janet was born, March 28, 1919. She was a brown-eyed baby with a mop of hair you would not believe a newborn would have. I did not see Joe for three days–he stayed away from me for fear I would get the flu. When he recovered, his hair had turned white.

In May, Mama sent us an announcement that she was getting married. They were coming to Cedar County to live. Her new husband's son was living near Wilton Junction and he wanted to be near him. Mama also wanted to come back.

They were married May 18, the same date Joe and I were married–only the year was different.

My new stepfather was John Buck, a warm-hearted and friendly man. He reminded me of Papa. I never could see how Mama could find such good men with the temper and personality she had. Papa John was brown-eyed, bald, and clean-shaven. He was about fifty pounds lighter than Mama, who weighed about the same as I did. When I looked at Mama, I thought, "Am I really that big?"

They bought a house in Tipton, and Mama let me know that she expected us to bring milk and eggs when we came to visit, so we tried to make it every week if we could. As time passed they got settled in Tipton, and Mama met some German friends. They seemed content.

The spring was a busy time. The boys were back from overseas and Arty was helping Joe with the haying. I was busy with a small Janet and three-year-old Jonathon. Maybelle and Buck got married; they moved to a farm that his father owned near Atalissa.

Sue moved to Davenport and got a job there. That left me with a house and two small kids to look after as well as the job of leading Gypsy on the hayfork. I told Beth and Lori to watch Jonathon.

The hay rope was run through a pulley and I told Jonathon to stay away from it, warning him that Sergeant, of whom he was afraid, would get him. I did not pay any further attention to him, for he had had several encounters with the gander and had a lot of respect for that old bird. I did not reckon with Jonathon's inquisitive mind, and the rope crawling along the ground and sliding through the pulley was a fascinating object. That fascination was greater than his fear. I had started the third fork full up the side of the barn when suddenly Art jumped from the hayrack, and ran toward the rope at the same time he yelled "Whoa." Gypsy stopped dead still in his tracks, the way Maybelle had so patiently taught him. The horse's obedience to the command perhaps saved Jonathon's life. Two fingers on his right hand were badly mangled. Doctor Werner saved his hand but it was crippled, a handicap Jonathon would carry to his grave.

Janet was a robust little girl about sixteen months old when she came down with the croup. I worried that she would get the same type that took little Bessie's life and I called a doctor in Tipton because Dr. Werner was away for a few days. Doctor Haley was a middle-aged man with dark hair and eyes. He checked her over, gave her a shot in her back, and told us she would be better tomorrow. The next morning she woke up feeling good and ready to play.

Beth had turned out to be the scatterbrain in the family. At school, she was constantly punished for misbehaving, mostly for fighting with the boys. She clawed the youngest Potter boy's face so badly that June called me on the telephone.

"Marty, for heavens sake, cut Beth's fingernails so she can't scratch. You should see Gail's face."

Beth howled when I got the scissors. "No, Mama, I need my fingernails," she protested.

"For what?"

"To scratch with, when I get in a fight."

"Shame on you Beth! You're a girl, why don't you act like one?"

"Well, Gail always starts it, he pulls my hair."

"That's because he likes you. He pulls your hair to make you notice him. Next time turn around and give him a big smile."

"I don't like him–he called me a horse face."

"What did you say?"

"I told him to 'Shut up, weasel eyes,' and I got him good after school."

"Lori doesn't fight."

"That's because she"s a coward . . . besides the boys don't pick on her."

When school started in the fall, we had to take Beth out. She caused so much confusion the teacher said it disturbed the other children. She had only completed the fifth grade.

Our last boy was born that fall, Joseph, Jr. Sue married a boy from the city, and soon gave us our first grandchild, a little girl.

The roaring twenties hit our community. Beth and Lori were wearing their dresses above, and their stocking rolled below, the knees, with brightly colored satin garters. Bowery and barn dances were the latest craze, along with the Charleston and the black bottom. All we could do was teach the girls right from wrong and hope they had what it took to keep them on the right path.

Beth went to work for a farm family as a hired girl. Time after time stories came to us about her wild escapades. She was going steady with Larry, the family's hired man, and they planned to be married in the spring, but Beth stepped out with other boys behind his back. It was not long before he realized it. They quarreled and broke up. Beth went from bad to worse. We breathed a sigh of relief when she got married Don, a boy she had been secretly seeing. A week after they were married, she was sorry and wanted Larry back. Joe had taken about all he could stand from her; he sent her back to her husband. "You made your bed, now lie in it," he told her.

Beth's life was a heartache to us. I honestly believe she loved Larry with all her heart. As for Larry, he was like a wild man when he realized what Beth had done and threatened to shoot Beth and himself and kill Don, too. After weeks of fear and turmoil over Beth's hasty marriage, we received the news that Larry had married a girl who was very much in love with him and who had been trying to break Larry and Beth up. By this time, Beth was pregnant and she settled down.

Lori finished eighth grade in our country school and started high school in town. She rode Gypsy the eight miles, leaving him at the livery barn during school hours. The old horse was beginning to show his age, but he faithfully took her back and forth, and we knew we could trust him to come home if anything happened.

I was not surprised when Joe brought a radio home one day. He had been talking so enthusiastically about this new contraption that let you hear people talking from hundreds of miles away. He worked all day putting up an aerial and hooking it up. That little crystal set was the beginning of a new way of life in our house. New ideas, entertainment, and news became a part of everyday. The next year we got a set with a loud speaker.

Joe was aging. I could see it in the way he walked; when he came in from chores, he did not rumple the girl;s hair or throw a light punch to Jonathon;s chin. That brush with the flu he had five years ago had really taken all the sap out of him.

We were worried. Prices were going down for hogs and cattle. There was talk about a new law enacted in Iowa requiring all farmers to have their cattle herds tested for tuberculosis. Joe worried about injecting our cows with a tuberculosis test.

"I don't think you have to have it done if you don't want it," he said, "and I don't think I'll have them test ours."

"Our cows are healthy–they don''t look like there's anything wrong with them," I said.

Joe was wrong. About three weeks later a couple of farmers from Muscatine County stopped to see Joe. They had a petition they wanted him to sign.

"What's that for?"he asked.

"Have you heard about the state wanting to test all the herds in Iowa?"

"I heard there was a law passed, but I don't think you have to have it done."

"They are trying to make it so everyone has to."

"Well, maybe the big dairy farms, but I wouldn't worry

about the few cows we have."

“We’re trying to get enough signatures to stop it. They can test your cow, and if it reacts they condemn it and it has to be destroyed.”

“How can they do that?”

“That’s what they’re trying to do.”

“Sure, I’ll sign your petition. They can’t just kill my cow and give me no compensation–they would have to pay you for the animal.”

“Thanks for signing. Your neighbors are all signing up.”

“Well, good luck fellas.”

Joe did not say anything more about it until he heard on the radio that the owner of the Muscatine station K.T.N.T. was on the side of the farmers, telling them to object to the testing.

Chapter Twenty

In the fall of 1929 came the Great Depression. Banks closed, businesses failed, mortgages foreclosed, men lost their jobs, and there were no jobs to be found. Men who did not have family lived by bumming their way to other towns and cities, sometimes just walking, more times catching a freight train and riding in a boxcar, sleeping in haymows and straw stacks when they were on the road. Many times we found evidence of where they had slept and even milked a cow. One morning a man came from the barn to the house and asked for something to eat. By that time it was nothing new to have a bum ask for a handout. The talk around the neighborhood was, do not give them anything because they will mark your place for other bums to find food. We thanked goodness we did not live near a town.

Jonathon turned sixteen in 1931 and Joe began to let him drive the car. By this time Joe had traded the Ford in for a bigger car, a Velie. Being a young man, Jonathon needed money, so he went to work for a neighbor who had bought the old Sheldon farm. He was breaking up rocks in a quarry across the road. He spent the summer in the quarry; and when it was time to go back to school, he did not want to go. Then we found out that Jonathon and Janet both had been playing hooky and had not spent much time in school last year.

We had also found out that Janet had a learning disability. The illness she had when she was a baby had left her unable to learn–she could not even write her name. Joe blamed the doctor for her disability because of the medicine he had injected into her spine.

With fall and the summer work out of the way, oats in the granary, potatoes in the cellar, full jars of vegetables on the shelves in the cellar, it was about corn-husking time. Jonathon helped with the corn husking, leaving the quarry for as long as the corn picking lasted.

Papa John had a stroke in October; it left him completely paralyzed. Mama could not take care of him. Papa John's son moved him to his house where he and his wife, Bertha, could care for him. Since Mama was getting up in age, she would soon be eighty-five, I decided she should come and stay with us.

Joe and I were picking apples to put in the cellar when I asked him if we could take Mama for a while until Papa John got better.

"Marty, you know your stepfather is not going to get well. If your mother comes here, it will be permanent," said Joe, with an edge in his voice.

"She can't stay by herself. She''s been complaining of having a stomachache after she eats and she can't go to Fred's to stay."

"Well, maybe she don"t eat right since John isn't there."

"That's just it Joe, she probably don't cook for herself. I'm the only one she's got, Joe. Pete's not her son, he don't care."

"I know, honey, but how would the girls get along with her?"

"Well, they would have to learn to live together."

"She's not like old Granny and we don't have room

for her."

I could see Joe did not like the idea of Mama staying with us. He picked up the basket and took the apples to the cellar. As far as he was concerned, the subject was closed. As the days passed, I tried not to think about Mama, and was content taking milk, butter, and eggs to her, seeing she had everything she needed. She got down to see Papa John twice. She was losing weight in the three weeks he was away and she looked thin.

"Marty, I tink I better go see doctor. I hurt in my bach," she said, indicating her belly.

"So do you want me to send the doctor to see you? There is a doctor in town and I can have him come to see you."

"No, I vant to see Dr. Werner. He see Henry when he alive and I know him. I tink I have somedings in my bach, not gute," she said.

Papa John died a month after he had the stroke. Fred buried his father in their country plot near Wilton Junction.

We closed Mama's house and brought her to live with us, even though Joe was opposed. There was nothing else we could do. We set a heating stove in the summer kitchen, and Joe and I slept there. Mama had a downstairs bedroom. When she was settled in with us, she seemed content. She always seemed to have trouble after she ate.

Lori and Mama did not get along. Lori had a boyfriend and they dated twice a week. Her friend was an older man with dark hair, hefty build, gray-blue eyes, and large full puffy lips. He always had tobacco snuff in them. James Swind was a very nice fellow and Lori had met him at a bowery dance in Rochester. He brought her home from the dance one night and he came in to meet her family. Joe and I thought he was a nice man. He worked in Iowa City and had a good job; he drove a Hudson. He was fourteen years older than Lori. He became a good friend and we trusted him to take care of Lori when she was with him. Lori was only sixteen years old and James was twenty-nine. James would take Lori, Janet, Joe, and me for drives in his big car on Sundays. He did not mind one night when Lori went on a date with him and she came home with someone else; he came back the next day.

"Did Lori get home all right last night?" he asked Joe.

"I think so, wasn't she with you?"

"I took her to the dance. She always dances and has a good time, but she disappeared when the dance was over. I waited and waited. The bowery got dark and everyone left. She was nowhere around. I had seen her with another man earlier, so I just left."

"Yeah, she's here."

When it happened a second time and James brought her coat in, it was nearly 3 A.M. when he rapped on the door where we were sleeping and handed Joe her coat. Joe dressed and went into the house; I put on my robe and followed him.

When she came home after 4:00 A.M., Joe was angry. He yelled, "Young lady where have you been?" We had been sitting in the dark and she got scared when he yelled at her.

"I went to the dance and then we drove around for awhile."

"You didn't come home with Jim," said Joe, using his nickname.

"Yes I did, he just left me out."

"That wasn't Jim. Jim brought your coat home over an hour ago. You get to bed and we'll talk about this tomorrow."

"Lori, who were you with?" I asked her.

"Just a friend I met at the dance who wanted to bring me home. I didn't think Jim would care."

"Did you ask him if he cared?"

"No," she answered and went upstairs.

When Joe talked to her the next day, he gave her to

understand she was to stay with Jim or tell him she did not want to go with him. Jim did not show up for a long time. When he did come it was on Sunday; he wanted to go hunting with Jonathon and he did not even say hello to Lori.

Weeks passed. Mama was really having a bad time with pain. Doctor Werner came and checked her, leaving pain medicine. He told me Mama had a growth in her belly and it would be just a matter of time until the cancer would get her. That happened sooner than we expected; a week later Mama was in a coma. I stayed with her all through the night and the next day. That night as I opened the door to go out, a gust of wind suddenly hit me so hard that I had to brace myself against it. Just as suddenly it was calm and I saw two balls of fire roll down the hillside into a thick blanket of fog. Quite shaken, I went back inside the house and closed the door. Sitting by Mama's bed that night, I dosed off; when I awakened, the room was in semidarkness-the lamp was turned down low. Mama had not moved. The doctor told us Mama would probably just sleep away. I got up to stretch my legs, picked up the lamp, and went up the stairs to check on the girls. The flame of the lamp fluttered and the black angel appeared leaning over the trunk. The light went out and I was in total darkness. In a panic, I called Joe. He hastily relit the lamp.

"I saw her again, Joe, the black angel."

Joe took hold of my shoulders. "Calm down," he said.

I made some coffee, and Joe and I sat at the table drinking the hot beverage, listening to the loud snoring coming from her bedroom. Suddenly it was quiet and I said, "Honey, Mama is awfully quiet. I can't hear her breathing."

Joe got up and went into her room. I think she's gone Marty," he said when he came out.

We buried Mama in the same plot next to Papa Heldt.

It was nearly a week before I could look at Mama's clothes and put them away. In a dresser drawer I found a metal box, which was locked. I looked for the key and found it in her pocketbook.

I had a strange feeling as I took several photographs from the box. The people in the pictures were all strangers to me. On the back were the names of the people written in a beautiful English script. The oldest picture was dated in the year 1875.

One picture was of Lord Frederick Montgomery Vaughn II, Lady Elizabeth Weldon Vaughn, Frederick Montgomery Vaughn III, Anthony Montgomery Vaughn, and Mary Welda Vaughn.

The second picture was Baron Charles John Westley, Baroness Elizabeth Bloomington Westley, Charles Bloomington Westley, Grace Jane Westley, and Maragret Martha Westley.

The third picture was Lord Frederick Montgomery Vaughn III, Margaret Martha Westley Vaughn, and Frederick Montgomery Vaughn IV.

The last picture was Charles Bloomington Westley and Dora Ann Westley.

As I looked at the pictures, I realized these people were my British ancestors. How had Mama gotten the pictures? She had only one picture that I knew of and it was of my father in his military dress.

I took a letter from the box, it read as follows:

My Dear Hannah,

My letter will, no doubt, come as a surprise. I hope you will read it through. Lord Frederick passed away a few weeks ago. Before he died, we decided I should locate our grandchild. As the years passed, one after the other, we realized, with regret, that we should have handled Frederick's marriage differently. However, what's done is done.

I realize your f eelings will not be friendly toward this

letter, but I hope you can find it in your heart to send me a letter as to the whereabouts of my grandchild. Fortunately, Mrs. Tremble had your address, and she gave it to me, so I trust this letter will reach you.

Your health,

Margaret Martha Vaughn

I sat holding the letter in my hand. Why had not Mama told me Grandmother Vaughn had tried to get in touch with me?

I picked up the other letter in the box. This one was dated August 22, 1907. I looked at the date on the other letter; it was dated June 10 of the same year. I took the letter from the envelope and read:

Dear Hannah:

I wrote to you some weeks ago asking that you have my granddaughter get in touch with me. As you know, the Vaughn estate is quite large, and my son's child can inherit a large share of it.

I cannot blame you. We were harsh with you, but please do not deny my grandchild the inheritance to which she is entitled. I am old and ill. It is hard for me to say "I am sorry." I know you will think I am trying to clear my conscience before I die. Perhaps this is part of it, but I also have a strong desire to see my grandchild before I die.

I am enclosing our family photographs. I trust you will give them to Marty. I have written the names on the back so she will know who they are.

Please have her write to me.

I wish for you,

Good health,

Margaret Martha Vaughn

I was shaken. This was the first inkling I had that Mama

had been in contact with anyone in England–certainly the first I knew that my grandmother had any interest in me. I wonder why she did not try harder to find me? She said she was ill; perhaps she had died before she could find me. What was the matter with Mama that she kept this from me? I had a right to make up my own mind. The date 1907–I had been married nine years when she wrote the letters. Joe and I were now getting ready to celebrate our thirty-seventh.

I put the pictures and the letters back in the box.

The more I thought about it, the surer I became that I had to find out what had happened to the Vaughn estate and the beautiful old castle Mama had told me about. The only person I could think of that might be able to help me was the Right Honorable Lord Mayor of London. I had no idea who the Lord Mayor might be, but it did not matter if I knew his name or not. I wrote him a letter. I waited with anticipation for an answer, but days went by without any word. Seven weeks went by and I decided my letter had been disregarded.

Just when I had given up hope, the letter came. It was from the Longerbeam firm of British Travel and Passport Service and Information.

The letter said the holdings and land of Lord Frederick Montgomery Vaughn III had reverted to the heirs of Anthony Montgomery Vaughn, since the direct heirs, a son, died in 1887, and a grandchild died in 1890, according to letters received from America. So that was it–Mama had told Grandmother Vaughn I was dead! I fretted about the letter for days.

"Forget it," said Joe. "There's nothing you can do about it now."

"But why did she lie?"

"Maybe she thought you would leave and go to England. You were all she had . . . she loved you in her own way."

"Mama always said the name Vaughn was dead. She was trying to bury me with her past."

As Joe said, there was nothing to do but forget it; too much water had run under the bridge. I tried very hard to forgive my mother as time passed.

Days dragged by. I could not forget the letters from my Grandmother Vaughn. Joseph was on my mind, too. He wanted to enlist in the Army. We did not think too much about it, but Joe was afraid he would do it. It was taken out of Joe and Joseph's hands when he got a notice from the draft board; Jonathon received one as well. They were both called up. Joseph passed the exam, but Jonathon failed because of eyesight, heart problems, and his crippled hand.

September came, and there was a great deal of worry among the farmers of Cedar and Muscatine counties. The state was sending veterinarians to test their herds for tuberculosis, and the farmers were standing pat and not letting the vets on their property. There was violence involved. Joe said they would not get away with the testing, but it got to the point where the governor called out the state militia. Officers were arresting the farmers and sending them to jail.

"What are we going to do, Joe?" I asked.

"What in the hell can we do? They are sending the National Guard. We have to do it–we'll just have to pray our cows are healthy."

Joe kept following the radio reports and they were getting worse all the time. Finally, the notice came: have your herd penned, so your herd can be tested. It was the next day that three truckloads of soldiers drove into our lane and pulled into the orchard. A car with two veterinarians also arrived. Joe went to meet them. I was scared that Joe would do something, but they talked a few minutes and walked over to the lot where the cows were penned up. Soldiers were picking apples that were still on the trees and they did not pay any attention to us. The next day they were back again; our cows were clean, they said.

With the Depression over, things gradually began to get better. Joe talked about retiring. With Jonathon's help, we bought a house in town and moved off the farm. Jonathon had two children and they needed the room. We had fourteen grandchildren by this time. Maybelle and Buck never had children, but Sue had four, Beth had six, and Lori had two.

December 7th, 1944, was a shocking and tragic day for America. Soon after, Joseph was drafted into the infantry. He took his training in Kansas and in due time was sent overseas. When his letters began to arrive, we found he was stationed in England. Although his first letters were those of a very homesick boy, soon he began mentioning a girl he had met. Soon Dora Westley became his main topic.

"Dora and I went dancing last night, and Dora's family invited me to supper," and finally, "Mom and Dad, how would you like to have an English girl for a daughter-in-law?" His next letter said, "Mom, I've asked Dora to marry me."

Enclosed in his next letter was a note from Dora. "I love Joe, Mrs. Mason. I hope you won't mind receiving this letter from a complete stranger. I am looking forward to meeting all of you. Joe has told me so much about his family. I am an only girl. I have two brothers, one is in Burma in the Commandos, and the other is in Australia in the Navy. We have an Anderson air raid shelter in our backyard, where I am writing this letter.

A strange feeling came over me as I read her note. Where had I seen that beautiful handwriting? The snapshot she had enclosed–where had I seen that picture? The photographs and letters in the metal box–I went to get them. The snapshot could have been a twin sister to the woman in one of the photos. The name was the same, too, Dora Ann Westley on the photo and Dora Westley on the snapshot, a younger girl in this than the one in Mama's box. Instinctively, I knew Joseph planned to marry his second cousin. Suddenly, things seemed right to me. The sun shone brightly on the rain-drenched garden, turning the drops of water to glistening diamonds; the birds sounded like clear beautiful notes of a harp. All about me was a glowing warmth of understanding. Yes, Grandmother Vaughn, your spirit can rest. I have been reunited with my father's family.

The old wooden trunk stands unopened in the attic. My will contains instructions to burn it unopened upon my death, for as long as I live, I will never have the heart to destroy it.

www.ingramcontent.com/pod-product-compliance
Lightning Source LLC
LaVergne TN
LVHW091041080826
845145LV00002B/577

* 9 7 8 1 5 9 5 4 0 9 0 7 2 *